Tender is the Gelignite

Elizabeth Harper

Tender is the Gelignite

ISBN: 9781978391239

First Edition.

For my Grandma, who will be horrified by the language used but only has my parents to blame.

Tender is the Gelignite
A novel of 2016

Gelignite (noun): an old fashioned word for a type of explosive substance. Please see 'There Goes a Tenner' for further reference.

0.5

Definitely not the best idea to stare at the rain when you're crossing the road.

First, no matter how calm and relaxed and dreamy you feel, your mug will form a snivelling sneer. Second, it's likely that a pretty-car will knock your block off. Unintentionally for once.

A black shiny pretty-car screeches to a halt right up by my hip and I blink and jump back onto the pavement. It careers off again straight away, with a tuneful 'fucking stupid, miserable, crazy, fat, dick-flapped cu-...' stringing out of the driver's window. I wrinkle my conk. The watchtower looms over the dim and dingy rows of red warehouses, prickly coils of barbed wire lacing over obtuse bleacher roofs.

In the UK there's what I call UMAY, laws where you literally may pick whatever Uniform you like. Any clothes any style any arrangement. Which is great. Freedom and choice and all that. I like knowing who and what I am. Just so long as you stick to it afterwards mind, that's very important.

Me

Feet: Laced-up bovver boots.

Bod: Black jumpsuit. Jersey.

Coat: Woollen, blood-coloured.

Choker: Scarf, like a blanket. Black, white, yellow.

I crunch my way through the downpour, the chopped fragments of glass, grit and sodden cardboard, squishing, mingling and munching in the thick soles of my bovvers, a firm barrier between my digits and the grindy, grimy slop. Careful: scantily scattered used condoms are a slippery risk, always best to avoid splurting skins.

Completely out of control Conscript.

This creeping crisis always begins when I first start walking to my Employment. At the beginning, I step into the hustling muscling city Centre-For-Work. Buildings are tall, sleek and clean. Dull sky is reflected beautifully, pavements are fresh and clear, streets are pedestrianised for bods, odds, sods, Conscripts, capitalisers, Employers and bods. Not many Poor Ones but they constantly hang about unseen. Clacking from the soles of hard-heeled shoes clash with snaps and spits coming from the Autogrammers, their portable ze-cams and ze-phones capturing the commute. Autogrammers aren't just some nuisance bods that you need to dodge with their flashes and their cracks; they fill the city Centre-For-Work, providing photographic evidentials of everything and every bod all the ploughing time. That's why you'd better stick to your all-important Uniform, especially during the day. Otherwise you'll be Unrecognised and, well, that's always a mess waiting to mong.

Walking through the city Centre-For-Work is void and impersonal; bods autogramming, staring at hologrammed ads or news stories on the roof tops or plodding along in a misshapen and miserable manner on their way to some office box or other. But there's some comfort in seeing other like-feeling shittos living out the communal curse, no matter how vapid and sophisticatedly superficial the surroundings.

But crossing the ornate nineteenth century old old cold bridge into Strangeways, like I do and did every sodding day, you want to see as few bods as possible. You can never trust anybod driving them BMW, Jaguar or Mercedes Benz around a god-forsaken No Bod's Land shit-hole dump like where I work. But you see them there a lot. What has a nice pretty-car got to do with a place so crap? A place so measly, oozing with muck, sweating like a foul ponging cheese or cold sore on the way out? Them BMW, Jaguar and Mercedes Benz form a clean, cool contrast to such a mildewed patch: the rotting decaying roads and alleys; prozzes clopping about in puffer coats, flashing over-worn underwear and grotesque kitten heels as they perch on corners or fumble after these luxury-wagons, these fill-your-bovvers cock-on-wheels succulently-leather-arsed motor machines. Drug dealers dally at an angle to the prison, the tell-tale trainers lobbed over the disused ze-phone wire, hanging in a still brooding manner over the grids of warehouses.

I hate to see those cars. I hate being mistaken for a prozz. They crawl up alongside you. Even though you can't see the toads inside you can feel the goggly woggly globes scanning your bod like you're a slab of meat hanging in a blood house. Except they want to fuck you instead of eat you. Same thing really though, no? Tell me I'm wrong. I fantasise everyday about smashing them up. In my head, I take one of the slippery slimy waste bricks that has been lying chucked about round here since who knows when and pummel it into the pretty-car. The windscreen doesn't stand a chance against my bricky blows, with Odious Toadious inside bricking his denim dick-casket as glass shards are cast in all the directions. He screams and shouts 'you crazy betch' and I shriek with delight at his panic, taking my big booted bovver foot to the hood and kick kick kick.

TAKE THAT YOU FILTHY FAT FUCK

No pretty-cars lurking today. I crunch on unwatched.

I pass the same bod every day. I think he must actually live in Strangeways or something because he's always hurrying down the hill, every fucking day. He's Asian, with a kind pleasant mug. We glance at each other every morning. I get the feeling he's a nice bloke. You can tell who the nice ones are around here. The ones who keep their heads down and plough on; not the serial strutters, the swaggering shits who are proud to be a big-shot in a piss-pot like this.

Welcome to the hub of the UK's fashion industry, the old Hell by wholesale.

1.1

Yikes. Get to the warehouse and the grates are still down. I stand shivering in the cold and wet, confronted with the big long line of prison wall that runs parallel to my Employment on the next street down. That big old chunky wall, made from red brick and its thin red watchtower. It is very impressive. In an overwhelming Stately dark shitshow kind of way.

9am. Official working time according to the tick tock puncher that I have to clock every time I shackle and unshackle myself from the desk. I am not not getting paid for having to wait for some bod to open the grates. But I don't care how long I have to wait, I don't care how cold I get or how much I need to pee, I am happy to not be working for as long as possible. It's their time. I hover underneath the building's pathetic concrete lip for cover, squidging myself on the damp step and take stock of the sour scene in front: a cold metal girder fence encloses a herd of rusty busted vans-for-hire ticking dormant, whilst the air is tinged with a sweet, bready smell from the brewery that towers behind the work-shack warehouse that is my place of Employment and occupation. The prison and the brewery compete for air monopoly and all I see is brick brick brick brick brick. Even the road has an acne mug with pockmarks of brick cobblies lying exposed underneath the worn out and tired tarmac paving. Metal, brick, concrete and grating. It is harsh, kind of stressful, all the shit complementing each other. I respect that. It's all appropriate. What's the use of pretty, like them cars? The whole thing is ruined by a stupid fucking tree that stands there all green and crisp and lively and hopeful. It has somehow managed to successfully grow up around all this crap and crud; or maybe it was there before the crap and crud. Well, I don't know, I don't care. It pisses me off and I like to imagine it catching some fungal rotty disease and dying a withering mossy death or catching fire and turning into a black singed mess or something other than stand there and smile at me and oversee while I wait to get pushed and pulled into the warehouse for another delightful day of Employment achievement. Fucking nature.

I scowl at it a little longer until Marissa approaches from the direction of the main road.

'Hey', she says.

Uniform

Feet: Faux sheep-skin bovvers.

Legs: Leggings.

Bod: Over-sized knitted cardigan. Belt at the waist.

Head: Covered with umbrella. Hair in braids.

'Hey'.

'Thank god Ah wasun' late'.

'I know right'.

'The X-bus, righ', it just didun' turn uhp. Then aftuh fifteen minutes, there were three. So dumb'.

'So dumb. You'd have thought they'd be regular'.

'Ah know'.

Silence.

'I wonder where they are?' I ask.

'Don' care, Ah'll stand out here for as long as possible. And theh can pay meh for it'.

I like Marissa. Same priorities.

'It's not like that's going to happen any time soon though', I start.

'Ah know. What is it now, a week late? Takes the piss'.

'I thought that the UK had made rules about this sort of thing'.

'Have theh 'eck, all the rules theh made are geared towards the Employuhs not the Conscripts. Dad knows all about this stuhff, he gets on realleh well with his Employuh so he gets to hear and understan' abou' all the legislations'.

I blink. 'A nice Employer?'

'Sure. He's realleh luckeh. Ah mean, theh're not friends or anythin. But for Conscription, it's as good as yer goin to get'.

5

'Yeah'.

She sighs and surveys the same slumpy scene.

'I think I'm going to ask Rich about getting paid', I say. 'We have been waiting a week and I've got shit to pay for'.

'Yeah', she says. 'Good luck with tha'".

We stand outside as the rain turns to a pathetic drizzle. Not even proper rain, as if the clouds couldn't be bothered and only wanted to do a half-arsed job. Can't blame them. Conscription, being forced to do shit, is boring, repetitive and time-consuming. Who could be doing with it? Even boredom is more fun. I'd rather be doing nothing, bored, procrastinating than pouring my poor little Conscripting soul into a spreadsheet or a lousy piece of contentious content copy. Boredom is the new radical, boredom is the new black, bitches. And I know. I work in fashion.

All of a sudden an old state of the art 4x4 Land Rover Discovery Ranger Wrangler Wagon pulls up. Our plump Employer Rich side-steps out. He jogs around the truck with his belly overhanging in a tight-fitting T-shirt with jeans and garish trainers, the hideous kind in black with a fluorescent yellow stripe and one of those see-through plastic bubble wedges in the heel from about twenty million years ago that helped bods do well at sport then but are now just worn by idiot fatties like Rich. Yuck. This is our director of fashion. There he is, his thumb blotting the buttons on his remote-control keypad thing that brings up the grates. Scratching his stubbly head, one hand on his hip, he's a style maven, a sartorial extraordinaire, suited and bloody well booted waving his wand and deciding what style will mean for others. Creep.

'Sorreh, gerrls, sorreh. Yous been thinkin about todeh's agenduh yeah?'

The grates creak up slowly and all at once, it feels like I'm going into an extension of the prison next door. Except this prison contains cute, sweatshop dresses. I leave at the end of the day but I come back to the same place everyday so I might as well be in Strangeways. It would save crunching and squishing and swaying through all the crap it takes to get me here.

'Come on then gerrls, inyaget, clock in straigh' aweh yeah. Don' want to cost mih moneh, this, bein late... '

Speak for yourself cunt. I am the essence of Conscript punctuality, can't knock my timeliness. I scowl. Marissa slights me a sneer behind his back.

'Get in then, uhp them stairs. Turn all the lights on and unlock the doors and then get started. Ah'm payin yous to ge' on with it yeah', he pants breathily as he struggles with an enormous padlock around the metal barred gate inside the porch. He says the same thing every day. Thinks we're really thick.

'Clock in and then shackle uhp, pleeeuse'.

Marissa and I tramp up the stairs. Rachel and Lauren are just getting in. Rich races ahead of us all and assumes the position of fucked-off Employer in chief, ready to have a go at anybod who arrives after him. We take it in turns to scan our fingerprints on the clocker. Marissa turns on the ze-CCTV screen and a huge booming sound system. That fucking sound system. With all the annoying flashing hologram ads and the same shite music that pisses all over the airwaves day after day after day. I wonder why they play that gunk, that pip-pap-crap with the constant bom bom boms, yeah yeah yeahs. I swear the presenters are these mad obsessive octopus children jumping around pressing repeat in a blind mad frenzy shrieking in double time AGAIN AGAIN AGAIN. That really is the only reasonable explanation for this damn death drive radio with the squeaky voices and their squawking parp parp parp playlists that don't change from week to fucking week.

I go for a piss then I sit down at my desk, attaching a ring of steel chained to the floor around my left ankle which bleep bleep bleep bl-bleeps as the lock clicks into place. It's not enough to just clock in anymore: we have shackles that bind us to our desks; ze-CCTV watching and listening to even the most innocent conk sniffle and ear scratch; no toilet breaks; no talking, nothing. We, like everyone else in the god-forsaken UK UPRAY, are on the racking wheels, keeping markets and economy and big Business and booms and busts and bonds and ball-sacks going. Once Conscription was just an army thing but now it's gone corporate: Official Workplace Conscription. I just call it OW.

Our enforced silence is golden because you can communicate on the sly with ze-emails. It's my preferred method of communication with the girls here. We interact in snippets which is enough for me. Doesn't mean I dislike them. Plus, ze-emails and their silence allow you to listen to the bollocks and bullshit that goes on in this, the shit-source of the beloved UK Fashion Industry. I look up and see that Lauren, who is sitting in front with her back to me, is virtual shopping on her screen. Another lazy dazy bones.

I start to type.

I work in content. I produce the content, I am not the content of the content and I am not content with the content. But I am the contents of the job that contains me and that is what I do. It's boring, constantly fast-paced and drains me whilst also weirdly addictive and pumping. I basically bung up the Internet with masses of endless blah blah blah about everything so that we can link everyone back to our website. Fun right. The best thing is that you don't even have to write proper sentences with the right spelling punctuation or grammar because as long as you have the right keyword in place for the right number of times then that's enough to boost your ranking on a search engine and there you have it, you win at Business. There's not much opinion shit that is allowed online and LAW FORCE watch everything and anything in the UK. Content is greatly encouraged because it's good for Business and helps make Employers like Rich rich. They all want any old crap writing to sell shit, just as long as bods don't get any ideas beyond shopping. I don't see why clap trap shitty pap I spew online shouldn't infect all areas of my lingo life. So that is what I do.

What's hilarious is that I've heard from The Money News that some ultra-exclusive Employers have bots to produce content now. Bods are no longer needed to write for them. Words and writing and content are so old fashioned that they can be produced by machines and mechanisms. I straddle this line beautifully, a fleshy bod bot blotting the plot. Rich saves money on expensive bots by using cheaper me: obedient little automaton. Plus he's dumb as fuck about tech. Doubt he could even think up a bot, let alone get it to work.

My digits tap rap clickety splat over the keyboard. Today my assigned keywords, straight from the horse's Dick himself, are 'wholesale fashion', 'wholesale clothing', 'wholesale dresses', 'wholesale sexy dresses', 'wholesale sexy fashion chic' and 'organic beauty'. I train my globes on the monitor but my ears are pricked for any impending chaos that may or may not involve me. You never can tell.

Also it's fucking cold in here. I once had a problem where the office suite was definitely freezing itself into a fridge but I was told to shut up or go home. Not a fiscal or institutional option for Conscripts.

Rick, Rich's enormous, sweaty second-in-command comes bumbling in about an hour later. 'Mornin'!' he says cheerily. We mumble a response. Rick is one step up from a Conscript. He is distantly related to Rich and is some kind of managerial mongrel but still has to grind more than Rich does. He seems like a nice, friendly bod on a good day but, you wait, he's actually a proper snide.

I carry on. My automatic stream of typing is wickedly relentless.

Half an hour later, Ryan scurries in with a slouch, clutching a cow-bound notebook and practically jogs to the clocker. He loves Employment and as a result he is Rich's favourite Conscript. Sometimes he stays until half seven or eight just so that he can carry on working, which is also why he's specially permitted to arrive late. A true Employer in the making. I much prefer being lazy. There is something to be said for the rebelliousness of laziness where I refuse refute and reject my ability to be properly productive. I just won't do it. Take that work. When it's over, it's over. It's best to know when it's time to go.

'Mornin Ryun', Marissa always says.

'Mornin', Ryan always replies nervously.

'How are yer?' she asks.

'Fine', Ryan always replies.

I don't know why she fucking bothers. I'd have given up expecting some kind of question about how I am ages and ages ago. He honestly doesn't give a flying fuck if she's good, bad or ugly. Either that or he's just so bloody absorbed in his Employment that he can't comprehend anything, any tiny weeny smidgy thing, outside of it. He sits down, shackles himself bleep bleep bleep bl-bleep with a happy sigh and is immediately under, his globes boring into the screen and he starts bouncing his leg up and down, as if he's some rabid dog humping his desk. When you love Employment that much I suppose all it takes is a new spreadsheet, a report doc or some backlinks to get you hot and heavy.

All of a sudden Rich bursts out of his cupboard office box barking down his ze-phone: 'Nouuh Ah don' fuckin care abou' that, you ge' that stockk here or this is off, totalleh off. Come on, be a man, be a fuckin man and let's do this propuh yeah? Let's do this propuh and make sure everythin is delivered, OK? What what what, what do yer mean Ah gotta pay yous Ah haven' even got it all yet! Everythin delivered and then we can put all this shit to fuckin bed. Are we coool? Yeah? We're coool?'

He pauses to laugh, a laugh loud and hollow. It takes his entire chest, choker and conk cavities to do it and the sound is coarse and cruel. There's not much to laugh about in the UK and any warmth has been sapped out of any laughs that still come from bellies, chokers, conks, gobs and arseholes.

He continues: 'Alrigh' and, yer know, Ah'm only doin'

what's fair yeah Ah gots bods askin abou' the Business and you know Ah think these things should be put to bed as soon as, yeah, put to bed. Marissuh, Marissuh love could you come heeyuh and help a minute? Thaanks love, come in heeyuh'.

Marissa unshackles herself with a bleeeeeeeep, keeps her globes down and walks to his office while Rich continues to whinge and moan down his blower. He slams the door to his office box loudly behind her.

Fashion is for the weekends, fashion is for your leisure time when you can float about the town wearing whatever you like. Conscript bods love fashion. You can look like Tiggy and Giggy and Figgy or whatever they're called; those Transcendents, the models that fill up the official UK ze-hologram boards all weeklong and then you can effortlessly emulate their effortless chic sexy style come the weekend. Little do all these fashionable foul-ups know about the bods, who are Conscripted all week for their chance to weedle into the next IT skirt at the weekend (a.k.a. official dress-down non-Uniform days), and that bulging bulbuous Rich has been pummelling my ears on a regular basis, deciding which wholesale clothes to buy and to sell onto everybod's favourite sweatshop-slave-style-shithouse retailer.

Congratulations boddos, you're wearing the fruits of a foul fat fart-arsed fuck-mug who likes to yell a lot and annoy me to death.

Marissa has been in there for fifteen minutes and Rich is becoming increasingly riled. From what I can tell, he's not on the ze-phone anymore but just berating her with an endless barrage of swearings and questions. Marissa isn't a pushover; every so often her fabulous, classic I-don't-give-a-fuck-but-don't-fucking-talk-to-me-like-that regional drawl can be heard interjecting or attempting to answer one of his spasmodic winding shouted questions.

I pop open a ze-email window and type out a message to Rachel in front. We all know that Rich can access the ze-email server and read all the ze-emails we send, but I don't care if he sees what I have to write. Every Business bod sees everything anyway because the UK and LAW FORCE grant Employers rights and laws to check and vet vital communications and in the end you stop giving a fuck because if they read something they don't like then it'll just be added to the lengthy list of other naughties you've committed and it's not like you aren't already chained to your desk. Oh wait. Irrational irritating sods, the lot of them. To be honest, I bet they'd be more pissed off if we weren't bitching about them. At least they're centre of attention now. Not being talked about, even by your Conscripts, is the real bind in Business you know.

- Can yuo hear that??
- *you
- *Yeah, what's he going on about?*
- Dunno. Poor Marissa though...
- *I know!*

All of sudden, she storms out and disappears out the door.

'Oh shiiit', says Rich, trying to bounce after her like an over-stuffed pooch trying to get up a hill.

Rich returns in ten minutes or so without Marissa.

'Er, Marissuh's on her lunch-break yeah gerrls. She's got a bit of a headache so Ah'm givin her some time to cooool off. Does that sound alrigh' with yous yeah?'

We murmur whatever.

At lunch, I unshackle myself bleeeeeep, clock out and then head towards the 'kitchen'. This depressing excuse for a culinary box is more of a crevice, located in the basement of the warehouse. To get there you walk through said warehouse, where rows and rows and columns and rows of cardboard boxes contain precious stock: the latest non-lined coat, a dress with more cut-outs than cut-ins, awful synthetic jumpers in too many arrays of gaudy colours and Old Groggy, the clapped up mechanical arm, who lingers quiet and rusty down one of the rows and you can see him looming about. Business is slow which is good for Groggy because he's all out of sorts. He can only manage to dash and grab a few boxes at a time, because he's all creaky and cranky and makes a fucking racket and then he can pretty much only pick and pack one box every two minutes or so. Way way slow. If he doesn't up his game, he'll go the same way as his wife Skeggy and she ended up in a skip.

I walk through the warehouse's half light and listen to the loud hum of the heater in there. It makes me laugh that the bod temperature of the clothes is more important to Rich than his poor Conscript things who have to shiver in that office suite all day. I walk down the stairs to the kitchen, with walls pasted a crispy, crusty white and turn into it. To compensate for the anti-social underground location, the kitchen is awash with metallic white lights, clinical and porous, the sort of lights that aim to make you look your very worst. If there had been a mirror to look in you'd be gaunt, verging on a grey/purple colour, your globes dull and dead and your hair lacking shape and life. A grimy old hob sits oozing and stinking of all sorts of old mouldy crap so nowadays it's the microwave that sees the most action. A breakfast bar runs along the length of the long white wall and there are no windows, not even boarded up ones. Think about a room box so white, so bright, so boggled down and effervescent with some kind of all-consuming crisis and you get the feel of that kitchen.

Marissa is sat in the corner facing the wall picking at her salad. I always have lunch with her. I'm not allowed with Lauren and Rachel. Rich is a divide and conquer type of Employer, no more chatting or Conscripts mingling than is necessary.

I get a tin of vegetable soup from the cupboard, heat it up and sit two chairs down from her.

Neither of us says anything.

I'm too curious about what happened earlier.

'What happened earlier?' I try.

'Ugh Rich', groans Marissa shaking her head. 'So fuckin stupid'.

'What do you mean?'

'Well Arch didn' send the right pictures through. Or wait, no, theh werrrre the right pictures, but Rich didn' like them. And then Arch is havin to re-shoot the new luxe boho tramp chic dresses and Rich was tryin not to peh him for the extruh Employment and then obviousleh it was all MAH fault that Ah hadn't spotted that the dresses weren' righ' in the first place. Ah think he forgets that Ah work in Customer Services and that Ah'm not his PA bot'.

'And what was all that about stock?'

'Well, Ah'm not entireleh sure, even though everythin's my fuckin fault these days', she says, stabbing a potato. 'It sounded like Rich hasn' received the stockk from some suppliyer or othuh and is refusin to peh them and theh're completleh mad with each othuh. Realleh professional right'.

'That is so dumb'.

'Did yous hear the bollockin Ah got?' she says, slamming her fork on her plate.

'Yeah'.

'What is his fuckin problem. Pisses meh riiight off...'

'I know right'.

'You know what he said before Ah left the office box?'

'What?'

'Don' get upset and leave because then that makes meh look bad, alrigh' love?'

'He didn't'.

'Yeah'.

'What a twat'.

Most of mine and Marissa's conversations revolve around Conscription, Employment, Rich and his fuckery. But I don't mind: there's always ample material to discuss. Plus it creates the resemblance of cool Conscript camaraderie between us which is nice.

I don't like to spend too long having lunch because I know Rich isn't paying me for it because he can't afford or be arsed to. So what I do is down my soup, clock myself in, shackle up bleep bleep bleep bl-bleep then turn my monitor as far away from the ze-CCTV camera as possible. I then use the remaining twenty minutes I'd have being unpaid on my lunch break, surfing and scouring the Internet for buzzy click click articles and still get actually paid for it. I don't feel guilty. Procrastination and laziness put two very large fuck off digits up to productivity and I will get away with it as much as I can. Plus, Ryan normally slopes off for lunch at around about the same time so there are fewer bods to pry. Can't do much about the ze-CCTV in the corner but whatever.

Rick comes in on the ze-phone theatrically feigning some accent. He gets 100 off an order and wheezy laughs a lot. Scammy jammy git. He sits at a random desk and starts clicking and flicking through some files on his computer.

The front doorbell buzzer thing peals throughout the office with a harsh electric peeeyarp.

Rich crashes into the main office suite again. 'Is Marissuh back yet love?'

'I think she's making a call'.

'Alrigh''.

Marissa comes back into the office.

'Hiyaaaaaa love', says Rich.

Marissa's shoulders flinch. 'Hi'.

'There's someone at the door, yeah, who is it?'

'Ah don' know, Ah was havin lunch'.

Rick is running his globes from top to bottom of Marissa's bod and is unconsciously chewing on his chops. Rich tramps to the ze-CCTV screen. He has about fifty different cameras on one screen in his office box so he uses the one in here to zoom in proper. It's a bit mad and paranoid and excessive to say the least all this filming.

'You know who tha' is love?'

'No'.

'Well, go down and have a look yeah?'

Marissa rolls her globes when she has her back to him and he calls after her, 'Thaaaaaaanks love'. Rick continues to gaze her down, his globes firmly glued to her arse.

She returns. 'It's a pizza bod down there. Ah told him to wait until Ah checked with yous-'

'Oh yeah', Rich cuts in, 'go and get it for mih then'.

Marissa's jaw tenses as she turns around again. 'And bolt the door after yerself love, make sure it's bolted tigh' yeah, we got to be careful who we let in yeah'.

Rick laughs at her.

Marissa returns holding the pizza box with a purposefully limp wrist.

'Thanks love, good gerrl'.

Lauren and Rachel in front of me are silently squirming. Marissa returns to her desk to shackle herself in bleep bleep bleep bl-bleep.

Rich comes back out. 'Marissuh Marissuuuuhhh. Any calls or messages or anything love?'

'No. Nothin', Marissa snaps, not looking away from her screen.

'Good work love, yeah, good work'.

He slams the door shut to his office box to gobble up his pizza. We all relax a bit.

*

At about 4pm we still have two hours left to go and I decide that, yup, this is an opportune time to ask Rich about getting paid.

I unshackle myself bleeeeeep and knock on his office box door.

'Yeahhh', he moans.

I open the door carefully.

'Come in love yeah. What's uhp?'

'Soz to disturb you-'

'It's OK love go on. What's uhp?'

It is so fucking cramped in here with all those fucking screens.

'I just wanted to ask you someth-'

'Go on yeah'

'Just quickly, you're probably bu-'

'Ah'm actualleh realleh buseh yeah love, Business takes a lot of time and effort yeah. It's alwehs non-stop, realleh importan' bein an Employuh yer know'.

'OK. I was wondering if you had managed to look into us lot getting paid yet?'

'Ah have paid yous', he says, sticking his bottom chop out and goggling his globes.

'No, you haven't. I haven't had a confirmation through from the Bank'.

'How is that MYUH problem, huh?'

'There hasn't been a confirmation because we haven't been paid. That's how it works'.

'RICK come in heeyuh pleeuse'.

Rick ambles in and immediately stares at my tits. I wish supernatural lazer beams could pan out and melt his globes into nasty bloody gloop and I could stomp all over them with my bovvers.

'Yeaaaaaah?'

'Have Ah or have Ah not pehd the gerrls?'

'Ah don' know, it depends...'

'Has Arge sorted out the accounts?'

'Ah'm not sure... what could have mucked things a bit was that big delivereh load from-'

'SHUT IT ABOWT THAT', Rich spits, giving me a ruthless glare.

'Sorreh mate, Ah don' know, Ah don' know...'

'Look, yous got to speak to Arge', Rich turns to me. 'Ah am makin it yer responsibiliteh to speak tah him. It's on you now that yeah love'.

'Arge comes in once a month, I barely see him'.

'Well you have a ze-phone, the ze-emails. Come on now love, yer want to get paid, yer need to talk to the accountan', simple as yeah, it's on yous that is'.

'I don't have the responsibility or the authority to sort out pay. You are our Employer'.

'Ah don't have time for this yeah', he barks, his globes narrowing impatiently. 'Is it just you who has a problem, yeah? Any of the other gerrls? Have yous all been talkin abowt this?'

'No, it's just me...'

'You sure it's just YOUR problem yeah?'

'Well, it's not just my problem-'

'Well yous can sort it out now yeah. Speak to Arge. Off yer go, back to work, both of yous. Stop wastin time. This is mah moneh yeah'.

Rick nods and immediately goes back to his desk to sit on his fat arse and grin about.

I pause. I bring the door to a close behind me but purposefully not enough for it to completely shut. It bounces back open with an eeeeeeeeeerrrrrrrkkk. Rich growls and groans and heaves himself up and slams it shut after me.

Teeheehee.

It's 4.30 pm and a car pulls up at the front. On the ze-CCTV a group of men get out of the car and press the buzzer. We all turn to look.

'Marissuuuuhhhhh', bawls Rich on cue, once again bumbling breathlessly from office. 'Who is it love?'

'I don' know'.

'Go and have a look yeah? The door's bolted riiight. Don' bring them uhp, tell them to wait yeah?'

'OK'.

Rick comes to the office. 'Do you think it's...?'

'Shiiit', says Rich, pulling out his ze-phone, scrolling through for a number before pressing it to his mug. 'Get her back uhp yeah, tell her not to let them in, no one's heeyuh'.

'Marissuuuuuuuuuuuh, Marissuuuuuuuuuuuh don' tell them we're uhp heeyuh yeah?'

'Wha'?'

'Don't tell them that yer Employuhs are heeyuh, OK, we don' know who theh are'.

'Oh, OK'.

'Well, technicalleh, Ah'm her Employuh Rick', mutters Rich, jabbing at his ze-phone. 'Yer jus' her managuh or somethin'.

'Alrigh' Rich', strops Rick. 'Marissuuuuuh tell 'em yer Employuh and yer managuh aren' heeyuh'.

I pop open a ze-email window to Rachel and type:

- What's going on?'
- *Dunno*
- All seems a bit dodge
- *Dunno, but I'm going out this evenign so it had better be alright.*
- Yeah.

(I wouldn't want to put it past them though. Rich probably has all sorts of things going on the side...)

- *evening
- *Yeah, he's so dodgy. Can't believe he's sending Marissa down to deal with them!!*

- I know right. Bloody chicken shit.

Marissa comes back up. 'Who is it love?' Rich asks, the ze-phone still squished against his ear and mug.

'Karl and Ford from one of the suppliyers-'

'SHIIIIIT don' let them in, alriiight, don' let them in. Say Ah'm not heeyuh OK, yeah? Thanks love, go on'.

Slightly unnerved, Marissa turns around and goes back downstairs.

The men hang about for a bit before jumping in their car, looked like some kind of pretty-car BMW or Audi, and then they just drive off.

5pm. Still an hour to go. I think about some of the luckier Conscripts who are permitted to leave their Employment right now and angrily grind my bovvers into the ground. I'm going to have to watch the minutes literally creep by as stupidly and sinfully slow as possible until I'll be able to burst into the night sky and sweep my way to the tramsmmuter. Why do we have to stay here until fucking six? Anybod who thinks they're being productive in the eighth hour of the working day is having a fucking laugh. You might be jamming away at the keyboard, sending all the ze-emails, counting stock, clearing your work space or doing a host of other inane items but you might as well be doing it in that dreamy space between being dead and alive and you're making a fucking mess I think you'll find.

6pm rolls round and I'm the first to jump up and leave. I unshackle myself bleeeeeeeeeep and bowl over to the clocker, my coat already on and bovvers ready for the standard crunch crunch crunch.

'Byeeeee!' I call cheerily.

The girls give a mumble jumble lukewarmish reply. Ryan says bye with wide bemused globes, unsure as to why exactly I'm leaving on time.

Best part of my bloody day this.

I open the barred indoor-gate that has kept us penned in and who bloody knows what penned out all day, and step out into the night air. It's dark outside with a crisp wind to lightly batter you in the mug. I shove my digits in my pockets and march past the rows, careful of the streets I take in case any pretty fat-cat-rat wagons are loitering and lurking about. I'm clomping and clumping along and I'm practically flying down the hill next to the main road while lanes of gridlocked traffic snake around the city Centre-For-Work into the outer burbs beyond the warehouses. I sweep into town to catch the tramsmmuter to take me south of the city Centre-For-Work. Every time I cross this bridge I feel the earth shift. Up loom the gleaming and glistening glass towers, still ablaze with artificial blue as Conscripts carry on at the mill, and hologrammed models on huge multi-dimensional rooftop billboards like Lily, Milly and Tilly who all wave and skip about from building to building. The clean streets are quiet and virtually empty, not even the Autogrammers are out for a cheeky snap. Conscripts and other lowly bods don't live here anymore because it is an exclusive Work Safe and Centre-For-Work zone. I keep my head down as I plummet and plough through the ravines and caverns, skating round the dark corners that unnerve me no bloody end but that are much less harsh on the globes than those bright, burning buildings and hologram boards. Why go down Turner Street and Thomas Street when you can go down Back Turner Street and Back Thomas Street? Inversions are so much more relatable and easier on the globes, even if they're a bit mucky. The wind whips around them creating an eerie ethereal whistling. I stop for a second and realise that I'm panting and my back and armpits are getting hot. I want to carry on because the burn in my leg muscles and the built up nervous energy in my bovvers after a long day of being shackled are eager to stomp, stretch and gallivant through the deserted streets. For all its brite lites and buzzing hives of glass and steel, Manc looks and feels cold and vacant. With an unnerving pang, I long for the weird tangible reality of the grim and grubby red bricks of the warehouse, prison and brewery of Strangeways. The holy trinity of Grub. I look up, let the wind whip my mug and I feel like I might as well be standing in a graveyard made of glass.

I board a tramsmmuter home and wank all evening.

1.2

Back again.

I splish slip splosh and squish my way back up into the gaping arse of Strangeways. It's like the evenings don't even happen, completely unconscious. I've crossed the bridge, nodded at the Asian dude and scurried down a side street. A pretty-car is lounging with a shady figure inside. I scan for a brick but there are none when you need one to fulfil your greatest frisk. I slouch past, my knuckles tightly clenched in my pocket. I glance out of the corner of my globe into the darkened window and see the silhouette of a lanky head bobbing up and down and a toad gurgling with his goggly wogglies rolling. Can't help but think it's a bit early for that shenans.

No imminent fuckery coming my way from greedy yuck-fuck so I keep on.

Rich is late again. I wait. Marissa is late too. Rick eventually pulls up in a pretty-car that's too small for his fat arse and lets the grates up.

'Alrigh'?' he smacks his chops into a swarmy smirk.

'Yeah'.

'Good deh of work comin up, yeah. Good good good'. His brows wobble. 'Very brave to bring uhp peh to Rich', he says following me up the stairs trying to catch my bum at the best angle.

'What?'

'In his office yesterdeh, when yer asked abou' moneh'.

'Oh, yeah'.

'Need yer moneh don' yer'.

'It's my right'.

'Well yer know yer rights don' yer. Good thing too, so you can get what yer want'.

I don't really know where this conversation is going. I nod anyway, clock myself in, march to my desk and I shackle in bleep bleep bleep bl-bleeeeep.

'Good to see yer shackled Ah think', Rick clocking in and ambling over. 'Don't want yer gettin too into yer rights, don't want yer to get all riled'. His globes are wide and his tongue lolls a bit when he finishes his sentences. I grind my gnashers and fix my globes on the screen. Type tip tap tap tappy-dappy-doo.

One by one, Rachel and Lauren arrive and shackle up. Rachel gives me a slight smile and I nod my head. Ryan slopes in too.

There's no Marissa for the morning routine:

'Mornin Ryun'.

'Mornin'.

'How are yer?'

'Fine'.

Rich bumbles in on the blower, yelling and swearing 'shit fuckin fuckin fuck'. He sees us sitting down and glances at the sound system. He taps off the call on his ze-phone, turns his screen to a remote volume control and yanks it up to the max. He does that from his office a lot too. Fucking terrifying when you don't expect it when your churning out your content and all of a sudden it's like WAAAARGHHHHHH. Maybe it's those bods on the ze-phone again from yesterday that he doesn't want us hearing or knowing about.

Five minutes later Marissa enters with a limp. Rich has finished on the phone and practically pounces on her.

'Where you bin love? Late arrren' yeh'.

'Sorreh'.

'Didn' say yous could be late did Ah? What am Ah supposed to do when yous are late?'

'Sorreh'.

'Well, can' happen again love can it. Though' you was bettuh than that. Yer gonnuh have to knock some time of yer lunch. That or it'll come out of yer peh yeah'.

'OK'.

This isn't like Marissa, who can hold her beef with any

doss twatty stunt that Rich or Rick try to pull. For some reason the salt has been knocked out of her. She doesn't look at anybody as she shackles up and starts to check her ze-emails. She's sad.

'Aneh messages Marrisuh? Aneh messages love?' Rick pipes up.

'No'.

'Alrigh'. Good gerrl'.

My globes flick constantly to Marissa. I don't expect her to look at me, and she doesn't, but I'm trying to work out what's going on, what happened.

'WHYUH isn' the fuckin screen on?!' Rich suddenly demands. No one answers. He's talking about the huge 85 inch screen that fills the left wall of the suite, right next to his office box. On it is an analytics page that has a map on it and graphs and statistics, showing site traffic and views. Normally the numbers are pretty low so Rich likes to use it to incentivise us to work harder, even though we're already chained to our desks and we're not allowed to chat.

'Come on gerrls, we need the screen yeah', he scolds, punching buttons and gaping at the screen as it flashes on. Nothing much happens. A graph pops up with a spotty UK map with dots that show the whereabouts of bods who are looking at the site.

'Keep an eye on the numbuhs yeah Ryun'.

'Oh yeah, Rich, yeah', Ryan jitters back.

Seems pretty bloody pointless when apparently only twelve bods are online. Every other bod is otherwise Conscripted. I suppose my copy content crap isn't having the desired effect but it's hardly my fault when everyone we're trying to sell to is busy Conscripting and it's nowhere near lunchtime buying time yet and actually I don't care anyways. Rich rarely takes notice of his figures however much he hammers on about them. I'm safe.

The sound system is booming and I'm boredly whizzing through my content. Keywords today: 'bandage dresses' 'sexy fun dresses' 'tight skirts', 'hot wholesale leggings' and 'ethical fashion'. Makes for some lively copy cat.

Rick ambles about constantly and keeps glancing over. Marissa pays no attention and just carries on typing emails and quietly answering any calls that come her way.

At lunchtime, I find Marissa sat glum and quiet on the far corner of the breakfast bar dangerously close to the white grimy wall. I rummage about for some veg soup for two moments before sitting next to her whilst it stews, simmers and spits in the microwave.

'How's your mornin goin?' she asks.

'Fine'.

'Good'.

'How's your morning going?'

'Been bettuh'.

'Oh. What's happened?'

'Got shoved abou'. Nothin major'.

Ah. That figures.

'Again?'

'Yeah. Ah mean, it's not like Ah'm not fuckin used to it. But yeah. Things got a bit scarier todeh'.

'What do you mean?'

Marissa pauses and keeps her globes firmly on her food before stating, 'Theh threatened to Unrecognise meh'.

Seems pretty bloody unfair and OTT. I get my veg soup out of the microwave.

'Why? They can't just Unrecognise you'.

'Well, yesterdeh Ah was carrying an umbrelluh and todeh Ah wasn't, so theh though' Ah was obscurin somethin yesterdeh'.

'But it was raining. LAW FORCE can hardly stop you from doing that'.

'Yes theh can'.

'I don't get it'.

Marissa smiles bitterly. 'Well you wouldn' because yer not black. Yer not always 'up to somethin''.

'I'm more up to something than you are'.

'Ah fuckin KNOW, it's so unfair', she laughs bitterly. 'You come into this place lookin like a bloodeh rag sometiiimes'.

'Thanks'.

'No worries'.

'I just didn't think...'

'Yeah, not menneh white bods do'.

'Sorry.

'Whatevuh'.

'So are they watching you all the time?'

'No, but there's a scabbeh stupid Autogrammuh bint who likes to foller meh for a bit when Ah'm on the weh to work. He's workin for LAW FORCE like most of the rest of them, but he's realleh snide with it. Sees it like an opportuniteh to prove himself or somethin by pickin on meh. He was lurkin about when LAW FORCE dropped in on mih on mah way to work'.

'Ew'.

'Yeah. But it's fine,' she says turning back to her lunch, 'Ah can' let that rule my life because that means theh'd be winnin'.

'Sounds pretty difficult to me'.

'Well what choice do Ah have?'

'None I bet'.

'Right. And especialleh after my crap deh yesterdeh as well. Just mah luck'.

I slurp some soup.

'So, are you feeling better?'

'Ah am actualleh,' she nods, 'Ah've been lookin into this suppliyer business with Rich and Rick because what happened yesterdeh was just too weeyud'.

'Oh. Found anything yet?'

'Well Ah'm just goin back through the old orduhs and bills but Ah don' have access to the accountin email inbox, so Ah'm goin manualleh through everythin on the e-commerce platform'.

'Sounds complicated'.

'It's not too bad. Ah think it's goin to take a little while but I should get it done by the end of todeh. Sayuls have been pretteh quiet, so it's not like Ah'm bizzeh'.

She pauses.

'Plus Ah realleh don' mind. Ah know that one deh, Ah want to be an Employuh'.

I gulp.

'Why?'

'Ah want to have my own Business and run it fair and propuh, like dad's Employuh. It's not like Rich is goin to show meh any of this stuff so Ah migh' as well learn it for mihself'.

'You know how rare it is that Conscripts become Employers?'

'Yeah'.

'You have to be given one of those Donations and an Appointment. Not just anybod can do it'.

'Wha's that suppose' ta mean?' she snaps.

'Nothing'. I shake my head.

'And anyweh Ah fuckin know, OK, Ah know', she mutters frowning. 'But Ah will, Ah bloodeh will. Ah realleh want to, Ah want to learn, get mihself out of this shit'.

'What do you want your Business to be? In fashion?'

'No, not at all. Ah think probableh somethin to do with health, like a physiotherapeh thing or bod conditionin', sellin treatments, Ah don't know'.

'That's interesting'.

I am not convinced that being an Employer makes you any less miserable or a dog to the UK than being a Conscript. But at least Marissa would be in charge, able to take control of something. I would want the same too, but I really just don't care about Business or any of that shit.

'Well at any rate', she smiles to herself, 'at least that fuckin Autogrammuh would leave me alone! Him and all those LAW FORCE fuckers'.

At around 2pm things are apparently looking up in as busy a Business sense as possible. All of a sudden there's a big sharp spike in the number of bods who are on the site. It turns out one of my articles on 'sexy Friyay dresses' has gone viral because Flo, Clo, Ro or one of those other models snapped themselves in a similar style somewhere someplace last week and hashtagged our keyword and now the rest of the UK wants to nod to the same inimitable style once the next weekend rolls around. Rich looks like he's going to sing or something else mad when he sees that the number of hits reaches above 50. Can't believe his fucking luck.

'Riiiiiiiiiiiiiiiiiiiiiiiiiick', he pipes, his globes goggling wide and his tum jiggling about as he hops from one foot to the other. 'Come and look at this mate. Keeps goin uhp!'

Ryan is hovering over his chair in excitement and looks like a pooch with worms whilst the rest of the girls uniformly turn their heads to look at the screen.

Rick eventually wobbles in and assumes a Knobby Know-It-All stance, his globes are a similar size of goggle, nodding, pointing, rubbing his cheeks and saying, 'Well, hum, yeah'.

'This is great yeah, Rick, Ryun, gerrls, there's some bods down South, look down there'.

'Yeah Rich, yeah'.

'This is so good, nevuh had this before have we yeah?'

'No, yeah, no'.

He turns to me. 'You did this didn' yer, what was the keywords?'

'Um, 'sexy Friyay dresses''.

'Ah knew that was a good one, Ah knew it! HahahahaHA good gerrl good gerrl, yer've done a realleh good job yeah Ah'm impressed with that, you could go real real far. Sky's the limit love. Yeah we gotta get a lot of sayuls offa this yeah?'

He whips out his ze-phone and starts taking snaps and vids of the hit-ticker's numbers going up and up.

'Well, yeah, I suppose so yeah', says Rick.

'HohoHO this will keep that lot off our backs with all these sayuls, we'll ring Arge up straigh' and tell them we can transfer moneh before the rest of the stockk even arr-'

'Rich Rich, them, the gerrls...'

'Oh right, yeah, sure. Stop listenin gerrls, rude to be noseh innit, watch yerselves. This is Business, Business. So, Rick mate where should all the sayuls be appearin huh?'

At this, Ryan jumps up and lollops over to the screen, eager to get in on the praise and recognition. 'Heeyuh, Rich, HEEYUH!' he garbles pointing at a plain pathetic black bag icon in the bottom right hand corner. When a purchase is made, it jiggles about.

'Alrigh' then, so how do we know when the sayuls have been made and gone through and all that?'

Rachel and Lauren glance at one another, raising their brows subtly. The fact that the Employer of his own Business doesn't know how his own sales go through is pretty hilarious.

But for Ryan, it's a perfect opportunity.

'Well Rich, it's quite simple', he says, demonstrating flamboyantly with outstretched hands and digits. 'Images of ze-pound signs will juhmp into the bag, effectiveleh visualleh indicatin that moneh has been spent and a purchase has been made'.

'What?' Rich turns to Rick.

'Look yer'll see it when it happens', he replies.

'Well it's not happening yet Rick!'

'It will, it will yeah'.

'But Ah can' see aneh ze-signs or pound bags doin nothin'.

'Yeah well, it will Rich, theh're probableh lookin now anyways'.

A few minutes pass. The number of hits peaks at around about 112 and then slowly starts to drop off. The black bag remains still and silent. No ze-pounds come anywhere near it. Rich is getting a little fidgety, still clutching his ze-phone and training it on the lifeless non-jiggly icon.

'Come on, theh're all goin. Whyuh aren' theh spendin?'

'Well maybeh there's a problem with the system...' Ryan says, sounding slightly panicked and returning to his screen to roll up a report page of statistics and graphs and shit.

'Whyuh aren' theh spendin huh Rick?' Rich turns threateningly on Rick, even though Rick is much taller and rounder. The smug stance has wavered and now his digits are in his pockets and he's scuffing his feet into the floor, refusing to meet Rich's globes with his own. He's gurns grotesque instead.

'She's done her job Rick yeah bro', Rich points at me with his ze-phone, 'she's a good gerrl, did a good job, she got bods heeyuh in the first place. She got us them hits, so WHYUH aren' them, those bods, actualleh spendin? It's not hard is it, we got the website re-designed and everythin'.

'Yeah Ah know Rich but sometimes these things take time-'

'Nothin takes time no more alrigh', we have no time, there is no time for nothin. If them bods wanted to buy then theh would have done and now theh're all gone. LOOK', he snaps, waving at the screen as the hit-ticker reaches 68.

'Summin's not right bro, this is all wrong. I'm not happeh Ah am NOT happeh'.

'Well, maybe the links weren' workin or something-'

'If theh hadn' been workin, yeah, that means theh wouldn' have reached the site in the first place, yeah?' Rich looks to Ryan for reassurance and he nods and pants in return.

'Well, maybeh theh just don' like the clothes'.

'Well that's our fuckin job bro, we buy clothes so that bods want them and buy them, what's the fuckin point otherwise yeah? You fuckin idiot'.

'Now don' talk to meh like that Rich'.

'That was a golden opportuniteh Rick mate and we haven' even sold nothin'.

Ryan pipes up timidly, 'Well maybeh it's because we sell

wholesale and the only bods who came through aren' retailuhs'.

'Yes you got it!' Rich squeals before double-taking. 'But how do we get them retailuhs to come to the site?'

'Um. Ah'm not sure'.

Rich is about to burst.

'Look yous two, your fuckin jobs are about buyin clothes and marketin them yeah, WHYUH isn't it workin? If yous don' fuckin know then what the fuck are we suppose' to do. This is a fuckin shambles and Ah'm goin to have to realleh think about the future now, what to do next, yeah, because this is not good, not good'.

'Now there's no need to seh that', says Rick as a single bead of sweat begins to skim down the back of his big thick choker.

'Ah mean Rick, it's not like Ah can' replace yous yeah, if Ah don' know what yer doin all day, pissin mah moneh all over the shop... we have BODS to peh for fuck's SAKE. Get out my sight Rick yer a fuckin twat'.

With that Rich storms into his office box. Rick goes after him and bangs on the door, 'Open up yeah, Rich, mate. Come on, don' be like that'.

Ryan looks like he might cry. I glance at Marissa and her chops are curling up. Rick glares in my direction and flumps out of the suite. Probably gone to wallow in some dingy corner of the warehouse with all his crap clothes. Fat prat.

I hope my so-called good work keeps me out of the spotlight for a bit. I hope they ignore me, just let me get on in peace. I want my Employer to have as little to do with me as possible. Remote please remote. You know I'm doing a good enough job for your shitty pile of wack so back the fuck off.

A couple of hours slime by and I decide to go for a piss. Rich's office box is on the other side of the wall so you can try to listen in to the bitching and gossiping on the other side (us gerrls are normally the reasons why things are going too well in the Business) and sometimes I like to push harder than usual when I fart and shit so that my parps and plops are as awkwardly and embarrassingly audible as possible. That's right you fucks, gerrls shit and fart fart fart too. I unshackle myself bleeeeeeeeeep.

I leave the office suite and turn left towards the toilet box next to Rich's office. As I stomp through the rails, I catch a glance of a dark shape hunched up amongst the clothes. I carry on towards the loo but can't believe what I think I've seen so I turn back to the rack of bright and bubbly sequinned party miniskirts. Rick is curled up like a cross between a goblin and pluffed up plump chicken, his brow wrinkled and his chops pouting. Pathetic. His dark tracksuit forms a dark and fugly contrast to the eye-watering shades of the miniskirts, heightening the absurdity of whatever this is. I mean, if you're in a mood, go outside, kick some windows in, stab a pillow, scream in your wardrobe or switch some other bod's radiators off, don't just boil and bubble in the fucking corner like a fucking gammy brat. Our globes meet and I avert mine instantly so that I can try and skim over this very weird and repulsive sitch. Rick clambers up, 'Not shackled uhp no more eh'.

This isn't exactly a question so I decide to raise my brows in agreement and swivel away towards the toilet box.

'You think yer so damn clevuh don't yeh. Now Rich likes yer bettuh too'.

'OK'.

'Didn' use to, you know, said you was only temporeh and had to prove yerself in work. Rich said that, he did'.

'Right'.

'Well, looks like yous done that now yeah and now Ah'm in trouble. Rich doesn' want mih aroun in work no more instead. Not realleh fair now is it'.

'Um'.

'You think yous so clevuh, so smart, with yer rights and yer hits but yer not bettuh than meh, yer hear, you are NOT bettuh than MEH'.

I'm at the door of the toilet box. I turn and look him dead in the mug. He's much much taller than me but I fix my globes straight and stern.

'Let's put this to bed right now YEAH let's put this to bed. You bettuh watch yerself from now on yer stupid little twat'.

I pause for a moment. I bare my gnashers and snarl at him.

'I don't give a flying fuck you fat choud. I need to piss so go fuck off and fuck yourself'.

I turn into the toilet box and close the door.

A second later, before I've had a chance to lock it, he barges in after me with a muffled crash and a thump, slamming a big sweaty paw over my gob and pushing me back into the toilet box and the sink. I think I know what's coming and I really really don't want it to happen. He brings his mug right up to mine and hisses, 'Need to teach yous a lesson don't I, you little piece of Conscript shit, yous no bettuh than mih, yous no better than mih, who the fuck do you think you are, bitch, rat, little muckeh shite'. I try to gnash my gnashers against his palm but they just slip right off. I scrape at his arms and hands, feeling his skin and hair getting caught in my nails as I flail manically at this hulking heft of man-beast. He smacks my head into the grey mirror, crunching my whole mug hard with his paw and then yanks me round and starts undoing my jumpsuit with one hand, hissing curses and insults at me like some I'm some manky witch, 'slut slut slut Conscript scum'. Jumpsuits aren't easy accessibility which is one of the reasons why I like them so much but my protective back fabric is nothing compared to his groping clumsy fat greedy digits and I'm horrified and scared and I want to scream and yell as he undoes his chunky belt and rubs a hand down my back and uncovers my arse and I'm shaking with rage and fear and I meet my own desperate strained globes in the mirror and we're trying to blot out the image of his pulsing purple disgusting thing that bounces and throbs and seems so pathetic and meek compared to his bulging hairy scabby arms that gag me and catch my gob and strain on my hair and choker so that I can hardly breathe and I hate him I hate him I hate him I hate him I hate him I hate him I hate him I hate him I hate him I scrunch my globes shut as he grips my hips and rubs his thing and prepares to shove it in, his thing, his stupid stupid stupid thing, brushing his fat club digits over my cunt and I'm at the brink, I'm at the fucking brink and I squirm and scream but there's nothing nothing left to do so I scrunch my globes tighter and tighter and tighter, absorbing the dark and I imagine my cunt, my cunt is a vice and it is squeezing and crushing his useless thing a nothing a nothing to my steely steely cunt and I can see him he's confused and upset because I'm squishing and squashing his thing, nowhere to go as it ends up a pulpy purple mess that splats on the floor and he's crying and howling and he's calling me a bitch and a slut and a Conscript but I keep my globes on him and squelch my bovver into the squidge and I don't care because his thing is gone and my cunty cunting cunt did it.

He starts to moan but it isn't a moan of propsective pleasure or dominance or power or control or enjoyment. And coming to think of it my pelvic muscles are feeling really fucking tight. It's disgust. He's disgusted. 'What the fuck...' He pulls back his digits from my cunt and we look at them at the same time and he freezes. Blood covers his digits, thick clotty blood, not a gush not a rush but a kind of ample blobby blood that screams PERIOD. I reckon that I am about due and the sudden onset of my period probably explains why I had such a rampant and charged and absolutely fucking satisfying wanking session last night. I don't know how he's going to play this. Rapists and assaulters and violent pigs I'm sure are so patho so gobbly that I can't imagine a bit of blood would freak them out and make them stop but then again I'm not so sure. I stare at the blood and he gapes at it in horror, 'ugh ugh UGH UGH' he breathes headily, his globes popping at me a glorious abject cunty woman and he can't deal with it, he can't deal with my rosy red discharge and he's flinging his thing around and there's no loo roll because Rich always forgets to keep the women's toilet box well stocked and he releases my gob and hips and I collapse against the sink and turn slowly starting to creep my pants and my jumpsuit back over me as he's still flailing about and before I zip myself up I slowly reach a hand down my pants and rub my cunt and bring it up to my mug and see it smudged and smeared with sticky warm and friendly blood, my blood my smell my thickness and I look from my blood to him and his mug is contorted in disgust because he can't deal with me and my own so I look at him in fear, in anger, in defiance, in powerlessness and I slowly dip my tongue into the gloop and I love its sweet tang so I lick my palm and lick and thank the fuck of fucks for this period that stopped him and his horrible thing, I lick I lick and begin to smile and laugh as I coat my chops in beautiful bloody gore and his brows are raised as I laugh and I choke with laughter and shriek to freak him out and now he thinks I'm completely fucking crazy and he might hit me in fright so I raise my palm in front of me to ward him off. GET BACK. BACK BACK BACK. He scrambles out of the bathroom box with a dithering, vengeful shocked and appalled expression and I shut and lock the door firmly behind him.

I breathe.

I brush some stray tears that have crept from my globes with my sweet bloody hand.

I look at my reflection and see our mug half covered in red.

I bite and chomp on my tongue.

I fill the basin with warm water.

My tum groans.

I piss.

I wash my mug.

I leave the toilet box a few minutes later and venture back

into the office suite.

Everything is as delightfully dull and silent as usual, except for the booming music. This must have obscured the noise of what just happened and must be why no one came to help. Not that anybod would have helped anyway. Would I have helped? I had my own precious bloody cunt.

Rick is sat at a desk pale and paltry staring at his computer screen, his big bland bulky back is hunched and insecure. He notices me walk by him. I get past him as quickly as I can. I still have a few fragments and flecks of blood stuck under my finger nails and feeling them, knowing that they are there is quite comforting. His globes dart side to side as I walk past.

I get back to my desk and shackle myself up bleep bleep bleep bl-bleep. I get my digits out ready to start typing but they're shaking. Shaking too much to do anything. I lower my head and rest it in my hands as that stupid music pounds and pounds and pounds.

My womb really really hurts.

I squirm about in my seat trying to crunch it to a stop then I lengthen my hams out in front of me to try and stretch out the pain. But then I'm glad I'm in pain, I'm glad I'm hurting because concentrating on this pain is the only thing stopping numb shock and fear and disbelief from taking over everything.

I don't know how long I sit there, feeling the cramps spread up my back and down my thighs and there's nothing else for it.

'Marissa?' I whisper.

She keeps on typing nodding her head from side to side in time with the music.

'Marissa!' I hiss.

Her globes flash at me.

'Got any ibu?' I gob.

She nods, rustles about in her bag and whips out the painkillers. She pulls out a tampon as well and raises her brows.

I nod in reply.

She passes it and the pack of ibu into my shaking hand.

She frowns inquiringly.

I shake my head.

Ryan has caught sight of the tampon and is gaping at us like a fish.

Marissa rolls her globes.

I inch my chair back and unshackle bleeeeeeeeeeeep.

It's like a siren call. Rich launches out of his office clutching his phone 'What you doin unshackled from yer desk love yeah? Ah know yer did good todeh but there's alwehs more work to do yeah alwehs more and Ah know yer've done real well yer got them hits, all them hits, but this is a platform yeah we move uhp from this. We got much more to do much more to do yeah for the Business, we need sayuls. No time for not workin. No time for standin abou".

'I need to put this in', I mumble quietly, showing him the tampon.

Ryan gapes more. Rick audibly gags. Rich's brows have disappeared into his stubbly head of stubble.

'Ah right, love, yeah Ah see, Ah um, yeah, off you go, yeah, Ah mean you sort yerself out yeah ok Ah just, Ah, Ah am going to call them lot again'. He backs into his office box.

I return to the toilet box, which feels cramped and close and trapping amd my tum feels like it's going to practically plunge out of my arse. As soon as the tampon is in place, I slam the door and scarper out as quickly as I can.

*

5pm. I feel bitter and ultra-shit. Most of all I feel hollow and empty.

These are new: my tum has settled into all kinds of strange knots. Never ending or beginning, they're winding and winding, in and out and deep and dark into my gut. They're setting off all kinds of creaks and groans and I feel sick sick sick. Never felt anything like it. All my sickness and pain is being wrung out in my belly and I feel like I might shit and vom all at once.

The sun is setting fast and the dank murky dark of Strangeways will soon gobble me up as I walk away from this shitstore. It makes me want to quake even though I normally like the idea of stretching my legs and stompy crunching in my bovvers down the hill and across the bridge.

The ibu has kicked in so the ache in my womb is going away so all I'm left with is the numbness and fear.

I see Rick sitting there like a fat old useless lump and his thing has been out and about ready to stab and jab me and even though my gorgeous cunt got him back I feel nervous and sick and anxious and furious and all I can think about is the Irwell. I want to wade and wash and sink away all this fucking horror.

Ryan is humping his desk again whilst tapping his feet to the latest crap coming from the sound system and I want to throw the whole fucking thing, speakers and holograms and all, at his thick fat fucking head so that his brains run all over his keyboard.

I see a flicker in front of me: Marissa has leant back, is looking at her screen and giving it a confirmatory sigh and a nod. She looks at Rick, then back to her screen, then to Rick again and then back to her screen. She puffs out her cheeks with disbelief, hits the keyboard for the printer and then unshackles herself bleeeeeeeeeeeeep.

She goes to the printer and takes what looks like a report in her hands. It looks like she's onto those fuckers. I would wait around for a while afterwards to hear what she's found out but she takes more time to leave than me and I don't hang about for anybod and plus I've got some serious shit stifling and stuffing my mind and guts and I want out even more than usual.

At 6pm on the dot I'm unshackled bleeeeeeeeeeeeep and give one last withering scowl at Rick's fat back as I shuffle towards the door. He's sweating again. There's dark marks fanning out and spreading in the creases of his choker and under his pits. He doesn't even notice me because he is too absorbed looking at some kind of stocklist and email thread with loads of exclamation marks and asterisks and capital letters all over it, which pisses me off because I want his mug to turn green at the thought of me and my cunt. I want him to feel my disgust and pain and numbness but he's nowhere even close.

I patter out of the place.

I step outside and the wind rattles the warehouses. The brewery behind looks fucking grim and the prison is a perfect match. I feel sick and tired and angry. This whole bitching bitch isn't my fault it's not fair, it's not fair and I feel guilty. But I don't want to. I won't. I decide a freak act of violence will settle my tum and so I don't head straight for the trammsmuter but circle around Strangeways in the dark for a while looking for inspiration. I see it. A mangy mouldy cat struts stealthily in front of me in the pompous and preened way only a cat knows how. I grunt at it and pounce into its pathway. It sneers at me with its fatty cynical globes, knowing I'm more disgusting and dank than it is. I hiss and hold its gaze. It blinks, pauses, then poshly places a paw in front and tries to prince and ponce off, its tail in the air and flashing its arsehole at me.

You twat, I'll fucking have you.

I take a sudden run up and boot the blinking blonking block off of that fowl fucking fuck and it MAAAAAAAAAAAA-AAAAOOOOOOOOOOOUOOOOWWWWWWWWWWS SSSSSSSSS into the night arcing pathetically and not as high as I thought I was capable of and lands with a thud and skid about 5m down the street. It scrabbles and limps off and I exhale. It feels good but nowhere good enough. I still feel the guilt. I still feel the shame.

My knots, these Rick-induced knots, squirm and tighten in my tum.

There's only one thing for it: Montmorency and Monk.

I need Memory Foam and I need to brush my gnashers.

1.3

Montmorency's flat is about a twenty minute stride from the city Centre-For-Work and it is almost guaranteed that Monk will be there too. Montmorency is fairly flexible about flakey friends dropping by so I make headway in the direction of his block.

He's a lucky bugger who was chosen to go straight from the Academy to the poly-versity, bagged exclusive Employment at the poly-versity after grad and now he works in the Policy Marketing department. It's an educational interest corporate Employer that affords extra luxuries and status to alumni Conscripts so, for example, they actually let him work remotely. This means he always has the flat ready and welcome for any fleeting visitors who rock up in all manner of states and dress every night. The ideal host and hilarious to boot, no wonder he's Popularity Knocks. I need to be looked after and he is a great go-to in a crisis.

Instead of heading to the trammsumuter, I dodge my way past Shudehill, clutching my tum to relieve the knots, barrel through the fronts and backs of the glossy and grimy inversions of the NQ and bound across the aggressive concrete jungle of Piccadilly Gardens, with the holograms and interactive advertising boards for the kids to play with at the weekend. There go Taylor, Faylor and Waylor skipping over the roofs, swishing and swaying in their summery textures and hues while the rest of us shake shiver rattle and roll in the damp dank drab. Where once Times Square and Piccadilly Circus were mere novelties, now every city that thinks itself a city has granted itself specially certified advertising attractions that fill the city Centre-For-Work with bright and bursting boards. I cast a wary glance at the Autogrammers clustered outside the Starbucks mega-shop and dip down the rich tasty backstreets of China Town. The thing is, big shiny buildings cast the most illustrious shadows. They fester, they're ripe, full of down and outs and gurgling gutters but you can exist safely out of the light with whatever dreamer's disease you've opted to wallow in. Darkness and obscurity can be the best friends you'll ever make: thank fuck for shimmery shiny office blocks and shotels and scrapers and drinkies pricking everything in sight and creating good alt-sport for the rest of us. In China Town the pungent delicious smells of food clashes and commingles with the foulish stench of the drains and fisheries. Sleeping karaoke bars lounge idle until later at night when the snappy neon lights will punch the dark night and a healthy hefty bright glow rings around the quarter. China Town plays with the senses in a blinding hypnotic way: one street the most blinding bright bottomless bit you've ever seen, with scrummy bakeries and takeaways and drinkies and everything else; then off again: dark, drains, shadows and parlours, shifty and guttural before the lights snap back on. Not yet though. Too early. I scooch past the dramatic ornamental arch that is already lit up with bright orange lights.

I emerge onto Portland Street and wait to cross with a horde of other shuffly Conscripts, some with dead globes, some with not, some with dark circles denting their cheeks, some not, some with tired and worn hair, some not. All in their Uniforms. Streams of pretty-cars are passing by ferrying Employers and other officials home and then there are the stuffy trammsmuters and coaches laden with Conscripts who are heading out to the burbs. After a while, an automatic lollipop lets us flood across the street and I dip out of the crowd through the backstreets of the Village which, unlike China Town, knows no semblance of an off switch. The lights are on on on and the drinkies never close and the clubs always boom and there's constant noise and commercial chaos. Here's the thing. Capital UK loves and hates its gays in its own particular way that is different to the way it treats other Others, like Marissa and her brushes with LAW FORCE. This is a fragile place. Sexually fluid bods are totally commercially viable, the men more than the women obviously, and I don't know any bod who doesn't get with any bod and every bod. But still, they, we, are boxed into this bright narrow patch of Mancunian earth where there and there alone we can actually mingle and move safe and happy blinded by all the lights. Montmorency rarely goes there. He thinks it's fun but oppressive. Easily invaded by thugs and phobes and capital. I go wherever. Wherever's right on the night.

I move past the clubs and shotels and underground spas until I emerge onto Princess Street. I cross the canal which is lit up and on fire itself with neon lighting and rippling bods. From there I shoot down towards Montmorency's block. It's next to the infamous Factory which forms the last post of the Village's noisy eternal patch, constantly humming and thumping in steady steady time. The Conscripts there have to work for much longer, sometimes only emerging from the Factory three days after they last went in. It's OK though because they get paid a lot and it's the choice some bods choose to make.

Montmorency's in the closest block a Conscript can possibly get to the city Centre-For-Work. Nothing for us straight out of the Academy into Conscription bods. I am always slightly jealous of Montmorency because he is a bit older than me, went to the poly-versity and is a graduate of the arts and humanities area and knows a lot about a lot and a lot about bods in general. I swear he can speak a different Academic language and is always taken very very very seriously by other poly-versity bods. But I just know him as fun old Mont. I first met him legless at Satan's Hollow and I was having a shitter of a night on my bloody one and he scooped me up, he was generous, fun and up for a laugh. We kept seeing each other out and about and so we decided to be party bods together.

Having said all this, Montmorency and I actually tread similar paths of the not-so obscene copy cat, the content curator, specialising in endless spiels of bull bull bull. So you know, we all end up in the same place.

I reach the door to Montmorency's and remember that I've forgotten the code to get in so I hover about near the entrance until some bod comes along to let me in and I tailgate that shit. There's another keypad at the lift because you can never be too careful about who's decided to get into the building to have a wander about or a sleep. I don't want to waste any more time waiting for another bod to let me into the lift so I go towards the stairs. The Conscripts here keep the door to the stairs perpetually unlocked which throws shit in the mug of the lift keypad any way and it really is very tiring how the Landlords try to make the little bods sweat and I think they're all a bunch of fuckers.

Montmorency's flat box is on the sixth floor so I start to heave myself and my big big bovvers up the fluorescently lit stairs, you know, those bright blueish lights that make everything look crap on purpose and the breezeblock walls make you feel like a piece of breezeblock yourself as you trudge up up up forever and a fucking day. By the time I get to his floor I'm panting ever so slightly and enjoying the sharp burns that are rippling up and down my legs and back because they're distracting me from the Rick-knots. I crick my choker on each side and stomp up to his door. I ring the electric bell and on cue five seconds later, he opens the door graciously.

Uniform

Head: Top hat perched elegantly

Bod: Undecipherable T-shirt underneath a richly knitted black jumper.

Legs: Navy jeans

Feet: Bosch bovvers.

'Oh HELLO lav', he squeals beaming at me. He puts his arms around me and I pat him slightly on the back and when he starts to pull back my hair gets a bit stuck in his mug stubblies so that when he's on the move I'm pulled along after him but it's kind of nice because it happens every time.

'Hi'.

'Cam right on in. We've just had dins I'm afraid, but I've got some left ovah staff from yesterday'.

He takes my coat off for me and leads me into the flat. It's a standard size but the floors are covered in an array of throws and blankets and rugs and mats in a variety of different colours and lengths. The lighting is, like everything Montmorency does, moody but on point, complete with vintage standing lamps he's scavenged from some antique shop or auction or something or other. It is a higgledy piggledy homey chaos and there is something alcoholic constantly bubbling in the kitchen. Monk is there too, sat at the table in the middle and chowing down on a big fat burger in one hand, that's bulging at the sides and making an impressive ring of foody gunk around her gob, and glaring down at a magazine she's holding in the other, the skully mug of a skeletal model (I think it's May or Ray or Fay) pouting up at her with acrid red chops, globes closed and cheeks jutting with something of a buzzcut on top.

Uniform

Head: Messy bun that's actually a mess

Bod: Hoody

Legs: Ripped skinny jeans

Feet: Loafers

'Hi Monk'.

'Hmmm', she says, nodding at me. Before turning back to the magazine and flicking it open with a globe roll and a gulp. She is very primal and I respect that.

'We had burgers with gwac and salsa and jalapenos and loads of ANYANS...' recalls Montmorency bustling about, bringing some glasses down from a well-stocked cabinet over the sink and getting some zesty ingredients ready for some cocktail concoction or other. I take one of the plush seats at the table next to Monk. 'But how's your DAY been? What's been going on? I was so reLIEVED to stop working today, I swear the amount of bloggers I'm having to blackmail to feature on the site, well I suppose legally it isn't blackmail anymore but I feel like such a BARstard about it, but it's not my fault. UGHHHHH but it's fine we have a very VERY exciting evening planned'.

This sounds good but I need to cut to the chase right away.

I place my scrunched up digits onto the table. 'Montmorency, I need to brush my gnashers first. If you don't mind'.

He stops what he's doing and swivels round.

'What happened?' he asks, shooting to the remaining empty chair.

'Well, Rick, this awful manager man-bod at work-'

'Not your actual Employer?'

'No, but related to my Employer, but anyway the fuck shoved me in a bog and got his thing out and he was going to stick me and I want to rip his head off and I feel sick and disgusting and I want to brush my gnashers to get rid'. My Rick-knots squeal and squirm as the words come out. That disgusting disgusting bod.

Montmorency nods.

'I'm so sorry. Are you OK?'

'I want to brush my gnashers'.

He pats my arm. 'If you really think it's going to help', he sits back and waves his hands, 'that can be arranged RIGHT AWAY'.

'Do you have any Memory Foam as well?'

He winces. 'I'm sorry lav, that went last week sometime, can't remember the last bod who used it but ANYWAY they wore it out and I'll only be getting some more in a few days. I'm sorry about that'.

'OK'.

He gets up and starts rustling in a draw for a tube of paste. 'I'll get you a new brush OK lav, just for you'.

I glance across at Monk who is sort of gawping at me with cow falling out of her gob, and she's evidently forgotten about the magazine because it's lolling out her hand and swinging very close to one of Montmorency's decorative candles.

Montmorency returns to the table and places the paste and the brush by me. He presses his digits to his chops.

'Please don't ask me to talk about it'.

'Lav, whatever you want, WHATEVER you want. I just, I really do think that you should EAT first'.

'But you've had dinner already'.

Monk nods vigorously starting up her chewing again to make the point crystal clear.

'No, no, it's fine', Montmorency continues jumping up. 'Look I've got some bread and some carrots and here's some cottage cheese...'

'That's OK'.

'I mean, I could make you pasta or something?'

'The bread and carrots will be fine. Just leave the cottage cheese'.

'A bit much?' he asks earnestly.

'Yeah. A bit much'.

'OK'.

Monk casually and silently offers me her half chewed burger.

'No. Thanks though'.

She nods heavily with understanding and shoves it back into her gob.

We all sit in silence for a few minutes apart from the fact that these carrots are super crunchy and Monk is still slurping and smacking her burger about so we've got a right squelchy mix of foody noises going on and it's sort of adding to the awkwardness instead of taking it away and I really really want to just brush my gnashers. It doesn't help that Montmorency is looking at me as if I'm going explode and I know it's because he cares but I really just don't like all the attention.

He opens his gob to speak then closes it again and then shifts weight from elbow to elbow as I look at him and carry on crunching.

'Just say whatever it is you're dithering about'.

'So, awright, I know you're not going to talk about it, and that's fine I get that TOtally,' he says shaking his head, 'but is there somebod you want to call, or tell who could actually bring him to task?'

'Not really. My Employer wouldn't care'.

'OK'. His mug crumples. 'It's just so sad because I would suggest that you call a support group or I could take you down to St Mary's, they're AMAZING down there, but they're swamped all the bleedin time, you'll just end up some numbah. I don't even know if there would be enough bods to help you. With as much help as you NEED. But then I think maybe it'll be WORTH the wait and it's just up to you, whatever you want lav, whatever…' He flaps his arms about and he's in a right tizz.

'It's fine', I say, 'I just want to brush my gnashers. I think that will do the trick'.

'Alright'.

Crunch. I think for a moment. I feel safe saying it.

'I will say this though'.

'What? Anything,' Montmorency says leaning forward generously.

'He grabbed my cunt and I started my period on him and he freaked out. Literally squawked like some fat over stuffed shit thing with blood dripping everywhere'.

'You're JOKING'.

'No'.

'Lav, I mean, that's GREAT'.

'I know'. My Rick-knots squirm. I look down at my carrots. 'I don't think I've ever felt so powerful and it was an accident and now I feel empty and sick and angry'.

Montmorency nods. 'Well. Here's hoping he'll never do it again, now that he knows there are all sorts of magical and mystical things going on in a cunt'.

'I don't know. Rapists are sort of, patho aren't they? They

don't give a fuck about anything?'

Montmorency leans back. 'They would give a fuck, if the fuckers knew it would be taken seriously. And that they'd be punished'.

'Yeah well. It's not going to happen. LAW FORCE don't give a shit about things like this. That's why I came here'.

Montmorency nods understandingly.

'I mean', he says shrugging his shoulders, 'we could beat him up for ya?'

'Mont, you wouldn't stand a chance. He is huge'.

'It was just a thought, lav'.

'I just want to brush my gnashers, please. Plus I'll need more tampons. I'm not very well prepared'.

Monk casually slips one from her pocket and holds it out to me.

I admire the resourcefulness. I take it and she grins at me with stuff hanging out of her gob all over the place.

I can't help it. The right corner of my gob twitches up.

'Monk you are a mess'.

She smiles smugly. 'Right back at ya. De nada', she says in her deep husky voice.

Montmorency roars with laughter. 'De nada de nada de nada'.

'De nada', I say in agreement.

I get up. Montmorency leads me by the arm to his bathroom box and lays the paste and brush by the side of the sink. 'I'll go after you', he says.

I look at him.

'Thanks. I mean, really'.

'I'm GLAD you came over my sweet', he says kindly. 'I'm just so angry for you. I want to make sure that you're ABSolutely OK'.

'I just didn't know what else to do. I just want to stop feeling shit. I've done nothing wrong. And now, I feel so sick and dirty. I'm so twitchy and a nervebag all at once. I've got these knots, in my tum…'

'You've done nothing bladdy NATHING wrong', he says gripping my shoulders. 'And don't you forget it. I will help in any way I can and if you want to brush your gnashers you jolly well BRUSH your GNASHERS'.

'Cool'.

'Cool. I'll leave you alone for a minute'.

'Right. Thanks'.

He leaves softly.

I look at myself in the mirror and I look tired and pissed off. First thing first: tampon. I take Marissa's out and put Monk's in and set about freshening up. Thank god that fuck didn't spray his mess around because that really would make me sick but luckily all I can see down there is my rich red and I take some and rub my digits together. I take a deep breath.

Good.

I wash my hands and look back into the mirror. I take the brush and squelch a healthy amount of paste onto it, drip some water and start to brush.

My gnashers immediately begin to ring and rattle as though they're going to shimmy right on out of my gob. My thumper is getting faster and before it starts to beat right out my chest I swill the paste round my gob and spit the rest of the water out.

My constant overriding impish impulse for kickings and bovvings and lobbings starts to slip and slide and slope away. Hmmmmm. All anger and hatred is pluck-a-ducked out and everything is fluffy for once. I am out of myself and it's kind of disorientating and nice. The knots start to relax. They're going, not gone, but there's no tension in my tum. I feel much much lighter.

Nada de nada de nada nanana. Hmm Hmm Hmmmmm.

Deep breath. Shhhhhhhhhhhhhhhhhhhhhhhhhhhhhhhhhhh.

I glide out of the bathroom box and Montmorency instantly swoops down over me like a graceful goose. 'Daaahling'.

'Hmm yes?'

'Have I been an irresponsible friend getting you all buzzed on durgs?'

'Nommme'.

'Well I hope not coz you look GREAT'.

'Thanks. I know'.

'Feel great?'

'Feel great'.

'Excellent!' He passes me a glass of clear. 'Wash it all down with this'. I gulpgulpgulpgulp. YUmmm.

I look across at Monk and she smiles tooooothily at me. She ambles over to the ze-phone in the speakers and puts on some music or other. I don't know what it is but it's stirring and fun.

'Hola', she waves.

I nod my head heavily.

'You look messy', she whisps with glee.

'Fankyouverymuch', I say.

Montmorency has disappeared into the bathroom box and I loll about on my chair waiting for him to come back. A pencil has materialised out of Monk's hair and she's scribbling and scratching on a piece of paper.

Montmorency is back jack and he slinks into the spare seat. Tripping triumphant trio.

Monk blinks and grabs the brush and paste.

'Don't get it on the table silly fool', Montmorency grins.

Monk manages to miss the table but compensates for it by ending up with froth and foam all over her cheeks and her conk.

'Charming'.

She pouts back and rolls her globes.

'You are the QUEEEEEN of BEASTS', Montmorency declares. He takes his hat and slams it on my crown. 'You are the BEEEEEAST of QUEENS'.

I wipe my conk. I don't quite know what to say. I settle for, 'I have always admired your hat'.

Montmorency's globes immediately begin to shine.

'Thhhhank you' he whispers with real emotion.

Oh the merry merry merriment.

'Now', says Montmorency, casually shaking himself back together and getting down to the business of excitement at hand. 'This is the thing, *the* THING. You'll never guess who's in town'.

Monk nods knowingly.

'Who?' I ask.

'And this is really cool, I mean he hasn't been back here in YEARS'.

Nostalgic Monk smiles smugly.

'Who what dammmit?'

'Malga'.

Now that IS interesting.

'Have you ever met him?' asks Montmorency.

'No, I haven't. Heard a lot from you lot. Obviously'.

'Yeah he coasts around a lot, doesn't want to be pinned down. Which I GUESS is understandable'.

'Yeah'.

'So, he's here in Manc. In Big Hands as far as I can tell... he still talks weird'.

'I love it', says Monk decisively.

'Me too', says Montmorency.

'I wanna fuck him', she quips.

'Yeah, me TOO' says Montmorency taking a swig of clear. 'For a bod so BLADDY weird he's sexy as FUCK'.

'That's the point', says Monk, shaking out her messy bun before re-doing it extra messy for the occasion. Very on point. I scuff my bovvers together.

'What do you know about him, C?'

'Not much', I reply. 'The basic gisssst that most bods have. He was on The Money News. Unrecognised'.

'The FIRST to be Unrecognised', squeals Montmorency clapping his hands together.

'And now he's an underground hero', I continue, 'something about his hair? I dunno I didn't go to the poly-versity'.

'Lav that really doesn't matter, neither versity nor no versity education will come in handy when it comes to him', says Montmorency. 'I've met him a couple of times at a couple of thhhhhhings because he was a couple of years above me at the poly-versity but it was all bladdy weird'.

'Why?'

'Well, they were both totally unofficial events and it was all HUSH HUSH and then everyone was clamouring around him, so I couldn't really get a look in. But then I don't know what the EFF happened. One minute I was a sulky shitshow at the bar and then the next I was with Malga having a smoke and a DMC. Random. It must have been fine and cool and stuff because he got in contact this morning for meetz. I don't remember much but he was verververy interesting'.

'Cool', says Monk boredly, leaning over to the fridge, grabbing the tub of cottage cheese and spooning it into her gob.

'That's GROSS', says Montmorency.

'BLEEEEUUUUGH', says Monk showing us the spitty cottage cheese rolling around her gob before laughing at herself and chugging it down even more ravenously.

'I mean really', cringes Montmorency straightening up his back, 'why is it ALWAYS the munchies with you?'

'Got no legs'.

'You mean you've got hollow legs'.

'Something like that'.

'Right'.

'What's the plan for this evening then?' I demand.

'Well, I think- ooh more clear?' Montmorency asks.

'Please'.

'Hmman'me', says Monk with her gob full.

'So', Montmorency continues, effortlessly pouring clear into glasses and it's looking pinkish pearlescent to me but I'm not entirely sure. 'I suggest we let all the rest of them have a go with him, let them converge and disperse, solve et coagulate or whatever they want and then we'll biff on down when the novelty is ovah. I mean it'll take us long enough to get there knowing you two'.

'I don't know what you're talking about', I say.

'Nnmmeneiver', gobbles Monk.

'Oh right', barks Montmorency, 'not like the time when you dropped all your shit on the floor Monk, or the time you fell out of the tramsmmuter, or the time you ran into a glass door or when *you*', he points at me, 'when you nearly punched those bods in the MUG. All on the same night'.

'Hmmum', grunts Monk as if to say calm down Mont that's slightly unfair. I agree.

'Well they were fucking fucks', I say.

Monk gulps, 'And they ruined my milkshake'.

Montmorency waves extra-extravagantly, 'Regardless. You are a pair of twits'.

'Fine', says Monk shrugging and grinning.

'Fine', I say.

'So what do you think'.

'Good plan', I say.

'I know', says Montmorency. 'In the meantime… intermediary bevs at Sandbar?'

'Hmmmmm', I say.

'Let's GO', says Monk, slamming the table.

'Monk, careful of the woodwork for gawd's sakes', whines Montmorency, clutching the table legs.

Monk shrugs. 'Soz', she says.

Coats on and we're about to go charging and gliding and spilling out of the door. I feel a twinge in my tum and I know that it's one of the Rick-knots threatening to weedle its way back into my immediate consciousness. I grab Montmorency by the coat tails. 'Montmorency?'

'Yes lav?'

'Can we take the paste, you know, just in case?'

'Isn't it working?'

'It's been a really difficult day and without the Memory

Foam... I don't want to take any risks'.

Montmorency nods, 'You're right, that makes absolute sense. Mind you', he says nipping back out of the bathroom box and pocketing the tube, 'none beforehand, this is for emerrrrgencies only. OK?'

'OK', I say.

'OKIIII', shrieks Monk from afar.

Three quarters of it has gone by the time we hit Sandbar ten minutes away for a clear pick-me-up. The sun and moon are shining out of my fucking arse.

The usual Conscripts are out, wrangling for bubbles or clear or brown, most have brushed their gnashers. It goes a number of ways depending on the combo you're consuming. You can end up wet like a wet thing, happy as Larry (whoever he is), fucking fucked off or a miserable lonely turd. It's too early to tell which way we're going right now but we're all feeling frisky and fun. You can always tell because Monk starts singing.

> *'Bincy bu-boncy bu bibbity bong.*
> *Fink you're wrong cos you're always wrong.*
> *Fuck the boys and give 'um a fright,*
> *Cos life's for living and living is shite'.*

We howl with laughter like the trash pack of wolves that we are. Nobod pays attention or gives a flying fuck.

Old Big Hands. Right next to the florist, both kind of jammed in next to each other in a strangely cohesive muddle. Been here for about a hundred years. The slow thud thud thud of music thumps out of the doorway, which is dim and dingy. It is busy tonight. There are bods having smokes outside, the queue for clear, bubbles and brown is thick and there are bods swaying and wobbling to the music. I am hammered.

We elbow our way in. The floors are never not sticky and the walls are slathered with posters for musical Conscripts and Musicians and this that and the other, with mugs and block capitals jumping out all over the place. The light is low and scattered around on every available surface are candle pots and flowers. Big Hands refuses to set up all the hologram and interactive rubbish that most of the drinkies and shotels have in the city Centre-For-Work, keeping things moody and mystical in this lovely little hovel. It's much easier on the globes and you're less likely to run into the sorts of bods who want to stare at themselves in automatic videos all night or pretend they're dancing with some dead singing musician from the past. Monk starts throwing her arms in the air and immediately catches the attention of everyone because she is kind of diddy and mad and a very enthusiastic dancer.

Montmorency scans around the dark for bods we may know and I'm temporarily in awe and dazed because I can't see a bloody thing because my globes haven't adjusted to the gloom. But it's OK, I feel warm and merry of thumper and I want to stamp my bovvers in time to some of the very lovely music that's jamming my eardrums.

Montmorency sees Immy.

'Immy, IMMO', he bellows, barely making a sound over the noise and music.

Immy turns to him. 'Jaaaaaaaa darling?'

'Where is he?'

'What?'

'Where's MALGA?'

'I don't know Mont, I lost him hours ago'.

Montmorency bats his globes wide. 'How?'

'Because it's really fucking busy darling and he spurned my advances'.

'Gutted', yells Monk.

'Yeah quite', she says. 'Long shot I guess. Have you seen the dog yet?'

'The what?'

'The DOG'.

'No we haven't'.

'I heard it's called Henry'.

'OK'. Montmorency glances at me and laughs. 'That bloody dog'.

'What dog?'

'Oh you know, the dog. 'Henry' apparently'.

Immy nods.

'I don't know what you're talking about'.

'How many times have you been here?'

'Manymanymanymany times'.

'And you haven't seen the dog?'

'Stop winding me up you fuck'.

Montmorency frowns a sassy frown. 'It's TRUE'.

'I don't care'.

'You're not trying hard enough'.

'I hate trying, it's useless'.

'We're not going into *that* right now AND it's beside the point. Let's see where Malga is'.

'A curiosity', sings Immy, casually flinging her bev over some bod's shoulder. 'Probably licking a poster somewhere or something'.

'Fanking youuuu Immoooo!' yells Montmorency enveloping her in a gracious hug.

Monk has disappeared but she said something about needing to piss a while ago so she's probably in the bog somewhere.

The crowd of bods is swinging and swaying and is almost impenetrable and the only way to get anywhere is to swing and sway with them. We are washed about by them all for a while keeping our beady globes open for Malga but we have no luck and the only thing left for it is to top up the buzz. We get an average four drinks each to keep us going and to avoid joining the bank of queue again, a strong hefty sustainable mix of bubbles, clear and brown with straws and then allow ourselves to get swept away again on a sea of elbows trying to get to the bar. There is no concept of time and space. Only the length and breadth of a song and the motions I am pulling. I think I might be getting quite warm from being jammed up to other bods from all the dancing and nodding about and gulping pops like water and I definitely think I wiped a bod's forehead at one point, Monk revisited us like a ghost before spectrally skipping off again to get with some guy or girl bod, I couldn't tell. I haven't got a fucking clue what's going on until I realise that Montmorency is dancing in front of a bod he likes called Gabe with a chair on his head and that Immy is hanging off my choker and she's laughing and crying and blithering on

'Ijustwanttoseehimithinkhethoughtiwasreallycooooooolandi neveractlikethisbutireallyjustwanttoFUCKandworkjustsucksss sssssssssiwishiwasntdoingwhatimdoingiwishiwasatversityagain IREALLYWISHIWASATVERSITYAGAINughbecauseireall ytrulywasthehappiestiveeverbeenandisitsowrongtowishforthep astbecauseifuckingWISHiwasthreeyearsagoimeaniwasthemost confidentpersonintheworldandseriouslyistillamobviouslyandi mhappppppybutyouknowijustwantsomebodtokissmeonthefor eheadireallydojustakissandtheniwouldbereallyfuckinghappylike thehappiest...' Most of it is incomprehensible and fucking ridiculous and I would just laugh at her if I didn't want to smack her so much. All of a sudden Montmorency flies by all sunshine without his chair 'looooooooooooooooooooooooook ouuuuuuuuuuuuuuuuuuuuuuuuuut foooooooooooooooooooorrrrrrrrrrrrrrr   Henryyyyyyyyyyy-yyyyyyyyy', he hoots, scooped off into Big Hands oblivion by tender loving digitss and I am totally alone with fucking Immo so I drop her to the floor and she's swept away and I'm alone and it's cool for now but I really don't stand a chance against all these bods. I get pushed and pulled around by the choppy current and I feel like my legs are complete jelly and I surf my way over to the side, opposite some cracked and cracking red leather sofas. I slam against the back of the wall harder than I think I will and it sort of knocks me back to my big fucking sticky reality and I realise that no amount of brushing my gnashers is going to sort out the knots that are pulsing in my guts. I find it hard to breathe as tears start to prick and stab my globes and my conk fucking hurts so I turn around and slam the wall a few times with my fist.

It's only then when my hand is bruised and a bit of the plaster has come off and stuck to my stinging digits that I realise that there's a bod stood next to me facing the wall too. I pull my fist down slowly. My globes are fuzzy and I'm not entirely sure what I'm looking at but it looks like it's staring at a poster of the The Malchicks or Cabbage and nodding its very tufty hairy head. I take a step closer and snarl at it:

'What are you doing you fuck?'

'Hmmm'.

'Bad night?'

It, he, opens his gob. He closes it again.

'Yeah well you're not the one', I say, rolling my globes and leaning heavily against the wall again.

He gulps.

'Wetar?'

'*What?*

'Wetar?' he says again, brandishing a glass full of zero-clear in my mug.

'Um...'

'Lokos lkie yuo're hnviag a bad one'.

I stare at him for a bit. It's like it makes sense but then it really really doesn't. I've taken strange drinks from strange bods before by accident but this practically screams odd. He turns his head to me. His hair is epically tufty and it has spread across his mug into a thick biblical beard. It looks, almost, purple, but the light in here is wacko so it's hard to tell. A pair of bright black globes peer through inquisitively and he's dressed in some kind of tweedish suit that again, seems oddly at odds in Big Hands but also as if he's never fitted in anywhere better. Maybe it's the slouchy way he's standing or that fucking weird lopsy hair.

'I don't think so you creep'.

'You hvae sikn lkie csutrad'.

'What?'

'It's iresitneng I lkie it'.

'I don't know what you mean'.

He shrugs.

'OK. Well you're fucking weird'.

He blinks and nods.

I'm not entirely sure what to do now so I stare at him for a while, really trying to wear him down but he only gazes back at me in return, like he's looking at me but he's definitely got other thoughts running around his head that are more important than getting freaked out by me. I am angry and sad and pour all of that awful bollocks into one obnoxious glare but he just sighs and moves his head from one shoulder to the other like a smug kitten.

'You're an arsehole' I say.

'Taknhs'.

'Fuck you'.

'How deos taht mkae you feel?'

'None of your business'.

We carry on the staring match.

I get bored after a while.

'Ugh', I groan 'you are such a slob'.

'I rneset that'.

'What?'

'I rsneet that'.

'Why?'

'I am mnay tghnis but I am not a solb'.

'How am I supposed to believe that?'

He wags a digit at me and then finds a little space in front of me and The Malchicks.

He starts nodding his head in time to the music keeping his globes firmly on me. Something in him ripples up from the ground and courses up his legs bod arms choker and finally up to his head which bounces down and back up again. He keeps his big black globes on mine and starts doing all sorts of movements noddings twitchings and poppings, seamlessly moving his hips left and right and forward and back and isolating the movements and then swirling them smooth like silk stuff again. His arms pump forwards and back touching his hips sporadically and his globes are no longer on mine but drifting between closed and creased looking through his lashes or peering over the length of his conk as his head is flung back and his hair shimmies and shakes with each flick and swoosh. It is ridiculously mesmerising and I wish he was wearing a lycra suit instead of that heavy tweed because then I'd be able to see him curving and curling properly, playing with the beat and rhythm by now accenting it, now skimming over it or push pushing against it with his bum. And all the time as his arms flex BEAUTIFULLY and his shoulders move seamlessly, his neat footwork weaves between cute precise steps and lengthy arching strides to suit whatever musical happenings are occurring, his globes and mug are completely engrossed in the rest of the various movements that are going on elsewhere, so many many movements to make this whole, sometimes with a casual bite of the chops or with furrowed brows and nods and shakes so you don't know where you stand in this conversation. And then it clicks: he's talks weird and I really want to fuck him. This must be Malga.

The song ends and with one last ripple up his bod. He walks back over casual as fuck.

'That was, uh, beautiful', I say choking up.

'Tnkahs', he says.

'Really, how do you do that?'

'I dno't konw. I konw ectalxy waht I'm dinog all the way tugorhh but I've aslo sptoepd tiknnhig and ciarng at the smae tmie. It's wired'.

'It's fantastic, it really is. Fuck, god, why am I crying?'

'It's OK'.

'No I've been crying all day it's, not good, it's fucking not what I do normally', I say, wiping the tears that are effortlessly stream down my mug.

'Cyinrg is fnie'.

'Yeah, no'.

'It rlleay is. Ciryng is aulsetbloy fnie'.

'It may be for you but it's not for me. I am rough and tough. I'm not myself today'.

Malga blinks at me inquisitively. He's so cute I can't keep my fat gob shut.

I scrape my sticky hair off my mug. 'Well, the thing is', I mutter, 'something terrible happened to me today. This man, my Employer's sub-manager or whatever, tried to put his thing in me and now I feel disgusting and angry and sad and afraid all at once and I don't know what to do about it'.

'Siht. Are you OK?'

'Yeah, I'm OK. Thanks for asking. It was really fucking weird, I sort of fought back, didn't really mean to but then I kind of did and obviously I'm fucking thrilled I did but, I don't know, even though I fought back and stuff I'm just feeling awful, fucking awful. And I'm sick of it'.

'I'm not sruipesrd'.

'Fuck. Why am I even telling you this. You should be chatting with, I don't know, Montmorency…'

'Yuo know', Malga starts, 'trehe's olny so mcuh we can fghit'.

'OK…'

'Eevn if taht's all we do. We fgiht buacsee tehre's not mcuh esle we can do. But taht dosen't maen it mkaes us feel good or altculay gtes us ahernywe'.

'Right. Absolutely'.

'But tehn what? Do we jsut let tehm get aawy wtih all teh siht?'

'No'.

'Three's nhtnoig esle we can do. De nada'.

'Right'.

'Rghit'.

'So we fight'.

'If adn wehn it's rhigt'.

'What's right?'

'De nada. Yuo konw tihs aelrday fool'.

'Oh dear', I say wiping my conk.

We stand in silence for a second.

'But of course, you must know what I'm feeling a bit but differently', I say. 'I mean you were actually Unrecognised. What happened with that?'

'Sretrnawgys got me and truend me idisne out'.

'Well, what does that mean?'

'Mroe tahn ayhinngt, I hvae a cnstonat haed ahce and I lsoe moreimes. I hvae to fnid mroe dclufifit wyas to htae and fghit them bcasuees tehy konw how to fnid me at all tmies'.

'That's shit'.

'Tckreas are in me ehwvreyree. Boold, serpm, sipt, fkincug all of it'.

'That's just so shit'.

'It's bad but tehy are siltl rvelltiaey new tloneohgcy. I aaylws hvae a 48 huor haed sratt if I've been up to smeoinhtg nhutgay and need a sdepey gte-waay'.

'Oh.

'It's OK. I lkie taht I sitll hvae my wyas. Divres tehm mad. But it's sad. All eneovery eevr wtnas to do is fcuk me'.

I gulp and feel guilty. 'Soz but I wanted to fuck you. Soz'.

Malga smiles, 'Oh taht's OK. I wenatd you to wnat to fcuk me'.

'Oh. Cool'. I smile back.

'And it wroekd'.

'Yeah. You are a bit of a tease'.

'I'll tkae bnieg a tseae over bieng a solb any day'.

'That's a good way to look at things actually'.

'Why not'.

'But I enjoy being borcd, I like not being productive'.

'Bineg berod is sltil bnieg and taht sillt mkeas you a

pbolerm to tehm'.

'So what can I do?'

'I dno't konw for srue. I'm tynirg too. All we can do is jsut tinhk aoubt it'.

'OK. I'll think about it'.

'And I ralely am srroy to haer aobut waht hppnead to you. Tehy're all scuh fkcuers'.

'Thanks'.

Malga casts a globe around restlessly.

'What's the matter?' I ask. 'Are you looking for somebod?'

He snaps back to look at me and his globes are glinting. 'I hvae an ieda', he says, 'an ieda for the gertaset hcak'.

'Greatest hack?'

'Yaeh. I'm not the bset at tceh but I'm gonig to do it, ginog to mkae it hpeapn'.

'What is it?'

'I'm giong to barek the Irenentt'.

After such a fruitful conversation, I kind of want to roll my globes at this.

'Bods have tried to do that before, doesn't sound like anything new'.

'Rpeates and rotipeiten and rvlunoiets rlue tihs wlrod dlnarig, dno't yuo freogt it. New is daed. New is ntnhoig'.

'Right'.

'The tihng is: so mcuh dpdenes on the Iretnent. It's the way we cmatcuonmie, ietfdiny, wlolaw in slef-dubot and slef-mseiry, ze-peonhs run on it too. No. I'm ginog to braek it and baerk it itno btis. No one will be albe or hvae to wrok or be Crniectospd or wahveretr or do any of tiher siht Eonpmtymles eevr aigan'.

'How?'

'Igainme no Csotcinioprn, no Bisusesns, no tiol. Wtih the Intneret premnlantey and puplalreety boekrn, terhe wlil be nointhg for aynnoe to be bsuy wtih. Oh the ferdeom. The wlrod wulod snatd slitl and it wlil hvae to cnofnort waht has been linyg bhiend tihs suiptd Ctapial dtcsiitaorn for so lnog.

No mroe Itnneert. The Irnetnet is trhugoh. If the Iretnent geos, 'wrok' wlil dpeaspair feroevr'.

I look at my bovvers. This all sounds crazy. Frightening, exciting, but a world without Conscription, could it really be? And could the Internet simply be broken just by hacking? Surely not. Deleting Conscription wouldn't stop Employment. It would take us back, to old types of Employment: 'work'. Less opportunities to be bored and lazy. Still...

'I can do tech', I say quietly. 'I can't hack but I can help?'

I look up and he's gone.

I stay hunched up against the wall for a while, kind of annoyed and mesmerised that Malga has ditched me so unceremoniously. Maybe he didn't want my stupid lame-o question and maybe I should feel embarrassed and it's just so typical of this stupid poly-versity lot to make you feel shit. My knots begin to squelch and squeal.

Breaking the fucking Internet. As if. He's an idiot and I'm an idiot for buying into it. He was just so convincing and fascinating and hot...

After a while I notice a pair of bright black globes blinking up at me from the floor. I can't see a bod yet so they are sort of just hanging there and it's kind of weird. I step closer. 'Malga?' I immediately rebound so that I don't stand on the kind jet black paw that is in front of me. I kneel and see a big tail thump the side of the sofa behind us. How silly of me. 'Hello nice pooch pooch', I say and it sort of grins up at me with a lolly tongue and takes a step forward to nuzzle my weary confused bedazzled and befuzzled mug. It understands my fuckedness because it has seen it a million times before. His black furry back is matted and patted and smoothed and firmed from the hundreds of hands who have eagerly cuddled him this evening alone. His head dips as I stroke it a little too forcefully.

'Soz', I mumble.

It smiles up and sniffs my mug in return.

Montmorency materialises out of nowhere dragging along Monk who is trying to continue snogging some other blonde.

'Heneryyyyyyyyyy', Montmorency booms and Monk drags herself away from her blonde and starts to snuggle against the dog's mug. He blinks at me apologetically and leans graciously into Monk's cuddle. Montmorency cradles the dog's bod yelling cutie things which I think he thinks he's whispering but he's actually yelling but at the same time he probably doesn't care how he says these things just so long as they're said. After a few minutes, Henry gently tugs away from us and backs back into the still swaying and stopping throng, greeting friends everywhere he goes.

'Look you cunts', says Montmorency flinging his arms around us. 'Ray is going to play anytime now. Time to go home. You', he says pointing at me, 'are staying with us'.

He steers us through the warm wild crowd and out to the nearest scummy dive shop for some scrummy late night snack snacks. It takes longer than it should do for us to stumble back to his block, even though you really shouldn't hang about in the darks for too long at night, but we get there eventually.

Home. Collapse into one warm and puffy bed and we sleep sleep sleep. I'll probably get into trouble for not registering at my building but who fucking cares. I wish these knots wouldn't come back so quickly.

1.4

I wake up in the morning as one set of a mumble jumble of limbs in a right old muddle of Montmorency and Monk. Considering all the consumption I took part in last night, I'm not feeling too bad, only ever so slightly Groggy. The alcoholic dogs have shone brightly on me today. If only I didn't have these fucking seething and clenching Rick-knots in my tum.

I grab my shabby ze-phone which I've carefully reconstructed with masking tape and the first news item that pops up on my hologram is about Strangeways. Even when I'm not bloody there that place peels into my private life. Apparently a bod escaped from the prison and the whole place is in a right hoo-ha with coppers and choppers and pooches sniffing out the area for the runaway. Almost twenty seconds later I get 'WORK IS ON AS USUAL' from Rich, which is obviously the bigger priority.

I slither out from the bed as Montmorency is groaning and rubbing his globes. We're no longer fun loving criminals, we're Conscripts, Conscripts all along and it's time to start peddling time and patience once again, the twats. As Montmorency and Monk are still staggering about looking for clothes, I give my gnashers one last quick brush and then stomp out the door. I march back past the thumping Factory, through the recovering streets of the Village and China Town. I stick to the gutters as the Autogrammers begin to snap and pounce. I cross Piccadilly Gardens and I can't believe I'm making this stupid fucking journey again. I'll have to see Rick again.

I cross the bridge into Strangeways with my head down but with my globes scanning about. What isn't surprising is the lack of pretty-cars out and about on the prowl this morning. Whilst LAW FORCE vans and vehicles have amassed en masse everywhere, with whirring LAW FORCE brutes in their armoured outfits patrolling the streets and lots of big flood lights illuminating the warehouse fronts and long lines of tape cutting off all my favourite short-cuts and metallic tinny voices ringing out of ze-megas and swarms of drones buzzing about, all I can think is that all the BMWs Jaguars and Mercedes Benzes are missing and it's proof that they shouldn't have been here in the first place and all deserve a good brick to the gob.

I can feel some of the support coppers looking at me as I make my way to the warehouse. They're not as scary as actual LAW FORCE but I march on with the old crunch crunch crunch with my fists forming tight balls. You'd have thought that coppers would see a place like this and think 'Ooh what a dump this place doth do, maybe we should sort it out', but then again it's easy to want to ignore a place that is so confusing, old-hat and mucky. It's easier to stare at the poor shits Conscripted to work there. I pass the Asian bod and we give each other the briefest of looks. I get to the warehouse. Outside, perched in a tiny car and squashed up like an over-sized squid is big fat crap-jack Rick. My tum turns over and the knots clench and churn and I feel the sickest I have felt all morning after having brushed my gnashers. I have to do something. I approach the car but he hasn't seen me yet. He's staring at the door of the warehouse looking like he's deciding whether or not to go in. I want to chuck everything up all over the place and leg it down the hill. Conscripts aren't allowed to take medical leave unless you've given 5 hours notice or you're in hospital, but I don't care. I could just vanish into the burbs and sleep and collect myself together. But I remember that aggressions might help so I stomp right up close with my guts in my gob and whack the window causing him to jump and hit his head on the roof of the inside.

'Yeeeeeahhhhhhguuuhhh', he shrieks with fright. He fumbles around with his car keys before screeching off round the back of the warehouse.

I look after him and I'm still angry and sick and scared and unsatisfied but I also feel calmer.

Rich is already in today it seems because the grate is up, so I slowly thump straight to the office, clock in and shackle up bleep bleep bleep bl-bleep. Rich is on the ze-phone in his office box with his voice thankfully muffled.

Marissa turns up. Rachel turns up. Lauren turns up.

'Did yous see the news this mornin?' asks Rachel.

'Yeah, scary right. I wonder who he is and where he is. Do you think he's cute?' says Lauren, cutting the ends of her hair with some scissors.

'Ah know, it had bettuh be OK and safe for us to walk home this evenin', says Marissa, ignoring her last question.

'Ah'm suuuure it will beh', nods Rachel. 'LAW FORCE and these coppuhs will be aroun until theh've been caught. Ah think it'll probableh be the safest time to evuh walkabou' round heeyuh!' replies Rachel.

'That's true…' says Marissa. She doesn't look convinced.

She looks at me.

'Dude what did yer do to yer hand?'

I look at my bruised and battered digits. Oh yeah. I hit a wall.

'Nothing', I say.

'Ah'm surprised there aren' aneh Autogrammuhs or journos or news crews though', continues Rachel.

'Oh they're ALL camped around the north of Strangeways', reports Lauren. 'Apparently the guy who escaped was last seen round there, so that's where they are. I think LAW FORCE are trying to keep this side as decontaminated as possible'.

Rich leaves his office box sheepishly and starts pointlessly shifting papers around Rick's desk.

'Makes sense. Glad theh weren' hoverin abou'', says Marissa.

'I don't know, if you get scouted by the Autogrammers, that's your ticket out of here. I could so do with getting out of here', muses Lauren.

Marissa scoffs but Lauren doesn't seem to notice.

Rick clears his choker and it sounds like he's hacking up oil.

'Hey, yer'll never guess what Ah foun' out yesterdeh-' Marissa starts.

'Gerrrrls is everythin OK?' asks Rich.

'Yeah', we mumble.

'Can we keep it to work then yeah. Ah don' want you to waste mah time and mah moneh, OK yeah'.

You could practically hear Marissa's globes rolling.

Once again silence reigns. Apart from the sound system. There goes our verbal interaction of the day.

After a soulless soupful lunch, I shackle myself back up bleep bleep bleep bl-bleep and then all of a sudden the same Audi from a couple of days ago pulls up outside the building.

Four men jump out and start hammering on the door as well as releasing manic buzzes from the doorbell around the office. We all look at the ze-CCTV screen. Marissa runs into the room and comes round to see more clearly who they are. Rich slowly comes out of his office box running his stubby digits over his stubbled head, his globes bursting from the sockets and his jaw hanging in a gawping lopsided manner.

'Shiiit', he says simply.

No shit. You know you're in trouble no matter who you are and what your job is when crow bars start getting whacked against the first line of defence.

'Is the door bolted downstairs Marissuh?'

'Yeah'.

'OK good and where's Rick, can someone go and find Rick?'

I hope he gets sliced and diced by that lot downstairs. Rachel races out of the room to look for him before anybod else can budge.

'Check the warehouse yeah love', Rich calls after her.

If I was her, I'd leg it and I wouldn't come back.

The men outside have ripped the doorbell from the wall and are pummelling the door with their crow bars.

'Who are they?' I ask Ryan.

'Uh', says Ryan.

Useless.

'Rich do we need to leave through the fire exit?' gasps Lauren, clutching her handbag to her chest.

'No no no', says Rich fumbling around in one of the cabinets clutching an assortment of papers. 'Stay shackled uhp pleeuse. We've still got plenteh of moneh to make. No, we'll just pretend that we're not in and then maybeh theh'll go aweh. Where's fuckin Rick?!'

My tum gets into even more of a knot as the realisation kicks me in the boob. I stay shackled to the desk and try to carry on typing but the sitch gets even more fucked up when a gun is pulled out by one of the men downstairs and it glints momentarily in the ze-CCTV view. Rachel re-appears panting with panic. Idiot. Missed opportunity to get the fuck out.

'Rick isn't there', she gasps.

Of course Rick isn't there.

'What do yer mean Rick isn't there?' demands Rich, whose veins are now bulging from his head as well as his big horrid globes. He pulls his ze-phone out and tries to ring him up, his mug turning redder and redder as the men outside get increasingly ferocious with their crow bars.

'He's just not there... Ah don't think he came in todeh...' stammers Rachel, her globes darting between the ze-CCTV screen and Rich. Of course Rick didn't come in today. He knew exactly what was going to happen because he's seen the fucking emails threatening this. I didn't manage to frighten him at all earlier on, this Audi lot already had. Fat fucking snide bastard.

'Fuckin little prick', spits Rich, which I actually find quite amusing even if the first bit is physically inaccurate. 'Shackle back uhp then yeah', he demands. Rachel does so cautiously.

Outside, the door is lying in pieces and the men are

thwacking the metal bars of the inside-gate. Far too close for comfort. I'm getting increasingly stressed that I'm going to be waving goodbye to my gnashers and a chunk of cheek if those long metal rods are anything to go by. Rich says to keep working but I quietly try to unshackle myself...

BLEEEEEEEEEEEEEEEEEEEEEEEEP.

Dammit.

Rich rips round on us. 'Who unshackled themselffffs huh?' he yells, his mug turning a flattering shade of purple and globs of spit firing in all directions.

We stay silent. The only noise is of the men at the grate, still hammering.

All of a sudden, another BLEEEEEEEEEEEEEEEEEP sounds.

'Stop that, who was that?!' Rich yells, storming towards us. I couldn't tell who it was but it's nice to know we have the same idea.

'Shackle yerrselves uhp now, yer'll be sorreh yous won't be pehd for a week you little bitches'.

His threat is met with a

BLEEEEEEEEEEEEEEEEEEEEEP.

'STOP STOP STOP! Shackle uhp, don' stop workin. Keep workin until Ah say you stop!'

BLEEEEEEEEEEEEEEEEEEEEEP.

'How dare yous, HOW DARE YOUS?!' he screams, thumping his fists down on Lauren's desk. She jumps up with a frightened squeak and he makes to grab her arm. Marissa is right in there. 'Back OFF', she yells, slapping his back with a lever arch file. He howls with anger and Rachel smashes a hole-punch down on his digits. I grab a stapler, opening it up and charging over to the fray.

'Uh, I don't think you should do that...' Ryan whines.

'Shut it', I snap back.

'How DARE yous attack yer Employuh?' Rich says, clenching his fists. 'Ah employ yous, Ah pay yous moneh and yous should respect meh, mah properteh and mah rules'.

'Who are those men?' demands Marissa.

'Ah don't know...'

'WHO ARE THEH?'

'The suppliyers on the ze-phone, them ones that turned uhp, bastards want my moneh don' theh, but theh haven' given me stockk'.

'That's not true you liyuh', says Marissa. 'Aftuh what happened the other deh, Ah checked the latest stockk lists and we had a delivereh two weeks ago. That was from them wasn' it?'

'And Rick asked meh to book Arch to photograph them yesterdeh', Rachel chimes in.

'Gerrrls gerrrls, it's Business. Credit and interest and credit and stuff, this is just Business. Yous don't understan' things like this. We haven' sold any stockks yet so WHYUH would Ah give them moneh? That's just Business.'

'Oh yeah!' Marissa laughs. 'And that's the sound of bods who are readeh to do Business?' She gestures with the lever arch folder towards the ze-CCTV screen where the men are throwing their full force into breaking down the gate.

'I nevuh thought theh would actualleh come roun' and do this...' Rich grunts.

'So they actually threatened to come round? And you didn't warn us?' Lauren cries, exchanging a glance with Rachel.

'Yer didn' think we migh' be in harm's weh?' Rachel shouts, her hands shaking.

'Well no. With all of LAW FORCE round Strangewehs todeh, what with that runaweh and that, Ah didn' think that theh'd actualleh turn up'.

'When did yer realise this would happun?' Marrisa asks.

'Onleh when theh texted meh last nigh' when Ah got home and refused to transfer them moneh'.

Rachel, Marissa and I look at one another in silence. A huge bang goes off downstairs.

'They're getting in, they're getting in!' squeals Lauren,

pointing at the screen. The men it seems have managed to blow up the metal gate with a random homemade mix of bits and bobs in the time we've been having a go at Rich. The ze-CCTV screen is filled with smoke but we can hear them storming up the stairs.

Time to do what we should have done ages ago.

I boot Rich in the belly whilst Marissa yells to everyone to get underneath the desks. The men burst in and Rich is immediately shot in the back of the leg. The blood splatters all over the place, including my wide-eyed mug. Marissa grabs my arm and pulls me under her desk and we both cower with our digits stuffed in our gobs to stop any sound coming out. Rich is dragged kicking and screaming into the office by the men, who all look a vision in black balaclavas and they start yelling at him about the money.

'It's the gerrrrls!' he squalls, 'theh cocked things uhp, it's not mah fault, it's not mah fault-'

The door shuts behind them and we hop up from under the desks. For some reason, Ryan is still staring vacantly at the spot where Rich was shot, his gob opening and closing in a mixture of confusion and misunderstanding at how anybody could treat the beloved Employer, his royal Business bossiness, in such an aggressive manner.

'We need to get out', I mutter.

'The fiyuh exit, there's a fiyuh exit next to the kitchen', whispers Marissa, who's managed to remain impressively assertive and calm in spite of the muddling chaos unfolding.

Rachel emerges trembling from under her desk. 'Su-sureleh it would be bettuh to go out the weh theh came in?'

Lauren stays huddled under her desk crying and shaking and cuddling her handbag.

Thuds and groans are coming from the office.

'We don't have much time', I say.

'Righ'', Marissa says, deciding for the group, 'let's go past the front weh and see if we can get out there'. We all nod as howls erupt from the office. Ryan stays put. It wouldn't do to move him anyway. When you have a full-on freak out about the ease with which beloved Business reveals itself to be a dirty, nasty horrorshow then it's better to leave them to it. He stays. Shackled. I don't give a flying fuck what happens to him.

We scarper towards the stairs and run down them before confronting the back of a big man standing outside guarding the smoking door. Don't fancy pushing past him much so we scuffle back up the stairs, turn right into the warehouse and start running down the aisles of cardboard boxes and sweatshop clothes.

'Hey, HEY', a deep spiteful voice throws after us.

We lurch towards the door leading down to the kitchen. I'm behind the others to make sure Lauren doesn't freak out but then I realise that this is pointless because she's already started screaming and drawing even more attention to us than we need. She trips and drops her handbag on the floor with lipsticks and nail varnishes skidding off in all directions. She bends low to grapple about.

'What are yer DOIN?' yells Marissa.

'I need my ze-phone!' cries Lauren. 'I need to find my ZE-PHONE'.

'For fuck's sake move!' I push her and she goes flying.

Marissa yanks her up and I dart ahead, turning sharply down a different aisle because I panic and I think it's the right way to go but it's not and the others carry on stumbling down their same aisle with Lauren sobbing all the way and now I am on my fucking one stuck with a row of tapered trousers and belted coats. Marissa stays on the fucking ball though, heaving herself then pulling the others through the door leading to the stairs down to the kitchen and the fire escape. She slams the door shut behind them. I crouch in the gloom behind some boxes and try to calm my breathing down. The heater is still humming and I peer between the rows of boxes at the shadowy figure marching towards the door that Marissa and the others have disappeared through. I start to creep down the aisle, heading towards one of the big boxes full of big puffer jackets, all voluminous silhouettes and faux-fur hoods. But I'm not looking exactly where I'm going and smack CLANG BANG into fucking Old Groggy who was lurking about and idling in the half-light because there was no work to do. He hits me in the mug with a wang and hisses at me as I clatter to the floor. The shadowy figure stops and starts to head in my direction. My vision becomes completely blurred and I feel like there is a definite possibility that I will chuck everything up everywhere, for the second time today. The thud of big bovvers, not unlike my own, are rounding the corner and deciding which aisle to come snooping down. I pull myself up using the nearest box and chuck myself all whoozy-woo into it, thrusting myself under the big packets of coats to hide me from the view of the aisle. Before I even know whether thump-thump picked my aisle, I pass out.

*

I don't have a bloody clue how long I've been out of it but I do know that between the plastic packets of puffy coats, there is a thick honey drip drip dripping right near my ear. I peer through the packets but can see nothing but black. The day must have drawn to a close because sunlight has stopped feebly oozing into the warehouse. I wipe the honey stuff from my mug and place a finger tentatively in my gob. Tastes like what I can only imagine it is. Petrol oil. Fucking rank. I spit it out and start to claw my way out of the box. I feel my bod for a second to see whether or not that stamping brute had got to me and stuck his thing anywhere but as far as I can tell, my hide-out worked and I managed to remain untouched and unfound. Once upright all I see are specks and stars and I remember that I hit my head on stupid Groggy. A big egg is coming out of my forehead, crusted bloody courtesy of Rich, which I touch gingerly with the tips of my digits. After a couple of beats, my vision settles. I run my digits down my jumpsuit. There are traces of petrol oil but overall, I've been kept protected by the plastic packets of coats. I walk carefully down the aisle, one hand outstretched in the dark and the other running along the rows of boxes. All of them are covered in the same honey-oil. The warehouse seems to be deserted. The humming of the heater has stopped and there aren't any voices coming from the direction of the office or the fire exit. I get to the end of the aisle and take another step forward. My sole comes down and crunches on jaunty objects underneath. They must be some of Lauren's lipsticks. I reach down and pick one up. A lighter. I glance about and I can see loads of them, plus matchboxes. Looks like the suppliers are planning an inferno blow-out. Although shards of this lighter's plastic cover are now minced on the floor, I pocket it.

A few steps further and two large mounds rise in front of me. I can't tell exactly but they look like the dull outlines of bods. I prod one with my bovver and it winces and groans. I tilt my head and my globes meet Ryan's, puffed and bleary. His hands and feet are bound, the metal shackle still ringing his ankle, and he is gagged with some socks from the Christmas collection. He blinks at me. I turn to the other and shake it. Rich lolls round with a similar gag and his nostrils flaring. I smile because for once his big fat gob and the means for his bastard booming voice have been muffled. I crouch down slowly so that my mug is close to his and yank the gag out forcefully. I will have my way with you now bitch.

'Where are they?' I whisper breathlessly. I don't want to disturb the peace that has descended upon the warehouse, the calm before the inferno.

'Office,' Rich gobs. I notice that his choker is covered in blotches and splotches of purple. I realise with delight that his vocal chords are probably permanently damaged.

'Where's my money?' I hiss.

His globes grow wide.

'Not here', he gobs.

I lightly press a dainty pinky digit to his choker. He writhes agonised, wheezing and choking with pained splutters. Ryan whimperingly follows suit.

'I haven't even touched you, you stupid cunt', I spit at him.

I let go of Rich. He's trying to say something but his gob is still contorting with pain. Zughhhhhhhh is all that comes out. Zughhhhhhhhh.

I grip his chin in my hands and twitch his mug up so that he's looking into my globes. 'Money'.

'Arge', he gobs.

He's probably not lying. But I've had enough. I re-take the ball of socks, Santa and his reindeer grinning manically from the polyester, and push the gag further into his gob, causing the veins at his temples to bulge with anger and pain. I tip-toe past them and pad softly over to the door that leads to the fire exit. Bitch.

I open it gently. I peer down the stairs. Nothing much to report. Just silence and darkness. I get to the bottom. To my right is the ground floor of the warehouse, extending back into the black with the small kitchen crevice. To my left is the door of the fire escape that leads into a potholed backyard delivery area, closed into a small box by a tall wired fence. Skeggy has been dumped there for years, her mechanical arm hanging all jaunty next to the fence, almost like she's leaning back reclining and relaxing into the luxury of junk retirement. I might just join you sister.

I open the fire door and step into the night. It's still, the air slightly damp. There's no one about. The floodlights and the swarms of drones have moved further south, lighting up the warehouses and prison walls down the hill, towards the bridge into the city Centre-For-Work. A halo ring of light shines around them. The pretty Audi wagon is still parked outside the front door but there's no one in or near it. They must all still be in the office boxes planning the logistics of the blaze. I wonder why no one from LAW FORCE has heard the commotion coming from our Employment, or why Marissa and the rest haven't run straight to alert them and make them surround the building or something. No loyalties to Rich Rick and Ryan I suppose, but then again LAW FORCE never seem to care about what happens to little Conscript bods. What help would that be. Who knows. Some bod might have caught up with them by now and helped them or they're lying dead or Poor Ones are putting their things in them down a mucky side-street somewhere or they've been Unrecognised because their coats were left lying around inside the office. I'm not saying they're my best bods in the whole entire world but I care enough about their general welfare to hope that this is not the sitch they are now in.

The thought makes me shudder and the sickness and fear begins to creep back in and I have no cat to kick. The Rick-knots squirm and tighten in my belly and I feel like I'm going to shit or vom. I've had just about e-fucking-nough. A spark goes off in my tum, and my limbs ring and zing with nervous energy, like they do when you've just had a fucking fantastic idea.

I turn back into the warehouse and run my hands over the boxes. Same honey-oil. I grasp for the bashed up lighter in my pocket and flick it. It doesn't work at first because I have slippery oil on my hands, so I run them over my legs. I try again and the flame appears and lights up my mug. It isn't the strongest of fiery flickers but it really doesn't matter because it *is*. It's there. I hold it up to the nearest cardboard box of sweatshop and it immediately whooshes up into flames. I jump back so that I don't go up in flames myself. The plastic packaging takes a while to catch on but when it does, the smell is sharp and sweet and smoke fills the place. The next box catches, then the next and then in a glorious domino every single box in the warehouse salutes the dark with a rush of free and ferocious fire. Even though it's fucking beaut the fumes are horrible horrible horrible. It can't just be the packaging; this is what trashy sweatshop clobber smells like. It's a piercingly horrible smell, all those rotten synthetics and plastic jumpers and the rest, its sickly sweet, acrid, bitter, overpowering, like a punch in the mug, as if all the chemicals are oozing and stenching to high whatever in the air and I feel my choker tightening and if I stick about for much longer I'm going to choke in all the ways. It's already clogging up my conk and I start to cough and wheeze. I crouch as low as I can to get my head out of the smokey stink and leg it to the door.

I break into the fresh clear night and take a few deep breaths, spitting out all of the shitty foggy muck I've just inhaled. Skeggy is lounging about all 'sissssssss justttttt chillllll'. I head over to her and she gives me a generous helping hand as I start to clamber up the wire fence. I swerve and sway on the way up and swing my leg over the top and perch for a second or two.

The flames gash gold vermilion, ravenously licking the night sky. The whole warehouse is blazing ahoy: a daydream come to fiery life.

I linger with her for a few moments to soak and bathe in the light and heat. Then it's time to move and I start to scrabble down the other side of the fence and make to leg it down the nearest side-street. I'm just getting into my stride, splurting and splashing my way through the gunk with a good amount of speed when I round a corner and run slap bang into a bod running my way, all with an almighty WMMFFF.

2.1

The collision causes us both to crash backwards to the ground. I am less than happy with this sitch because I now have all sorts of pong and pap all over my bod. Plus being clattered does not help with my general state of whooze thanks to the egg on my head. I prop myself up on my elbows and look at the other bod. He, she or it seems to have been equally knocked back and is lying spread eagled and groaning. I try to get up but my vision is immediately blackened.

'Are you OK?' it asks. It's a he.

'Yes', I snap.

I'm worried that he's a copper working for LAW FORCE who could Unrecognise me without my coat and scarf. And let's also not forget that I'm covered in blood, honey-oil and I'm running away from a blazing warehouse. It's not exactly a good look. He could snap me up or chop me down with less evidentials to go on. I plant my grazed hands on the sloppy concrete and try to push myself up again even though my head feels like slop sploshing about in an old bucket. I'm also trying not to think about all the fluids squishing and sliming onto my hands that make me want to wretch and wheeze. I get up and juggle with my bearings as the egg on my head throbs and my globes see sparks. I shake my head roughly and he calls to me again.

'Are you sure? You look kind of out of it'.

He's panting and sighing but he's making better progress than me. He looks like he's coming over so I try to make a move but only end up veering dramatically to the side and end up smacking mug-first into the warehouse next to us.

Turns out he's not coming over. The ground is littered with cracked mini jars of Marmite and packets of crackers and tubs of what look like sunflower seeds and he's scrabbling about in a drunken manner trying to pick them up. I lean against the wall and end up sinking down to the ground, trying to get my head straightened out because I'm not entirely sure that the bizarro scene in front of me is actually taking place. If he'd been a LAW FORCE support copper he definitely wouldn't be accidently scattering snacks everywhere with dizzy momentum as he tries to wobble back to his senses. He looks over after shoving the jars and crackers and tubs into a surprising number of pockets and plastic bags and says, 'Hang on, where's your coat and scarf?'

I freeze. He's a copper. I try to push myself up up and away from the wall. But he comes over, shielding me from the light. For the first time since we crashed into one another I get a look at his mug and I'm slightly taken aback. He's not a copper: he's the Asian bod. The one I look and nod to everyday, the unspoken Strangeways buddo.

He Recognises me too for the first time and smiles. 'Fuck. Hi!'

'Um hi'.

Uniform

Feet: Trainers.

Legs: Black jeans.

Bod: Teal woolly jumper under cropped parka coat.

Head: Black beanie hat.

'What's going on?' he asks.

'Um. Busy'.

'No kidding, where's your stuff? And why do you have blood all over your mug?'

'At work...'

'Oh shit, look at your egg', he says, scanning my head.

'Old Groggy...'

'Old what?'

'Nevermind'.

'Anyways', he says shaking his head, 'that must be really painful dude. How did you do it? And why are you running away from your Employment without half your Uniform?' he asks, his brow arching. 'Are you fucking mad?'

'I can explain', I say faintly. But I don't. He's asking too many questions.

He listens and doesn't say anything. I look at him blankly.

'Is there anything I can do?'

'Maybe'.

He pauses and takes me in. I can imagine I look a fucking state and I smell like plastic poison fumes, mutt shit, cum, crap, honey-oil, sweat and whatever other gloopy gunk was on the pavement. I've got a big egg on my head, my globes are crossed and I can't speak proper. This doesn't seem to sway him.

'Come on, time to go. LAW FORCE are still crawling about. They're camped out with the Autogrammers and journos, you don't want to be Unrecognised'.

I think for a second about whether or not to trust this bod. It's the combination of snacks that does it: no nasty bod would carry around such a weird pack of goodies. Plus Marmite is a Monk thing. And his globes are warm and he's not a swaggering shit; generally inquisitive if not a bit of a busy bod, but all in all, I'm not put off. I decide to say, 'OK'.

I hobble up and he puts an arm around my waist so that I can lean on him. I can feel the packets of crackers being pounded to dust thanks to my ribcage. We limp and lunge forward back up the hill, towards the fire.

'Where are we going? Why are we going this way?' I say, my voice gasping a bit. I'm caught between wanting to gaze at my fiery handiwork and being five hundred miles away from this dump down the fucking hill.

'The brewery up the hill. My fiancé Rosée owns and runs it. We live there', he says smiling that smug satisfied smile that in-love bods do.

'Right', I say. In-love bods are nice but they are on a bit of a different planet.

'We're having a baby', he says heaving me up and smiling even more deeply. He might as well be on a fucking moon on the other side of Mars.

'Is that why, um, all the...'

'Yeah cravings', he says, grinning to reveal deep dimples in his cheeks and patting the jars, crackers and tubs. 'Weirdest fucking shit ever. But it's fun. I don't mind running around for her. Even if it does mean running into a mucky mess like you'.

'Right, yeah'.

'What the hell is that?' he says, the wind blowing his mug. He wrinkles his conk. I sniff too and immediately scrunch up my mug in disgust. The sweatshop smell has spread down the hill. Sam breathes in again looking confused to check if he really has actually smelt it and, yes, he realises he has and, yes, it really does smell like burnt bodies and rubber and bits. We round the corner and the glow of the fire reaches our mugs. I glance at him and it's lighting up his globes and washing all the warehouses, our clothes and bods in rich orange light. I have to say, as awkward as this is, I've made a good fucking job of the whole thing. The pong is fucking awful and there's a big plume of black smoke that will inevitably draw in swarms of drones and LAW FORCE and coppers any minute now. But I love my splat of burning mess.

Unfortunately standing around admiring it will spell certain Unrecognition and it's time to chop chop. This bod is undoubtedly my ticket out of this hot spot so it's time to engage trust. Plus, I do quite like him. In-love bods might be on a different planet but they can also be reliable when other bods are down and out and fucked over. And hiding out in a brewery doesn't seem like the worst idea in the world for obvious hop-related reasons.

'What's your name?' I ask.

He's, understandably, kind of hypnotised by the flames because, you know, they are pretty fucking magnificent, but he turns and says, 'Sam'.

'Sam. I don't know you at all but I think I sort of do and I think I can trust you'.

'OK good. Ditto'.

'I need your help'.

He looks from me to the flames.

'Sure. What's going on?'

'It's kind of bad'.

'You're not Conscripted there are you?' he asks.

Fuck. I burned down my Employer's Business. My place of Conscription. What the fuck does that make me now?

'Um, yeah but I don't know. Not exactly, anymore'.

He looks back at me. 'Were you running away from the fire?'

'Um-'

'How the fuck did you get out?'

'Not sure'.

'Look, you don't have to say anything now, you don't have to explain', he says with a warm voice. He nods his head slightly. 'Let's just get to Rosée, she'll know what to do'. That smile again. He is so in-love and it is sickeningly sweet, the saccharine sod. 'I'm not having you being Unrecognised by that scum. Come on get a move on you lump'.

'OK'.

I turn and look back down the hill and that sinister halo of electric light is beginning to creep up. My fire is a sight for sore swarmy globes and the perfect Money News hologram story for the night. Sam follows my gaze and he nods again. 'Time to hurry it up bud'.

I've almost given up by the time we get to the brewery behind the warehouse and Sam is dragging me along. I apologised once because it felt like the right thing to do but he said 'you're not heavy' and who am I to argue, even though I know big bovvers don't make you feather-light.

Sam gets us to the gate, yanks up the bolt and we stumble into a sort of courtyard. He lets go of me for a few seconds so that he can turn and close the gate behind us. This place is even bigger than it looks from the outside. It really is like some kind of fortress castle or something old like that. Even though the fire from the warehouse is in front, and the stench and smoke really does reek, we're safe from the flames.

Above the big gate is a brick arch and the dull lettering of MAGNANIMOUS BREWERY is stamped across it.

'Bit of a long name that', I say.

Sam comes back towards me after shutting the gate. 'Yeah it is. Rosée sort of inherited it from the previous Employers'.

I blink. 'She's an actual Employer?'

'Yeah but she's no snob. She calls the place Magna for short'.

'Less of a gobful'.

'Right'. He heaves me up and we traipse across the courtyard towards some plain stone steps with a metal pole railing leading up to a big wooden door. We get to the top and Sam starts to fumble about for his keys, patting his pockets and juggling about with his jars and packets and tubs, even offloading some of them onto me. I clutch them and turn back to the words on the wall.

'Why are they facing inside? Surely for purposes advertorial it would be better if they were on the other side of the arch?'

I am such a pro-marketer.

'It was Georg, our marketing bod. It was his idea', Sam says still fumbling about. 'He went to the poly-versity and I think this was supposed to be some sort of theoretical joke to appeal to new conscious customers. Subversive, ironic, you know?'

'Oh. I don't get it'.

'Yeah', Sam says, finding the key, 'Me neither. But, you know. Whatever. As if he'd listen to me'.

He opens the door. It's dark inside. And cold. I was expecting it to be warm but I shudder with a combination of chill and surprise.

'Cold?' Sam asks.

'Yeah'.

'There's no insulation in breweries so it gets pretty fucking chilly when it's cold'.

'Weird. I always thought that a brewery would be a warm

place'.

'Maybe that's because when you actually drink beer it makes you feel warm'.

'Yeah, perhaps'.

'It's as cold in here as it is out there. No escape from it I'm afraid'.

'Bit disappointing'.

'Although in the summer, this place is sweltering. When the wort gets warm, we all know about it'.

'What's wort?'

'Sweet sugary stuff that has been extracted from malt'.

'Oh. What's malt?'

Sam shrugs. 'I'll let Rosée tell you everything. She's a beast at brewing. I don't get more involved than the theory really'.

'So don't you do all this then?

'Nah', Sam says turning the key to lock us in and smiling another wide dimpled grin. 'I can explain it but I'm not a patch on Rosée. Everything I learned I got from her. Knows her shit, keeps the rest of us in shape. I help with odd jobs, you know, around the place'.

We're standing in a big empty space. On the left hand side is a long row of noisy things. My globes begin to adjust to the gloom and I can see the silhouettes of steel tanks and vessels in perfect rows standing shadowed and shady and there are all sorts of clinking and clankings from them. There are windows but they're high up, kind of like in the warehouse, and they're letting in a small amount of icy night light. Green lights blink everywhere in the gloom and on the far wall, a fluorescent blue light is humming, providing a moody bass to the weird plipping and ploppings in this eerie echoing spot. Sam leads me to the doorway of a small side snug where there is the sound of rampant talking and raised voices. I falter slightly, what with the egg and honey-oil and muck sitch, but Sam is already on it.

'No sweat buddo, stay here and I'll go and get Rosée'.

Sam slips into the snug and I'm left in the gloom. A loose

tap is dripping, the leaky slaps echoing and bouncing off the steel containers. It is louder than it should be. The chitter chatter and gassing hushes down considerably.

The snug rings with an orange glow, it is warm and inviting, much better than the ringing and plonking and donging going on in this cavernous bit. Honestly, the inner workings of a big clock wouldn't be half as unnerving as this; at least there would be some regularity in it. I feel all out of joint. This subtle racket ricochets all over the place and it's unnerving, it really is. Why did I even consider that a brewery would be a safe place to hide out? This place is busy with the workings of spectral suds, fermenting, leaking, expanding, squelching their gaseous guts and succulent chops up against the shiny walls of vats and vessels. The whole place might just spontaneously combust with the dark thick sod of ale and stout, the bottles ready for filling audibly quivering in the racks. Noisy nocturnal nightmare. This isn't a magnaimacious magfuckingness or whatever it is, fuck that shit, this is a ghostly horrid mess. The whooze is wearing off and the Rick-knots begin to squelch in my tum. My ears are ringing and ringing and ringing.

'Here she is. We can help her right?'

'Of course'.

The orange light is momentarily obscured by the silhouettes of Sam and two women coming my way. I can see all sorts of mugs and bodies trying to cram in my direction from the doorway but they swiftly close the door and step out into the gloom of the main hall. The first is some sort of fierce old woman:

Uniform

Feet: Scarlet bovvers.

Legs: Pleated leather black skirt over sheer tights.

Bod: Pale pink jumper.

Head: Long silver hair clipped back on either side with two tortoise shell clips.

Sam swings the door shut so that I remain obscure.

The full-formed bellyful figure of the second woman suggests that this is none other than the Employer Rosée. She's wearing similar bovvers to the older woman, except hers are silver, with sheer tights, a light pink dress with a fetching mid-length tulle skirt and a simple strapped jersey top and finishes the look with a snuggly grey jumper tied at her waist like a badass magical pixie.

She looks about my age. Her hair is an ethereal strawberry blonde, full-bodied like her bumpy physique and cascading in waves around her shoulders. I had heard that women who are expecting babs have a full on glow and Rosée seems to have actualised this theory pretty successfully. This is proper mermaid shit. The rest of her mug seems peaky and shadowed.

She approaches me and takes a long look at my mug.

'Fuck dude', she says. 'What happened?'

I shrug. There have been so many questions tonight from bods I don't know and it's starting to freak me out.

'Right', Rosée continues casually, 'first thing first: Sam pass me those crackers, I'm going to need a sterner stomach for this my sweet'. Sam scuttles over with crackers and Marmite in hand, sunflower seeds primed for scattering on top.

Rosée crunches her way through five before turning to offer me one. Very Monkish. She scares me but I'm instantly taken with her. She's very young to be a proper Employer.

'N-no thanks'.

'Come on, we're going to sort you out and you can't have eaten in ages. This is perhaps one of the best things you will ever eat'.

'Um'.

'Seriously, I can't get enough of them right now, I could eat this entire packet in one go'.

'Babe, this is the weirdest shit anybod has ever craved', Sam laughs, in-love. 'It's probably unlikely that your hormones are that much on level that she's going to think exactly the same'.

'I'm just saying, you're both missing out big time'.

'I think you're a crazy hormonal pregnant woman'.

'I think I've been sick seven times today and this is the only thing me and baby can keep down so you better shut the fuck up or I'll bovver you in the gob'.

They find each other very amusing indeed. There's plenty of chuckling and chortling going on and I'm not entirely sure why and I'm not entirely sure what they're chuckling and chortling about. It must be an in-love thing. Maybe in-love bods spend all their time finding one another hilarious, maybe that's how in-love works and before you know it you've spent your entire life laughing at one another until one day you're out of breath and out of puff.

Rosée is still munching and beaming at Sam but beckons to the old woman. 'Nana, come and take a look at her'.

Nana comes up and has a sharp glint in her eye as if she knows my shit better than I do. She takes in my blood-soaked mug and taps my egg making me wince. She comes right close to my mug and takes a big sniff. I'm kind of apalled, honoured and suspicious all at once. Who the fucking hell *are* these bods?

'You really don't have to do this-'

'Oh stop', she says, 'I've seen worse, you are nothing special'.

She puts her hand on my shoulder and I try to shake it off.

'Come on now', she says chuckling 'let me help and don't be a brat about it'.

She smells of sea salt and citrus which is a very trustworthy refreshing smell. So I go along with her even though I want to be the brattiest brat there has ever been. She seems like she could do enough talking for the both of us. In fact they all do. This is more than OK with me for now, I would just rather melt into a little sleepy puddle because to be quite honest I am fucking tired and I wouldn't be too bothered if I didn't wake up again. The past couple of days have been ridiculous and I am too tired to even be afraid that LAW FORCE will catch up with me and I have no idea who these fucking bods are, only a hunch that Sam is alright and I just want to sleeeeeeeeeeeeeeeeeeeeeeep. It really shouldn't be too much to ask.

Nana yanks off my soiled coat and takes my hand, leading me firmly up some stairs to the smallest bathroom box ever with the biggest power shower I have ever seen. As in the kind of shower that is going to rake my skin clean. I cower slightly.

'Oh come on, you're a big girl', says Nana. 'But first, let me sort your mug out'.

She plonks me on a stool in front of her and I really just want to fall asleep on it but she slaps my arm to keep me alert.

'You might be concussed missy, no falling asleep yet'.

I groan and stamp my bovver.

She has knelt down in front of me but leans back now with an incredulous look on her mug. 'Look at yourself. OK? Look at what you're doing. Cool it'.

'Soz', I mumble.

'It's OK. You've had a day and a half'.

She runs some warm water into the tiny little sink on the wall and puts in what look like soaps and antiseptic fluids and it smells kind of punchy kind of dreamy and I await the soft fluffy flannel she has poised ready to wash my mug. She gently dabs the main muck and I can see a murky browny red colour spreading around the flannel as all the grime gets washed away. I reel slightly when she touches my egg, so she begins to pat some strong smelling plant shit on it. After she's finished dabbing and cleaning my mug she starts rubbing oils and creams in her hands to cleanse it. I'm not entirely sure I want her to touch my mug with all that crap but she doesn't give me a chance to say no and she starts properly doing the whole massage thing and it's fucking weird because she's really going for it, pushing and squelching my cheeks and stretching my forehead and patting underneath my globes.

'This is weird', I say.

'Just go with it'.

'OK, Nana'.

She laughs. 'Vida'.

'What?'

'Vida, my name's Vida'.

'Oh. OK. Vida'.

After a few more minutes of my skin being smoothed and kneaded and wiped and rubbed, I start to relax. In fact, with just the two of us in here, away from all the clinking and clanking from the main brewery, it really isn't too bad. Granted, the box could be slightly less cramped but to be honest you can only really know where you're at in a small space, no surprises. Like when Rick...

I shudder and I sigh as twinges of sickness seep back into my tum and spread around the rest of my limbies and digits and all of a sudden this box now feels a little bit too small for my immediate liking. It's cramped, clammy and claustrophobic. Even after flaming fun I still can't shake off this Rick-yuck. Even though I am probably responsible for chopping Rich and Ryan, and I really don't feel bad about them because they are absolute fucking shites, it's Rick that makes me feel guilty and disgusting. Vida evidently takes notice, blinking wisely into my mug but not speaking for a few minutes.

After a while, she quietly asks, 'What's happened?'

I could carry on being a big babby bratty fuck but she's been really nice and has a certain sassiness about her that I really admire in other bods, so I don't see why I shouldn't begin to open up. Especially if I'm going to start making life difficult for them with the little lawful problemo I have created with my crummy lighter and honey-oil. This Vida's got her own fiery look in her globes. And she's got cracking bovvers.

'I am a Conscript, I have probably 2 or 3 friends in the

whole UK and I don't know how I got them but they're a bit mad and very fun and it is highly likely that LAW FORCE want to arrest me for a huge fire that has most definitely chopped my Employer and a fellow Conscript and has ruined an entire Business but it's largely not my fault'.

'Right', she says.

'Yeah'.

'I'm actually quite impressed'.

'Oh. Thanks'.

'I thought you had something sparky about you'.

'Um'.

'You don't need to worry about friends here', she carries on 'we'll keep you safe'.

'Why?'

'Because to be honest, you look like you need a rub-a-dub back into shape'.

'OK...'

'I would ask, however, that if you have a ze-phone, you give it to me for a sec'.

I scrabble in my pocket and pull out my ze-phone, flashing with all kinds of hologram notifications and messages from The Money News about the fire and the runaway. Vida promptly nicks it from my hands and crushes and smashes it underneath her surprisingly strong bovver, sending plastic and glass shit everywhere.

'Makes sense', I say.

She nods and starts to pick squashed and scrunched chips of my former ze-phone out of her rubber bovver. 'Those bastards can tap into all sorts with those things. Audio, visual, you name it. Don't want them knowing that you're here'.

'Thanks'.

She continues to massage my mug for a while whilst humming.

'Right', she says eventually. 'Time for a proper wash. I'll leave you alone for a bit. Take as long as you want and I'll find you some clothes'.

'Great. Also I'm on my period with no supplies, could you get me a tampon or something?'

'I live with my pregnant granddaughter. There isn't a leak I don't have some kind of pad for. I'm sure I'll be able to sort you out'.

'Right'.

She leaves and I am confronted with the monster power shower. I peel off the jumpsuit and clamber in so that I can get out of this small box as quickly as possible. Huddling in the chill, I contemplate the range of dials and buttons I could choose to press or twiddle. I swivel the knob and the water comes out scalding hot and I yelp and swivel the other way until the water is as medium in heat and intensity as possible. I let the water rush all over me and immediately sink to as close to a state of calm as I can. I always forget that shower time is some of the most valuable and productive time of the day. I take a good fifteen minutes mulling over the madness whilst all the muck piddles down the plughole. Large wholesale tubs and bottles of shampoo, bod wash, conditioner and other beautifications are lined up on the side opposite, so I take a little bit of each and rub it all over my hair and my aching bod. After a while, I turn the water off and step into the warm arms of a fluffy towel that Vida has left lying on her stool for me. She knocks tentatively at the door. 'Have you finished?'

'Yes thanks'. I huddle close into the towel.

She steps in. 'I didn't want to interrupt your singing'.

Fuck. I hate it when I sing without realising.

'Oh, thanks'.

'Here are some things for you to put on; I'm going to bin the jumpsuit because it's gross'.

'But it's my Uniform'.

'I think your Uniform is going to be the least of LAW FORCE's issues with you if you really did chop your Employer and set fire to a building and ruined a Business'.

'Yeah, but still it's my Uniform', I mumble, glancing down

at the mucky pile feeling a bit sick that it's going to be taken away from me. 'Can I at least keep my bovvers?'

'Sure', she says. She presents me with a new pair of underwear, a pair of blue jeans and a white T-shirt.

'You'll look perfectly non-descript. A Non-Descript instead of a Conscript', she says chuckling. 'I hope you don't mind'.

I do mind.

'I'm really not sure about this', I grumble, holding the jeans up. I like my Uniform. I don't trust other things, other clothes.

'It might be good for you'.

'What's good for me is a jumpsuit that is power black, allows for elasticated tum expansion after big grub and is utilitarian in form and composition'.

'Nevertheless, give these a go'.

'OK'.

'Don't forget your bovvers. I think they'll go with it quite nicely'.

'They'll go with anything because they are the best'.

'I mean, they're not red. But they're quite cool', Vida says breezily. She winks.

I scowl. She takes no notice and bustles about. 'Now, I've also brought you up some pads, tampons, painkillers and a fresh hot water bottle too. Take or leave what you want'.

'Thanks'.

'No worries'.

'I don't get it', I say.

Because let's be serious, all this weird fucking generous shit must have some form of an endgame.

She smiles warmly. 'Like I said, you look like you need some help. That's what I want to do. Neither me nor anybod else here has any form of love for this sitch. This society, this culture, the status fucking quo. You chopped your Employer? I bet he was a cunt and I bet he deserved it'.

'Yeah. He did. He was a cunt'.

'And I'll let you in on a little secret'. Her globes flash at me.

'What?'

'I did the same'.

'What?'

'Snuffed a guy'.

Ooh. I'm kind of not unsurprised.

'Cool'.

'Yeah'.

'Why?'

'It doesn't matter. I was young. I'd just left the poly-versity. The cunt had it coming'.

'OK'.

'But know that a little jab jab, a little boot in the choker, there isn't any harm in it. As long as you're alright at the end of the day, it can take you a long way. I get that'.

'Yeah'.

'Some other bods have different ideas, not least my own granddaughter, but I've been around a while, I've seen a lot. I know what I think and I know I can help you out, as the sitch seems fit. I don't want you to worry yourself'.

'OK'.

'Sort yourself out, there's some deodorant there, and come downstairs'.

'Do you have loads of bods down there?'

'No just a few, they mostly work here'.

'I don't like big crowds'.

'These are friends, don't worry', she nods.

I'm not convinced but I raise one side of my gob for her nevertheless because she is so ridiculously reassuring and cool and I feel like she deserves it. She leaves me with this wealth of supplies and I get myself dressed. I move as quickly as I can, trying to stop the walls from closing in and to keep the knots at bay.

After lacing up my bovvers, I inch out of this little cleanly claustrophobic sanctuary and bumble down the stairs into

Clinking and Clanking. Everything is still ticking and groaning but I zone in on the orange light that sticks out into the gloom. I peek into the hallway and hover at the end of it. I would rather nab a jacket lying around somewhere and leg it out the door and into the murky dark of Strangeways than to enter that small room full of bods I don't know and don't want to know. But then again Sam and Vida and Rosée have all seemed very nice so far. I moan quietly with indecision which attracts the attention of some bod inside who is sat right by the door, who then stands up and comes to stand right in my way.

I can only see its outline at first so I blink like a confused fool for a second as it says, 'Oh, right, sorry'. It steps back slightly so that I can begin to see its mug and head and it's a he and I don't mean to do it by my gob falls open. This bod has killer cheekbones and a kind of sallow moody mug with his scalp dramatically on show: his hair has been undoubtedly industrially singed which means that this must be our friend the Runaway who scampered and scarpered out of the prison. Vida, Sam and Rosée really are the kind of bods who will let everybod and anybod into their home, if you can call a brewery a home. They're mad. Like Montmorency and Monk but in a more of a barking kind of way.

He shifts uncomfortably. I'm gaping at him. We're wearing the same outfit.

'Er, hello', he says.

'Hi'.

'Come in'.

I inch in and I see a blur of mugs which are all smiling nodding and saying 'Hello hi hey hiya' at the same time. I see Sam sat in the corner and dart straight over there without making globe contact with anybod else. He budges up on the bench he's sitting on and I slam myself down onto it and hunch as much as I can so that all the attention can be diverted as quickly as possible. No bod says anything for a few seconds as I stare down at my bovvers. I think it's Rosée who picks up some form of conversation about music or other and I am determined not to get involved at all as a hum of chitter chatter gets going. I keep my globes fixed on the tips of my bovver digits until I can feel all of their globes not on me anymore. Sam gently lifts the digits of his trainer and puts it on top of my bovver and pushes down so that it squeezes slightly, leaving a little mark. I grin slightly to myself and respond with a slow dig into his ribs with my elbow. It might have been slightly too hard because he winces a bit but never mind. I think I might start to really like Sam. If he doesn't go on about all that in-love stuff too much.

After a while, I decide to unglue my globes from the floor and my lovely lovely bovvers and scan about the different bods in the room. It's a warmish snugly kind of box with dark wood benches and beams. An electric fire is what has created the orange glow and is aided by deep red curtains that hang on either side of a large window that faces into the courtyard. We're sat in two rows. There must have been a table in the middle but the scrapes on the floor suggest it's been moved out. Everyone's legs on the opposite bench to me are sprawled out into the centre in a sort of unspoken battle for space and they're all clutching nearly empty glasses of brown or beer.

I glance across closest to the door to the first sprawler and there the Runaway is, rubbing his digits across his singed head. I've heard that prison inmates have their hair permanently removed with this burning method that makes them instantly Recognisable because all that's left are scalds and dark tufts. Malga was different with his purplish barn, perhaps because he was Unrecognised, and I heard that what they do to your head depends on what you're in there for and what your punishment must be. Or it could just be Malga. I don't know. I wonder what this bod was in Strangeways prison for and why he ran away. Singe's globes flick over to me momentarily so I quickly train my own back on my bovvers.

The next time I look up I see him sat next to a bod on his left who is another sprawler leaning against the big yawning window. He looks like a haughtyish scabby looking bloke who's gabbing off big time: 'Yeah it was hilarious I started it off, me, just on like a whim, on a tangent started booing yeah and literally everyone joined in! The guy had to leave the stage for a few minutes because we got so loud and someone started throwing cans...'

Seems like a bit of a full of himself kind of swine.

Next to him and opposite Sam is who is sighing scornfully at what this bod is saying, rolling her globes at Sam and the bod sat on the other side of him. Rosée's also sprawled out in an obvious attempt to gain back the space that Big Gob is definitely invading. She pats her tummy and elbows the blue-haired girl sat next to her literally every other word that comes out of Gobby's gob and I think the other girl is blind because her lids don't open but she seems just fine, scratching at her blue fringe, sniggering at what the bod is saying.

I look back at the Big Gob they're both laughing at and he's got his hair coiffed into a perfect little bun at the back of his head and his mug is smooth and his brows are impressively bushy and he's jibber jabbering away about fuck knows what and it's all kind of cringe and the only bods who don't realise it are him and his singey runaway mate.

'These days, it's just like Adorno says', he rabbits, 'music and every other kind of culture is an industry, and it is just totally dead and devoid of originality and meaning'.

'It's because choice has become an illusion of an illusion', says Singe nodding his head and waving his digits. 'We are so far away from actually making any form of decision of our own that we're longing for the days when at least we thought we were being offered the choice of whether to believe in choice, now it's just so removed, *we're* so removed from it. We live as part of layers and layers of powerlessness and the same old shit just goes round and round and nothing changes'.

'Yeah, man, nothing changes. It makes me so *angry*', says

Bun Bun.

'It's the Market', concludes Singe rubbing his head and nodding along to what he's saying. 'It's the Market, that king of the last word in every argument. Fuck to every tangible thing of meaning'.

'I know right. The Money News is on every night and it's literally the bane of my life. They're such fuckers'.

Rosée is almost audibly gritting her gnashers. It sounds like this sort of conversation has been on repeat this evening and they are pretty annoying with all this spiely stupid jabber that doesn't make sense. The Money News is important. Everyone knows that.

The bod sat on the other side of Sam earnestly asks, 'Well we always get back to the same point though: what are you going to do about it Georg? Sat here in this snug, you feel so strongly about it, you think you're achieving something just by gassing. Surely you must do something, speak out, actually try to publically contradict the narrative that is being constructed for people'.

Ah, Bun Bun is Georg, the marketing man. Weird that he hates the Market so much when he works in marketing. I bet he doesn't hate it really.

Bun Bun looks like he's getting a bit hot under the collar. 'Well what more can we do?' he demands slapping his hands on his hams. 'I'm still part of the system, I can't help it, I can't break out of ideology. But *he*', he says, jabbing a sausage digit at the Singe, 'he ran away from *Strangeways* for goodness sake. He got in prison for his demonstrations and his writings and for that song he wrote and he actually managed to get out. It's fucking brilliant!'

I have never heard of this bod.

Bun Bun continues, 'That act, *his* act, of breaking and breakage and escape from entrapment and confinement reflects the beginning of a fracture in the whole shoddy spectacle. It disrupts time and meaning and it's the biggest chance we have. If any revolution is going to happen, any big *thing* any *event*, he has to be the leader, he just has to. He is the Breaker of power'.

Singe rubs his hands together and looks bashfully around as if he's expecting more praise. Smug fuck.

'Oh COME ON Georg', bursts the blue-haired girl erupting with violent laughter. 'Nobod gives a shit'.

'Well why then are there LAW FORCE and coppers and choppers and all that lot hovering around all the time huh?'

'Because it's a good story'.

'Stop thinking like that,' he thunders.

'Excuse ME, I will not', she yells.

He waggles his sausage digit at her. 'You're so annoying and stubborn. Why can't you stop thinking like that and saying things that are totally counterproductive? We'll never get anywhere and it's fucking annoying'.

'As if we're getting anywhere anyway! Georg you are so ridiculous. Drax is right. All you do is sit on your arse and rarararararara'.

The bod next to Sam who questioned Bun Bun looks sheepish, 'I didn't put it *exactly* like that-'

'Whatever, you might as well have done'.

Bun Bun smack his hams with his fists. 'Really? Am I? And what about you with all this story nonsense crap. No one believes the News anymore'.

How would he know? I believe in the News. What else is there?

'Honestly', Blue Hair continues, 'I think there are so many interesting things to say about our political and cultural zeitgeist, and I don't disagree with you and a lot of your ideas, but ehh. You're just a bit full of crap and I find you totally disingenuous and unconvincing and, I don't know', she says flicking her hands about, 'a bit of a knobhead'.

'Well luckily for you', snaps Bun Bun, 'I'm not important, you don't need me as a figurehead, we have Breaker'. He points at Singe.

Rosée groans, 'Oh cut it out with the Breaker bollocks,

he's not a fucking superhero'. Singe is looking pretty embarrassed now but at least he's not sulking like Bun Bun.

'No, you're right', says Bun Bun, 'maybe I did get carried away but he's the best deviant we have. Not even Malga managed to escape, he went through the rounds and was fucked over and over again and now I've heard he's nothing more than a headcase'.

There's a pause.

I kind of want to slap him for being so mean about Malga.

'I'd still fuck him', mutters Vida.

'Yeah, and me, agrees Rosée. Sam nods. He totally respects that. He probably wants to fuck him too.

'Aside from the obvious', says Rosée, 'Malga is a great person. I re-watch his video-essays all the time, he can articulate ideas better than anyone. He is critical and sophisticated'.

'Was, Rosée, was', says Bun Bun with a patronising sigh. 'But then he was Unrecognised and then he lost it. Even people who actually knew him can't even deal with him. You can't pin him down now, he's just one big postmodern mess. It's not his fault but he's not the person he was'.

'You are unbearable', says Blue Hair, 'I bet Malga knows exactly what he's doing. Just give him time'.

'I promise you, Lucy, there's no critical faculty there, no drive to spread the word and share his experiences, he just hides himself away', says Bun Bun with a fucking annoying air of finality. 'He's not the leader of any form of resistance needs, he can't unite'.

Singe nods.

Blue Hair Lucy raises her brows. 'Who? Malga? Oh, soz Georg, I thought you were talking about yourself there for a second'.

I involuntarily twitch with laughter. I can't believe what this stupid cunt is saying. He's a pompous thinks-he-knows-it-all because he's got a lot of shit to chat and spout and yap yap yap about. Defo compensating for something. I'm not saying that Malga and I are even friendish but at least I've GOT something of a fucking clue.

Sam looks at me and raises his brows with a smirk on his mug. I look back and blurt 'Fucking SSSHITstain,' by accident.

Bun Bun, Singe, Rosée, Lucy and Drax snap their heads to look at me. Vida coughs with laughter from the doorway.

'And who even are *you*?' asks Bun Bun, wobbling his head about like a loose pipe. 'Have you got anything to contribute?'

'No', I mutter.

'Are you a Conscript?'

'DON'T say that word', shrieks Rosée, flinging her arms out as if to physically stop him. 'How many times do I have to tell you? None of you are Conscripts, you're men and women who are forced to work for people who happen to have money and privileged economic status'.

'Fine fine', says Bun Bun waving his digits to dismiss her, 'what are you doing here?'

'Um...'

'Maybe it's none of your business Georg', snaps Vida.

'I-'

'Well? Come on?'

Humming has begun to resonate outside and we collectively look out of the window. The ring of electric light relatively distant only an hour and a bit ago is burning quite sharply outside the brewery walls casting weird twisted shadows in the courtyard. The night sky is slowly becoming more and more lit up with choppers whirring and clipping and swooping about through the heavy smoke still pluming from the warehouse. Slowly, through the black clouds, ze-holograms of Singe's ghostly pale mug emerge over the walls and are left sort of hanging in the air. Singe visibly shrinks in his seat and my Rick-knots clench and I wouldn't be surprised if everyone else's tums were convulsing too. The bleeps and tinny noise of whirring LAW FORCE are being raised over ze-megas and there are pooches barking. It's a little too close for comfort.

'Shit', Rosée grunts, thrusting herself up belly first and pulling a pair of big heavy drapes behind her together over the window so that it's completely covered. She makes sure no light is peeping through before whirling her hair and her bump back around with surprising grace and sinking into her seat again. 'Don't want any of those nosey LAW FORCE fuckwits peeking in'. In the meantime, Sam and Drax twitched up as if to help her before awkwardly realising that she's actually OK doing this on her own. Sam in particular tries to casually sit down again without anybod noticing but I definitely noticed. Sweet in-love sod.

The feeling in the snug box is less het up and angry now that LAW FORCE are camped outside, and even the gobbiest bods in our company are beginning to feel twingey nervousness.

'Are you on the run too?' asks Lucy.

'Kind of a bit'.

'Oh'.

I look over at Bun Bun who is almost leering at me with another fifty million questions perching in his fat gob ready to spew and hurl at me and I want to elbow him in the choker. Or snip off his stupid bun. Singe also seems interested in what's happened to me but is less aggro about it. I wish they'd both fuck off. I scowl and my egg starts to throb again.

Rosée rubs her hands together as the silence continues to hang over us weighty weighty. 'I think it's time to hit the hay', she says. Everyone nods and murmurs in agreement and in my humble opinion, it's the best fucking thing anybod has said all night.

Drax hops up and immediately heads to the side of Lucy so that she can lean on him.

'Thanks', she murmurs.

There is something very tender but reserved about him and his manner which is kind of less sickly sweet than poor old Sam. He tugs Rosée up and she in turn thrusts her hand towards mine and picks it up in hers.

I want to vom.

'Follow us', she says warmly, 'we'll make somewhere nice for you'.

Vida follows and gives me a quick push out of the warm fiery snug box, a push that isn't altogether unpainful but I respect that. Bun Bun and Singe remain sulking but as I leave, I can feel their globes flash at me. Scorn? Resentment? Curiosity? Any of the above. Ohhh I don't fucking care. I'm so tired.

'How are you feeling?' asks Sam, turning round to look back at me.

'Eggy'.

'Right', he nods.

'Here's a spot for you', says Vida gesturing up some stairs. The three of them have led me through Clinking and Clanking to the opposite side of the brewery to the Power Shower. Up the stairs and inside the cramped and bare little bedroom box is a big sky light in the ceiling and a smallish bed and a wardrobe.

'Uh thanks. Very much', I say.

'It's alright', is the general reply.

'Nana, help me with this', says Rosée, who begins to comically fail to reach over her big bump to pick up a large paisley shawl folded up and resting in the corner.

Sam nips and gets it for her.

'And the pins', says Vida following him and reaching down herself.

They set about pinning the paisley shawl over the sky light to sufficiently obscure me from anybod looking in. I sit on the bed like an utter lemon. Eventually after a lengthy amount of time of pinning and fussing and some last minute checking of my egg I am finally left on my one.

My egg is throbbing but I'm not going to waste what little energy and patience I have left caring about it. I take off all my clothes, notice that my period is significantly lighter, perhaps as a result of the stress of this whole shebang, and I nestle into the bed. I look up through the paisley sky light which stretches right across my line of vision on the ceiling. Choppers are still whirring around. I try to make myself feel better by imagining all their rotors ripping off all of a sudden so that they all wheeeeee to the ground in gorgeous red flames and that the night is lit up with them blazing and crashing and burning hard. But it's only a vague fantasy and it doesn't do much to dent my bad mood. Instead of leaping red flames the sky is lit up and peppered with nasty blue bright search lights. I haven't registered at my block in two days now, they're bound to know something's up. I wonder how long it's going to take for my mug to start hovering around up there with Singe's, all ghostly and ghastly above myself and all the crazy bods who have taken me in. The snipping and spatting of the choppers begins to mingle with heavy rain that falls with fat slops and splats onto the glass. That'll put a damp end to my beautiful fire. Thunder rolls in for good measure because Manc likes a good old shitstorm and the general rumbling flashing and slip slapping forms a chaotic and oddly satisfying lullaby until I'm just nodding off and Rick slinks into my mind with his sloppy rank thing swinging about.

I shudder. I can't help feeling, again, that if I don't wake up in the morning, it really wouldn't be so bad.

2.2

I'm unpleasantly unsurprised to find that I am awake again. New day, new old shit.

My head and bod ache, my knots are churning about and I feel sick and anxious but I reach up to find that the egg has gone down quite dramatically so I suppose that's some progress. My womb is also aching slightly but it's not the worst it's ever been and I don't think this month is going to be a particularly heavy one. Probably because of all the stress. Don't have a clue what time it is but light is trying very hard to peek through the paisley shawl. I stare at the shawl for a while and its strange patterns and wonder where it came from and why it's here. Montmorency has a few paisley ties for the weekend but I've never really looked at them before. The patterns are glowing against the light and I stare and stare at them. Fuck getting up and having to deal with the hot pot of mess I've landed myself in, I just want to stare and stare at these paisley drop drops until my globes are red raw and throbbing.

What does 'paisley' even fucking mean?

At least I don't have to go to my Employment today!

Maybe I'm not even a Conscript anymore?

I don't have a clue what I am or who I am or what I mean in the UK. Not a Conscript, my Uniform in the bin, my Employer burnt to a crisp. Shit. I'm no one and I've got no money to pay for my shit because Rich stayed a dickhead until the end. Got nothing.

I might as well just slob for a bit.

I don't know how long I lie there for, just staring upwards. I notice that all the noise from outside last night has pissed off and I can only hear a couple of choppers whizzing around. Hopefully those bastards from LAW FORCE have fucked off somewhere else to look for Singe. I have no idea if they're onto me or know about me and I don't particularly want to know. Staying in bed seems like the best possible option.

I lie there and close my globes and lie there and open them again and wonder if it's possible to just fade away if I just don't eat anything and I don't move and I just stare and stare.

Your stomach is always flatter when you've been lying down for ages and maybe the rest of my bod and I will just get flatter and flatter and flatter and then eventually I'll be a total pancake on a level with the mattress and just be calm flat dust. Flat enough to string out and dissolve these awful fucking Rick-knots.

It feels like hours skip and slide by.

I daydream about Malga and I wonder what Montmorency and Monk will say when they find out the naughties I've been up to.

I get restless.

I squirm and plonk myself down in a different position.

There's no shackle keeping me to this bed but I'm still starting to get trapped and uncomfortable and fidgety.

I roll around for a bit trying new shapes to get settled in; I kick the duvet about, stick my digits out the end and try the other side of the pillow.

In the end it's just a little bit too warm in here and I hate hate hate it but it's time to get moving about.

I find all my new clothes and pull them on and tentatively go to the door.

I can still leg it if I want to. They'll all think I'm sleeping and yes they have been very nice but I don't want to be asked any more questions because it's none of their fucking business and this whole thing is temporary and what would be the point in revealing everything only for things to go down the shitter like they always fucking do? I am starting to feel a bit bad about the fact that I've dragged them into the whole fire thing and it really wouldn't be very fair if they were to be caught up in it all. I should just go, just leave.

I peep out into Clinking and Clanking. Still fucking noisy. There's the empty space below and the vats in their row. I turn and I notice that there is an identical stairway going up the wall opposite to me, up to the Power Shower. I look over the railing and there are random room boxes underneath the stairs and then corridors leading in each direction out of the empty space, one way to the snug and one way to somewhere else I don't know. Even though this place is constantly noisy and frothing and bubbling and plopping, there seems to be an additional buzz of energy and activity about the place which is utterly fucking irritating and I'm exhausted just watching them. There goes that bod, Drax I think it was, the cooler one, leading Lucy around; Rosée can be heard directing and giving orders from the courtyard whilst even stuck up Singe and Bun Bun are thumping about making themselves useful. Vida is striding about gloriously, a pair of large bright earmuffs pinned to her ears and she's carrying a big cardboard box full of stuff backwards and forwards to the door of the courtyard. Those earmuffs definitely weren't part of her Uniform yesterday but I don't think anybod round here actually care about Uniforms much. It's strange.

I creep crouch down the stairs with the most bowed and bent posture I can to avoid being seen but apparently Vida's on the way back and she doesn't miss a fucking trick. She spots me before I can slither off and shoves the muffs from her ears down around her choker.

'Oh good, you're awake', she says. 'I have to say, you're up earlier than I thought you were going to be, but that's just great. How are you feeling?'

Just goes to show, you're never missed. Not for long. Fucking flat delusions of grandeur shit.

'Better thanks'.

'How's the egg?'

I pat my head.

'It's there'.

'It's gone a nice green colour'

'Great'.

'Are you feeling OK?'

'I'm OK. Not really feeling eggy'.

'Good. Great', she says. 'In which case, you can help me with this'. She thrusts a cardboard box full of a mixture of spoons and bowls and socks and fleeces and ladles and other sorts of things into my hands, picks up another for herself and then turns through the rest of Clinking and Clanking towards the entrance to the courtyard. I tramp after her and blink into the flat grey light. The sicky stench from the warehouse is still hanging about.

Once I'm out proper I'm instantly horrified and confused as to why there are literally hundreds of smelly bods who have amassed in the courtyard. Poor Ones?

Bods with thick purple rings under their globes, worn and dilapidated ensembles, well below the standard of UK Uniform policy, with high-end dirt sodden and sewn into them; gnashers missing, dewy damp hair, the enveloping aroma of brown, clear and bubbles, desperation about the whole sitch. Singing and swaying; they're not happy but they're not completely in despair. They are. They are them Poor Ones.

What does Vida expect me to do? What the hell am I supposed to do? I've just got up and all this lot are just stood there. Everyone knows Poor Ones just like to charge about and nick things and generally stink places out to high heaven, why the bloody hell are they here? I look down at my cardboard box and evidently we're handing things out to them. As the bods carry on groaning and gesturing and jeering and cheering, I edge over to Rosée who has commanded a rather impressive position in the middle of a long old wooden table that is laden with spoons and gobs and digits and bowls, waiting for the big vat of soup she's stirring to spew forth. Sam is gabbing through a ze-mega as loud as he dares, telling bods to stamp on whatever crummy ze-phones they still have, emerge from the chaos into some kind of sorry line and they all nod and smile but none of them pay attention. Dear fuck, I wish I was back in Clinking and Clanking, even with that fuck-awful bone-shacking hop racket.

I'm not being a twat but I didn't think that so many Poor Ones actually existed. Obviously you see random little clusters of them in the city Centre-For-Work, staring at the floor, cackling, howling, whimpering, lolling about not being particularly useful, which I honestly have quite a healthy respect for; but I've never seen anything like this, not even on The Money News. All I can think of right now are all the reports and holograms I've seen on there to reveal the facts about Poor Ones, how they make bad choices and it's no one's fault but their own for the shit states they're in and why the fuck should we help them out. Where have all this lot come from? They're not just here all of a sudden, they can't all be in the city Centre-For-Work like this all the ploughing time. I would have noticed them by now.

I look down at my box. How magnaniwhatsit.

For fuck's sake.

'Just go through and offer these to bods. They're waiting for grub and we can give them other bits and bobs as well', says Vida, her box half empty already.

'Where did you get all this stuff from?'

'Oh the wholesalers. They make deliveries with as much stuff as they can spare'.

I hugely repress my urge to break into my scowly snarl.

'Yeah', I say.

I wonder if these wholesalers are paying their Conscripts and suppliers properly and do they sell nasty sweatshop shit and do their warehouses get blown up and set alight.

'Off you go then'.

'What?'

I watch her as she starts up asking these lot for their names and where they've come from and what they're up to and what they'd like and who they're with and what they're plan is for the rest of the day and she sees what they mean and she understands what they're saying and she feels stressed about it too but she's sure there's some way she can help and on and on and on. I'm so unprepared for this and a hundred headlines and holograms keep tumbling on and on into my head because Poor Ones are a nuisance and a menace. They keep streets unclean and scary to walk down at night, they're not Conscripts so what do they do all day? This is common sense, common knowledge. You don't just invite a hundred of them into your place and let them make a ton of noise and make a load of mess. They'll probably steal stuff, get really greedy and take advantage. That's what The Money News says. I really really really don't want to do this.

I shuffle after Vida and wait until the Poor Ones she's talking to decide to shove off.

'Will I be safe with this lot?' I mumble.

Her rosy glow clouds over into a shirty but patient frown. 'These bods are in pretty dire straits. They have nothing. They are desperate, they are unhappy, grouchy, violent, rude and snide but they are some of the most experienced, world-weary and sensitive bods in the UK. No, you're probably not safe. But were you ever really safe to begin with?' She nods in the direction of my firepit.

Rick immediately flings himself full tilt back into my mind. I chew and bite my cheek. OK. Message received.

'Dive into a new perspective boddo', she says, calmly but forcefully thrusting me into the crowd on my tod.

I get stage fright. 'Can I pee first?' I turn back to ask.

'Oh, fuck, yes, come on!' she flaps, grabbing the edge of my cardboard box closest to her and yanking me back out of the crowd and towards Clinking and Clanking.

'I am slightly worried that all those choppers are still buzzing about', she mutters to me as we trickle through the crowd. 'I thought they'd have caught a trail somewhere else or given up'.

I want to say something snide and sharp because I have no

idea why she thinks they'd have caught some kind of trail somewhere else when Singe is in this very damn spot because they're professional shit sniffers and they're actually doing their jobs really fucking well but this woman is sort of blunting some of my stabbiness. She's too nice for my own good. I say, 'I suppose this is too much of a big deal for them to let go'.

'You're right', she nods. 'It's embarrassing for them'.

I nod too.

We get out of the noise, back into Clinking and Clanking and I put down my box. Vida points me to the direction of the loo so I stomp over and swing the door open. I sit down and get myself sorted and sink into a nice piss. Such lovely relief and respite. As I start washing my hands, Rosée clatters in bump first and greets me with happy surprise.

'I didn't realise you were up!' she smiles tossing her mane about as she shuts the door behind her and reaches into the cupboards for towels. 'Are you feeling any better?'

'Yeah, thanks'.

'Nana got you helping out?'

'Yeah'.

'Classic. She loves discovering a new pair of hands.'

'It's OK'. I decide to get a bit bolder because maybe she'll understand. 'I don't mind helping, I've just never seen so many Poor Ones just, you know, being there'.

'What?'

'It's a slight, um, shock to the system', I say.

'Right...' she says slowly.

'I mean, no one really helps Poors Ones usually, so I just don't know what to do with this lot, these, um, bods'.

'Yeah but helping is the least we can do', says Rosée sharply. 'The way they're treated is terrible'.

'Yeah but-'

'Have you got some kind of problem with helping them?' Her voice is getting louder and I realise that she isn't going to understand and this is about to get pretty fucking awkward.

'I don't know what I think about them. Only there's a lot of them and it makes me feel nervy'.

'These are PEOPLE', says Rosée with an arsey tone. 'You're not talking about monsters here'.

'Yeah I know but bods, uh, people, can be, you know, the fucking worst'. I'm getting really hot under the collar and I'm beginning to resent Rosée for it.

'I don't disagree', she concedes, 'but you shouldn't see Poor Ones so two-dimensionally'.

'I'm not. I can't help it'.

'I know, I know. But you should probably take some more fucking responsibility for your opinions'.

We stand in silence for a few minutes and it's a fucking heavy one.

I don't know what she means and it's getting frustrating and annoying. It's not like I'm ignorant or anything, this is just what I've read about and I can't fucking help it, I only wanted to get some fucking help and she's treating me like I'm fucking stupid. She realises that she's been verging on shouting so she coughs, swipes at her conk and extends the best of olive branches:

'Um. Dude, have you eaten?'

'No not yet. Vida, she, um, took me straight out to the courtyard'.

'Oh Nana', she laughs overenthusiastically, 'one track mind for fuck's sake. Come on'.

She leads me past the door and the rabbly raucous that is taking place out in the courtyard and straight to the kitchen where she starts whipping up some porridge. I lean against the edge of the table whilst she hums and whacks and continues with such graceful weightiness, perfectly in tune with her big round belly that counter-balances everything she does.

'Sorry to get annoyed with you, I don't want to be *that* person', she says after a while.

'What do you mean?'

'Oh you know, dogmatic and didactic'.

'Um, it's OK'. Don't really know what that means.

She pauses. 'Like a poly-versity fuck. Like Georg'.

'Oh no, you're not like them'.

I don't really mean that. It seems like everything with her is from the thumper which is OK and all but she doesn't seem to like anybod who has a different opinion. Very mirror mirror chicken dinner. I don't really want to say that to her mug though because I'm scared that she'll bite my whole fucking head off and shove it up my arse for good measure. Sam was wrong about her. She's a full on snobby snib snob.

'Oh thank god', she sings whipping round to me. 'I get angry but I would hate to think that *you* think that I'm on a level with them, they're so so irritating'.

'No you're definitely not as bad as them'. She really is the prettiest bod in the world when she's not pissed off with you.

'OK, good. With them, I think they only half believe what they're saying. The rest is just, you know, some kind of display and I'm never that insincere', she says beaming with all the sunshine. 'They posture and perform so much and I find it fucking annoying and I feel like the only way I can respond is by laughing at them. Laughter is the only way to shut them up!'

'To be honest though', I say, 'I didn't understand half of what you were all saying, let alone get into an argument about it'.

'That doesn't mean you're not clever'.

'I don't know. I don't care'.

'No this is important. I'm not having a young woman feeling like stupid big-headed fuckwits have elbowed her out a conversation because they use big words and long sentences'.

Lol. She does exactly the same bloody thing.

'It's not a big deal', I mutter grinding my bovver into the floor. 'I have nothing to say and even if I did have the words I probably wouldn't want to say anything'.

'You went to the poly-versity right?'

'No', I wince. 'I wasn't allowed. The Academy put me straight up for Conscription'.

'Oh', she pauses. 'Well, you're just like Sam then', she nods. 'He ended up here and, you know, he has more emotional intelligence than anyone I've ever met. He's the best person in the world'.

'OK'. I know she's trying to imply it but I am not like Sam. Sam is nice. I just want to trash and stomp and brush my gnashers and drink the clear and brown and bubbles and fuck shit up and flail about with Montmorency and Monk and watch Malga dancing, which is a pretty new development, and I very much like to kick the shit out of anybod who gets up in my mug.

'Oh god, I fucking hate this country', she sighs.

'There's nothing else', I say.

'No, I can imagine something much much better', she says firmly, hand resting on her bump. 'And don't worry about Georg and his runaway mate'.

'OK'.

'What's funny about him, about both of them, is that apparently they both used to want to be LAW FORCE when they were younger. There's something quite fascist about them still, even though they're on the right side now. That's why it's important to laugh at them'.

'OK'.

'The guy who ran away is Georg's friend from the polyversity, they were on the same course. So it made sense for him to come straight here to hide out. But I'm worried, he's full of trackers'.

'Trackers'. Sounds familiar.

'Yeah. I don't know if you know about it but I've done some reading at the Central Lib and they put all these nanotrackers into you once you've been incarcerated. It's a relatively new thing I think because you're actually given a 48 hour head start because the technology is still so new but still... they're everywhere in all your fluids'.

'Wow'. Trackers. Like Malga's.

'Yeah, it's disgusting. So invasive'.

'Yeah'.

'But the point is, he's been here nearly 24 hours and as soon as it hits 48, he has to be gone, because they'll be here, they'll find him and we'll all be in the deepest *deepest* shit. And what if it isn't 48 hours? What if it's less?' She shudders. 'It doesn't bear thinking about'.

Right, because that's helpful. Maybe she should just kick him out.

'Honestly', she says with a smile, 'I'm more worried about him getting us into trouble than you. So he will be gone soon, he has to. He can't stay here and put the rest of us in danger'. She pauses and starts to grin, 'And there'll be fewer annoying conversations without him and Georg encouraging each other'.

Oh fuck. I really am going to have to come clean to her.

'Rosée I burnt down my work and probably chopped two bods'.

She bats her globes in shock. 'What?'

'Two, um, people. I just thought you should know'.

'Are they looking for you?'

'I don't know. Vida broke my ze-phone so I don't think they know I'm here but they might notice I've fallen off the radar'.

'Nana knows?'

'Yeah'.

I pause.

My kind of antics are given a thorough go-ahead by Montmorency and Monk but you can just never tell with other bods.

She considers everything for a moment before sighing heavily. 'Nana really should have told me that. I mean, it doesn't look great, but that fire probably destroyed any DNA they might have been able to find. I suppose you could say that you covered your handiwork quite nicely'. She smiles.

'I'm just glad that Sam ran into you when he did'.

'I could get you into deep serious shit. And you've got a bump-'

Rosée laughs. 'Any more than we already could be in? It's fine. It's true, I have a bump, but I believe that we have a social responsibility to look after other people, especially when they're in the most trouble. I know it's very easy for me to say that, I've been so lucky that I've been born into Employment, my parents did so much better from the system than Nana could do. But I never want to overlook my privilege. It's really important that I do what I can for other people when I have so much'.

I know this is probably coming from the best place and I really want to like Rosée because she's with my mate Sam but she's verging on patronising and I want her to shut up and just get on with it, I don't want her fucking gladness. Thank fuck she's becoming a parent.

After gobbling down the porridge we head back towards the courtyard picking up my cardboard box of stuff on the way.

I look around and see that Sam is doing a good job of dishing out grub, with Vida mingling amongst the Poor Ones and the others scattered around at various points. I get a big encouraging push from her as I slouch past and I'm off, slipping and sliding on the cobbled floor thanks to the combo of rain, brown, bubbles and clear slopping about and also because we are in Strangeways of all places and there's no keeping the murk and grime out indefinitely.

I duck and dodge through the crowd. They are heaving around me, there are so many bods. They're all munching or squalling or having chats amongst themselves; some are crying some are laughing or yelling, some are swapping clothes others are reuniting with bods they haven't seen for ages; some are having a full on shouting match, some are elbowing their way to Sam's table whilst others are attempting to wash their mugs and hair.

I do a circuit of the courtyard and they all seem to ignore me, which I don't think is the idea that Vida and Rosée have in mind.

I go round again and for some reason, again, I just merge into the background and nobod wants to know or even realises that I'm there to help. I must look an awful lot like a Poor One with my big green egg which isn't what I was going for and it's actually a real fucking cheek.

After another circuit I think that it might be better to just approach some bod. I spot a young woman sat on some steps on the other side of the courtyard. She's relatively far away from everyone else, there aren't many Poor One bods around her and she looks like she won't punch my lights out if the attention and supposed help I'm about to give her is unwanted. I pick my way through the crowd and approach her. She is leaning against the wall cupping her long lank hair behind her ears and peering about in the crowd, kind of frantic. I stand in front of her. She smells acutely of brown bubbles and clear. She doesn't notice me at first so I growl shyly:

'Need anything?'

She blinks in my direction.

'Wha?'

'Need a fleece? Food?'

'Oh, yea sure', she flings her hand out towards me and lets it drop it to the floor again.

'Um, I don't know what you want...' I'm really not very good at this and she's making me look and feel like a sodding twonk. I want to scream and swear and kick her but she probably won't care and it won't be the help that Vida wants me to give.

'I don' know', she coughs.

Standing here in front of her isn't going to work. I step carefully closer, keeping the box firmly in front of me so that she can't get too close but she can still get a look in. She slowly blinks at me.

'Wha ya got?'

'Just, you know, some fleeces or-'

'SOCKSSSSSSSSSSSS', she screeches with wide manic globes, almost leaping into the box, and grabbing a scruffy brown pair. She sits down, whips off her scabby sandals and puts the socks onto her purple scuddy feet, sighing with pleasure as they're clothed in warm sweatshop knitty niceness.

'Oh wow', she smiles contentedly. 'Fanks, fanks so much'.

'It's OK'.

'Oh god, it's bin aaaaages since I larst had socksss'.

'No worries'.

'Aiaiai, d'you have ennything else for me? Can I brush me gnasheez?'

Good question.

'I don't know', I say, 'I don't think they have any here'.

'Pittty', she says.

'Yeah I know'. I would join in and all. I really want to fucking brush my gnashers.

Her globes fill up and she wipes them haphazardly.

'It's alright vo. I just wish Armie woz ere to see veeese'. She waves her feet around in the air. 'He knoaws I've wanted socksss for ages. He buggered off vo dinhe, and we can' actually stay vat long...'

'Who's Armie?'

'My fellah. Always buggerin off. He tries to be in ve sellins, you knoaw ze-TVs and telephoniccommunications and 'ere he can try and meet all ve bods. Niver bladdy works vo, silly barstard'.

We sit in silence for a bit. It's not nice to see her sad. I like her spunk.

I think of one of Vida's questions. 'What are you doing here today?'

She swings her head side to side. 'I needed some fings. Armie brought meay. But he's gone again and I don't knoaw ennyone and I don't wan to be here'.

I know that feeling.

'But ven you brough socksss', she continues, 'you made my day you did, you're anangel'.

I almost want to laugh in her mug.

'I am not an angel. Believe me'.

'You are', she nods earnestly her hair flying about, 'you're a God-send. You don't know'.

'I really really am not'.

'Do you believe in God?'

'No'.

'I do'.

'Why?'

'Becoz I always 'ave done'.

'I mean, that's not-'

'I try to go to Church and stuff but I carn't hardly evah make it, ya know? I'm busy or in ve wrong place. An there actually aren' vat menny left'.

'Right'.

'Wish I did vo, vat's what I should be doin. Vat's wha's importan'. My muvver's probebbly so angery that I don' know a Church to do my prayerz'.

I bite my chops. I should probably ask some more of Vida's questions. It seems to be working. I think of a good one:

'What's your name?'

'Wha?'

'Do you have a name?'

'Oh yeah, Mara. Nice to meet ya'.

She holds out a frail grubby hand and I take it gingerly.

'Do ya know what insidious meeans?'

'What?'

'Do ya know what insidious meeans?'

'Um-'

'I saw it on a trammzmuter when we were walkin on ve way 'ere and Armie fort it meant one fing and I fort it was someting else'.

'Well. I don't really know but I think it's something bad'.

'Like creepy and somefing sinister'.

'I dunno. Maybe'.

She starts clapping her hands and stamping her feet with delight. 'I knew it I knew it I knew it. I always said vat and I was really right. Much cleverer van over bods fink ya know'.

She lets rip a phlegmy cackle and grins and hugs her arms around herself. Her elbows are very pointy. I smile.

'Where are you living, um, Mara?'

She rocks backwards and forwards on the step. 'Dunno. Round and abou', norf and souf. Strangeways mostly really, wherever we can. Now we are here'.

'Right'.

'I move between the Tunnels and Arches quite a lot. I have two bruvvers as well who live round 'ere but I haven' seen them in ages. Vey always on the bubz braown and cleer, or ve owld spice ya know. I mean, I am too but vem lot are jus' out of contowl, so it's not like seein vem is a good nice fing. Hopeless cases'.

I wrinkle my conk. 'But how did you all get in this shit?'

'Vey lost us our spot in the accommodationz becoz vey's such knob'eds, nevver turn up on time, fings like vat. Vere's not enuff space ennyways at ve 'ostel and vey were bladdy late all ve time. Vat was the larst fing we hadz really'.

'Fuck'.

She shakes her head at me. 'But no no no, it's OK. I'm great! I go wherevah Armie wants really'.

'But why are you Poor Ones? How do you become a Poor One?'

She laughs. 'What you talkin bout? We're just Poor Ones, vere's always Poor Ones and vat's us, vat's just the way. Born vis way, told we carrn' do nuffing ven vat's it'.

'I… I don't know'. I pause. 'Why don't you just get rid of Armie? He sounds like a bit of a dickhead'.

'Ohh he's alrite. Your not ve first one to say vat darlin', she admits, contemplating a big insect bite on her shin. 'But ve fing is, you don' understand,' she says shaking her head.

'I'm not a victim wiv 'him or ennything, I know girls like vat. I just need somebod to sleep next to at night. I need a cuddle, a big arm. He's a dipshit but he knows how to keep ovver fucks away'.

'What do you mean?'

'Before Armie came along and I was on my tod, it was not good. Not good. No one lookin arfter you is the worst sitch in the world. And I had to fuck abat for maney. Anybod can hav veir fill. Being with Armie saves me from vat, I don' mind how much of a barrstard he is'.

My Rick-knots clench up. 'You mean, you've been...'

'Had samone's thing shoved in me? Oh yeah. It's bad. Once behind the pizza shop, once in the Arches, vat was the scariest. Loadsa bods aroun and no-one did nuffing'.

'Fuck'.

I think about that disgusting turd Rick, poised to put his flabby thing in me. My insides twist and crumple up. She must know something similar. I put the box down in front of me and sit on the step below her, curling my bovvers underneath my crossed legs.

'Yeah, I mean mostly I used to let bods put veir fing in for maney, but then sometimes I don' want vem to do vat and then they do it ennyway. But ven bods don' believe ya coz vey say 'well yous a proz so you wan to do vat' but then I actually really don' and no one believes me at all coz look at the state I'm in'.

'Fuck', I say again.

'An yeah', she continues, blinking at me, 'one time, one bloke shoved his fing in me and then his fuckin trout took all ma stuff. Pads, pants, SOCKSSS ve whole lot. Wha would vey wan my pants for? Seems a bit weird'.

I don't have a clue what to say to her. She's had the fucking worst time.

'No one would...?'

'No one would 'elp'.

'Not even, boddos, your mates? Could coppers help?'

She coughs with manic chokes of laughter. 'Are ya kiddin? Nah, nah way'.

Of course not.

'I didn't think so'.

'Vat lot, coppers, or even worse, LAW FORCE, vey actually scare me quite a bit'.

'Me too'.

'When they closed down awll the shelters and fings we were left to go to the Tunnels and Arches. Sometimes they come round and set fiyer to bods' fings because they have some sort of orders to get rid of dirt and poverteez but ven vey're just forcin us to go somewhere else. Not like we can get jobs nor nuffing, we couldn't even get Conscription after the Academy. Wha' we suppose tadoo?'

I gulp. I don't have Conscription anymore, what's going to happen to me? Why are Sam and Rosée and everyone looking after me? Is it because it's not too late? Did they think I could end up like Mara? Was stupid fucking Conscription with Rich and Rick actually the best thing for me? Because I really don't want to end up in this state.

She doesn't stop.

'I tried to tell one bod about the pants sitch becoz vey stole mah fings but no one cares. Everyone's got veir shit. And LAW FORCE's coppers are as likely to stick veir awful fings inside ya as mach as ve next fuck'.

I scowl at the ground.

I don't think I've ever felt this sad about another bod. I mean, I have the feels for Montmorency and Monk very occasionally but this is something I've never really felt before, ever. I've never had to and I feel heavier than ever because I can do a big fat fucking zero nothing to help her out. She's making me terrified for myself, about what happens next for me. The knots tighten more and more in my tum. I can't survive what Mara's trying to survive.

'Sorry'.

'Wha?'

'I'm sorry'.

'I don' understan you've done nuffing wrong, you've 'elped so so much. Made my day, you did'.

'You really mean that?'

'Absolulee', she nods. 'Fanks fanks fanks!'

I feel my mug getting hot.

'It's fine. You're welcome'.

'Also why's vat fellah staring at you?'

'Who?' I blink at her.

'Vat one over vere, he's been watchin you and us all ve time. Got no 'air'.

I snap my head towards where she's pointing and low and behold, Singe is stood at the side with an empty cardboard box looking over in our direction. Gawping fucker. What the fuck is he playing at?

'I don't know', I say.

'Who is 'e?'

'Oh just some bod who's staying here and helping out'.

We look back and he shuffles to the side a bit, he's looking embarrassed.

'Well, he shudn't stare coz it's rude. My muvver always said vat. Do you fink he has sum kind of problem?' coughs Mara her shackles raised slightly.

'Nah, just ignore him', I say.

'I must say vo, vey are so good to us 'ere. It's just nice to know vat somebod is finking about ya. That Rozée is a goddezz, MarymuvveroffuckinGod right'.

I think she is an Employer snob. But she has got magical hair and a bump. 'Yeah, she is isn't she', I say.

We look over and Rosée is directing bods and doling out food and clothing.

'I wan to be be like 'er one day. 'Elping ovvers. Not drinkin bubz and brushin my gnasheez all day, all the time. I mean, I'd still brush ma gnasheez but only keep it for specialz. Ya know?'

I nod. Totally agree, totally reasonable.

'I'll be with Armie in an 'ouse and with a babby on the way. Not stuckkk in this rut. Ven my muvver would of been proudame. Right now I'm a fuckin gam'.

Mara raises her digits to her gob as she gives a rattling and crackling cough.

'Kerrrrrrrrrrruhkkkkerrrrugh'

Then it begins to sound like she's hacking up oil.

'Kerrrrrrukkkkkyyyyughhhhhhhh'.

Guttural and phlegmy, the sort of cough where the lungs and guts might as well come up as the rest of the green and yellow snot stuff.

'Kerrrrrrrrrrruhkkkkkerrrrughkerrrrrrrukkkkkyyyyughhhhh'.

Her globes are half-closed and the coughs are raking through her entire bod and she's beginning to hunch over and keel because of the coughy stress and it's so sad and she's obviously in pain because she's clutching her choker and her thumper and I want to do something to help because she's looking at me with globes that are so so embarrassed and helpless.

'Shall I get something?' I yell over her.

She nods very slowly while she takes in a deep raspy rattling breath.

'Guuuuuuuuuuuuuuuuuuugh'.

She inhales another gulp of air to try and suppress the coughs only to be shaken and shorn by a barrage of splutters and spitty gobby mess. She's squirming on the step she's perched on, her hair catching in her gob and she flicks it away and all her crap goes flying with it and I leap up as she closes her globes and convulses.

'I can get you stuff, um, water, medicine. Some food perhaps'.

'Ggchhhhhhhyeccchhhhhh'

'Yeah', I say scrabbling up. 'Just wait here'.

'Aghcccchanchhaaangggggghelchhhhhh'.

'No I'm not, but I'll come back. Don't move, just a wait minute'.

I scuffle off and turn back just to check she's staying put and she's on her hands and knees on the step and her gob is horrifically hollow and wide open O O O, skin stretching over her cheekbones and her globes popping as she retches and all sorts of gunk goes splattering everywhere. No one goes over to help her and ask her if she's OK when she's obviously not and I feel firepit fire rage begin to flame up in my belly because bods are so fucking mean and her gob is gaping into fucking oblivion and her tongue is lolling and glistening and I turn to stride into the crowd, still slipping and sloppering all over the soggy cobbles and elbowing all the bods out of the way with all the force I can and they shout and swear after me but I don't care because I need to get back to Clinking and Clanking and back to the supplies that are stashed away somewhere.

'Is everything OK?' calls Vida, after I've barged through the line of bods who are swinging and swaying and waiting to get some grub from Sam at the table. I ignore her and thump my way up the steps and fling open the door. I gaze around Clinking and Clanking with that awful noise crashing and clattering and the heat rising from the hop and whatnot. I run back and forth from the toilet to the kitchen to the Power Shower and I can't find the medicine or a good cup for some water and some pads and tampons and painkillers and I'm getting really fucking frustrated.

'What are you looking for?' asks Vida quietly but firmly. She has followed quickly in my footsteps, not sure why I'm whizzing and stamping around but seemingly willing to help.

'I need the medicine and water and pads and stuff'.

'OK, follow me', she says walking past the snug and into a utility room box where there's a big stack of plastic cups leaning next to a pokey sink. I fill it up as she digs out industrial sized boxes of tampons and pads and painkillers. Juggling the water, I try to pick up the entire box but it's too heavy so I scoop out as much as I can into my arms whilst also balancing the water and I storm back off to the crowd.

Vida follows with a big brown bottle of medicine and says nothing.

I pummel my way through all the fuckers who are standing about like fat arsed shit fucker cunts when I need to get sodding through.

'Move, move, MOVE', I bark in front of me.

Where is she?

Where the fuck is she?

All I can see are thick, chunky mounds of sick, globby blood and mucus that have splashed all over the steps. The yellowy greeny reddy and purpley piles have skidded and slapped everywhere making a right old cacky shitshow and Mara is nowhere to be see. She's gone. Totally and utterly vanished and gone. There's nothing there. She's not fucking there apart from her sticky sorry mess. I swing about helplessly seeing if she's anywhere to be seen, huge enormous Rick-sized knots in my tum squirming and squelching and I'm scattering pads everywhere. I see Singe lurking nearby in the same spot and I lurch towards him flinging some of the stuff I'm carrying as I go. 'Where is she???', I shriek 'Where did she go where did she go why didn't you help her you sick disgusting scabby fucking fuckwit you cunt you CUNT you stood there and just watched you fucking freak...' and Poor One bods are yelling and laughing at me but all I'm looking for is Mara and she's fucking disappeared, probably with her fellah Armie who sounds like a no-good shit dummy and there's nothing better for her and I can't see her at all I told her to wait, if only she could have fucking waited and I screech and scream in Singe's mug AEEEEEEEEEEEEEEEEEEEEEEEEEEEEEEEEIIIIIIIIIIIIIIIIII IRRRRRRRRGGGGGGGGGGGGGGHHHHHHHHHHHH and throw the remainder of the pads and tampons and painkillers onto the floor right on top of his feet so that he bounces back because, why not, I've left a snail trail of sanitary stuff all the way behind me and there's not much left in front of me and I kick them and pounce on them with by big heavy hurly burly bovvers and I pound and grind them into the floor, they're turning brown and black and murky and muddy, destroyed, decimated fucking gone gone gone and I'm making a right old sodding mess and I'm seeing Rick's big fat mug and I'm killing him and killing him and I'm making his brains run free and I'm using my fists and I'm smacking and slapping the shit into the stones and I'm grunting and groaning because she disappeared and she's gone, thwacking and thwacking and thwacking the ground with my bruised and bloody hands and I suddenly feel Singe's arms round my waist and no he fucking DOESN'T and I'm pulled off kicking and screaming and lashing out at him with my bovvers and tears are running from my globes but I'm not sad I'm not sad I'm not sad I'm just angry so fucking angry and I've contorted my mug so horribly that there's no space for fucking tears they can fucking fuck off out my fucking mug and I scream and yell and slap him because he should have done something like the crazy boddos who are helping HIM but he's a slimy no-good shit muncher cunt and it's all his fault and and and I see Sam running towards me and he's trying to hold my mug still. Vida's with him, 'Stop stop stop, there's more, there's more just stop', and her mug is so tender and calm and I don't know why she's being so nice to me and I moan and moan until I'm just breathing.

We stand there for a few moments and the rest of the buzzy courtyard appears to be relatively quiet.

I look back and forth from Sam's mug to Vida's and their globes are open and wide. She raises her digits to her gob and bites her nails.

I'm glaring at them sadly and Singe's stupid arms around me are feeling quite tight but I feel like if they went away I'd just fall to the ground in a million different pieces.

I sink into them and feel drained and unsettled but calm.

I hear a screamy yelp.

At first I think it's me again and I whip my head up and see panic in Sam's globes. I don't think it's me, in fact it's definitely not me. Rosée is blasting down the courtyard with her bludgeoning bump leading the way and her rose-gold hair streaming behind her.

'STOP! Get her in, get her IN', she screams.

Poor Ones are scattering all over the place in a blur of building chaos and panic. Singe is dragging me over towards the door to Clinking and Clanking, my bovvers scraping and scratching the floor as we go. I am a heavy bod but there's no need to make it quite so fucking obvious you cunt.

They're trying to thrust me up the stairs when I turn and see it with a big old lurch, bigger than my Rick-knots; my mug *my mug* my ghoulish ugly mug is hanging in the sky over Strangeways.

I look gaunt and grey and I'm wearing my usual scowl and I'm looking right into my own lovely hateful angry globes and they know who I am and I know they're after me and I'm not going to escape.

Underneath, the Poor Ones are trampling on each other to get under cover as choppers whirr and whirl overhead. The only thing I can do is sort of half-arsedly snigger and snarl.

Vida, Rosée and Sam slam the doors shut behind me after we've tussled as best as we can up the stairs and we're all panting and shaking.

Outside we can hear choppers whirring and Poor Ones scrabbling and grunting, trying to get away.

Our chests are heaving. Clinking and Clanking has never sounded so obnoxiously loud.

2.3

'Fuck', somebod says.

'Fuck', somebod agrees.

'*Fuck*' hisses Rosée. 'Fuck, fuck, fuck'.

'I know', says somebod else.

'No really, fuck, I've fucking pissed myself all over the place'.

We all snap our heads to Rosée and sure enough there is an absurd little puddle in between her legs that's shining and shimmering under her bump.

I don't know who starts laughing first but suddenly we're all howling.

'No please, it's not funny', gasps Rosée who can hardly contain her own laughter never mind telling us to stop, all the while squirming as a few late drops dribble and drop about underneath her tulle skirt and bounce off her bovvers on the way down. It is ridiculous.

'What's going on?' a silvery voice pipes up and it's Lucy being led in by Drax. Drax immediately gauges the sitch and bursts into surprised laughter.

'Wait, what? No what, what's going on?' giggles Lucy tugging at his arm.

'Rosée, she's pi-pissed herself', he squeezes out between chuckles.

'Ohhh', laughs Lucy, 'Ro, you're a mess dude'.

'Yeah well thank fuck you can't see it right!' calls Rosée.

'Yeah well you won't believe the image I've got in my mind', Lucy calls back. It is fucking funny and I can't help getting swept up in it myself, maybe even too loudly but who gives a fuck, she's just pissed herself. Singe has let go and is rocking backwards and forwards whilst Bun Bun snorts like a stuck pig.

'Oh Rosée', says Sam, giddily lunging towards her and Vida, who's trying to hold her grandaughter up whilst honking with glee and dancing around to avoid the puddle of piss.

'Oh Sam', Rosée groans clutching her bump, 'I AM a fucking mess'.

'The best fucking mess I've ever seen', he continues, 'come on, let's clear this up you silly gam'.

Well, there's nothing like a bit of well-timed accidental pissing from a pregnant woman to help relieve things. But once she's hobbled off with Sam and Vida in tow, our laughter tails off meekly and we all realise how manic we sounded, how over the top our fucking shrilly hoo-ha has been and we all end up looking at the floor and listening to the Poor Ones who are still desperately scuffling about outside. Gnatty choppers are still buzzing around too. Fat lot of help we were when it actually fucking mattered.

'So what happened?' asks Drax quietly.

'Lost her fucking shit didn't she!' snaps Bun Bun with a cunty guffaw. 'I've never seen anything like it. You've got a fucking problem mate, you're like a fucking harpy'.

'Fuck you', I spit under my breath.

'HE', he says pointing an ugly fat fucking digit at Singe 'didn't even do anything wrong and you were aggro. Fucking schizo crazy. It was ridiculous'.

I'm beginning to boil at this bod's fucking utter shit for brains. This isn't about ME. Well it is but it's not the POINT. Lucy steps in and says, 'Pipe down Georg, were you even there?'

'Well, not really, but what I DID see was awful, absolutely outrageous. Is that REALLY an example to set?'

'Look, it really was OK', says Singe shaking his head huffily. I'm kind of surprised that he hasn't started bashing me too but maybe he's just in shock, or he's hurting, or he's putting up some masculine wall and is actually in crisis. It's very difficult to tell with hetero man bods, you haven't got a clue where you bloody stand.

But it's OK because Bun Bun is still at it, 'No, no, you

don't look alright mate, she fucking slogged you. I mean, I didn't realise we lived in a time where recourse to violence is the ONLY way to proceed...'

WELL WHERE HAVE YOU BEEN YOU CUNT?

But Singe has already jumped back in there: 'It was an upsetting, thing, OK'.

'What', Bun Bun tries to continue, 'you mean that-'

I've had enough.

'Did you see where she went?' I butt in and snap at Singe.

'Not really', Singe says scratching his singe. 'This guy just came out of nowhere and sort of scooped her up and then they scurried off into the crowd'.

'Must have been fucking Armie...'

'What?'

'It doesn't matter'. Oh fucking Mara, I hope she's alright.

Singe carries on, 'She was in a bad way, I, I just didn't know what to do'.

'And maybe it doesn't even matter', says Bun Bun, 'she wasn't the only person there in a right shit state'.

Wow.

I ignore him.

I turn to Singe again and say, 'Well maybe you should have brought her inside you big fucking dummy'.

'Hey, don't start that again, yeah, don't start!' says Bun Bun with his fat brows wobbling up and down in time with his stupid sing song voice. 'You need to be looked at, you're completely unstable'.

'Oh FUCK OFF Georg', hurls Lucy.

'How am I the bad guy here?' he squeals, 'she's completely off her head!'

'Just leave her alone OK', she replies.

But it's too late, I've leaned over and I've nutted him in the mug.

Serves him right.

He pulls back rubbing his gob which has a nice little cut-cut busting out. First blood is glorious. He lunges at me. I bare my gnashers and as he charges forward, I whack the palm of my hand up into his conk with a loud sickening crunch.

'OOOOOOOOOOGH', he shouts, his globes tearing up.

I stomp forward. I want to kick this cunt right in the thing but Drax snaps hold of my wrist and flings me to the side.

'That's ENOUGH', he yells. Singe pulls Bun Bun out of the way and Bun Bun repays him by shoving him off roughly and falling to the floor himself.

'Calm down', Singe shouts, brushing himself down. 'Just cool it alright'

'WHAT DID YOU DO THAT FOR?' Bun Bun yells at me.

'WHY DIDN'T YOU BRING HER IN?' I shriek at Singe.

'WHY IS IT MY FAULT?' he retorts.

'What the HELL is going on here?'

'Vida...' says Lucy.

She casts a long stern gaze over us all and we shut right up. Of course it's Bun Bun who speaks first, little snitchy grass fuck, no wonder he wanted to be LAW FORCE.

'That girl is a fucking psycho SHIT', storms Bun Bun, clutching his bleeding gob and lying in bits on the floor.

'Georg, stop shouting. Stop, please', Vida says calmly, 'let me help you up'. She goes over and pulls him up under the arm with surprising strength.

'Look, I don't think it's OK that she stays here. I'm bleeding'.

'Oh but it's OK that your trackerful friend- no offence dear- is here instead?'

Singe shakes his head.

'Yes', says Bun Bun, 'because he's a victim of a bigger system'.

'Don't you think we're ALL fucking victims, including HER', Lucy shouts pointing at me. 'You are such a privileged bollock Georg'.

'You are actually letting her get away with this', Bun Bun gasps. Looks like I've actually properly winded the stupid fucker.

'No but the way you're speaking right now is completely unacceptable', says Vida fixing him with a razor sharp gaze.

'And quite honestly Georg I think you kind of fucking deserved it', adds Lucy.

'Lucy, shut it', says Vida. 'You are a nightmare wind-up merchant and you're getting on my wick'.

Lucy crosses her arms.

Bun Bun exhales sulkily and sadly, wipes his conk and starts to head over towards the door.

'Now hold it!' Vida commands and he stops.

She glares at me. 'Don't'.

'OK', I say.

'Don't do that again'.

'OK'.

'You're sorry?'

'No'.

'Alright, I get it. But don't you ever do that inside the house again. You can take it outside if it's worth that much'.

'OK'.

'Promise'.

'Yes'.

'Oh great, that was great', Bun Bun snaps, 'justice is served'.

'YOU', says Vida, turning back to him nimbly, 'I am going to help you with that split gob and then you are going to come with me outside and start helping the last of the Poor Ones left behind and we are going to clear the place up'.

'Whattttttttttttt' says Georg. 'Are you kidding?'

'You bet I'm fucking not'.

'I'm BLEEDING Vida'.

'Which is why I'm going to clean you up too. Now, mush, let's get on with it'. She takes him by the shoulders and leads him to the door and passes him through.

She turns back to me with utter force and conviction.

'I've been more than fair to you. Don't you dare take the piss out of me. Understand?'

'Yes'.

'Right'. She fixes her beady globes on me for a few more emphatic seconds well and truly making me feel like the first class fuck I am before turning to follow Bun Bun, picking up a bin on the way out and pushing the door open with her hefty scarlet bovver.

Drax exhales heavily and Singe stares at the floor.

Lucy breaks the silence first. 'Right you lot, there's only a few things that will makes us all feel better and fortunately for you fuckers we have some in ample supply. Beer. Come on Drax, back to the tasting room please'.

She holds out her arm and Drax expertly laces her arm through his and they make off towards a door round the back of one of the big vats at the end. Singe hops up at the prospect.

'You coming?' he asks me.

Honestly, Singe, I would like to crawl into my bed under that swirly paisley scarf and curl up and die. I am scared and tired and I'll probably never leave this clinking and clanking hovel full of shits like you and Bun Bun, especially now that LAW FORCE are on my tail and I've completely fucked things up but I wouldn't and couldn't have done anything differently because so many bods deserve the shit they sling about to smack them back in the gob, including fucking awful me, but it's all so exhausting and my knots are still Rick-sized and growing and I feel so sad and disgusting. I hate everything. I hate everyone. I want to be left alone.

Then again. All things considered. Beer might not actually be a bad idea after all.

I snort at him in reply and get up and follow them.

They have gone into a warm wooden and coppery kitcheny box and there are loads of glasses and bottles and barrels and vats, fucking giants made of stainless steel, stretching from the floor to the ceiling all over the place. Towards the back is a tall wooden island with a long sink behind it running along the length of the wall. It feels really nice and homey, like in a ze-mag. There are a number of tall stools clustered around the big island. I pull one towards me and perch on it. Drax is busy unloading brown bottles of beers onto the bench and Singe is heading over to help him out. I watch them fluidly moving together to unload the crates and soon enough the bench is covered with bottles. I fix my gaze on Lucy as they work. She's standing at the head of the bench like some high priestess, all-seeing and all-knowing even though her globes are perpetually shut, flicking her cool blue fringe out of the way and smiling as the thuds and clunks of bottles sound the arrival of delicious bevs. She definitely has a cool area of Employment I have to admit, much better than being a Copy Cat. Imagine just tasting beer all day. Then you can regularly get off your mug and out of your mind until you feel like a comfortable empty nothing. Fucking ideal.

All of a sudden I notice for the first time that her lids seem strangely stamped and scarred; there are funny marks specked all over them. I frown and lean closer off my stool. I know she can't see me so it's not like I'm being rude. And yes, there are, there are pale scars and burns on her lids and I shudder because it looks like something seriously fucking fucked up has happened and I bet there's some kind of horrible nasty story there that I kind of don't want to know about but I bet will also be horrifyingly intriguing.

Drax looks up and catches me gawking and starts to laugh. 'Ohhhhh Luce, looks like we've got a Blunter!'

'Ooh who? Which one?' she laughs in return, clapping her hands against the surface of the bench.

'Fire Cracker', he says. He turns to look at me.

I don't appreciate the nickname.

'What's a Blunter?' I demand hotly.

'Well, there's three things you can be', says Lucy nodding

her head. 'One, a Blunter, two, a Dancer, three, a Glosser. A Glosser like him'. She points to Singe.

'What?' he says.

'You gloss over it because you're *all liberal*'.

'Over what? I don't know what you're talking about'.

She cocks her head to the side. 'My blindness', she says.

'Well', says Singe, shifting uncomfortably, 'I don't see that as a bad thing. If you excuse the expression'.

Lucy laughs, 'Yeah. That's the problem'.

'I don't understand', I say.

'It's the three ways in which people respond to me and my lack of sight', says Lucy grinning. 'I have to say, a part of me thought you'd be a Dancer'. She gestures in my direction. 'You know, skirting around and avoiding the issue. There is something slightly and silently out of control about you, if you don't mind me saying'.

'Um'.

'But you being a Blunter makes even better sense. You know, you also barge your way through stuff, making a point of me being blind and demand to know what happened'.

My gob creeps into a grin because yes, I like it, I *am* a big bolshy barger. But then again:

'I didn't actually demand anything'.

'Yeah, but you were staring', says Drax raising his brows and folding his arms.

I scowl and look down feeling embarrassed. 'I didn't think it would matter, it's not like she could see me'.

'HELLO', shouts Lucy, slamming her palms on the table. 'Rule number FUCKING ONE, don't talk about me like I'm not here. My globes might not work but I am still in the fucking room and if you have any comments and queries about her, she, me, then direct them my way buddy. OK?'

I twist my knuckles into my thighs and nod.

'OK?!'

'Oh yeah, shit, sorry, yes'.

'OK. Right, now let's have some fun please, this brewery

is turning into a right morbid boneyard'.

'Yeah sorry about that', says Singe.

Lucy waves a hand in his direction. 'Ugh, I have no time for self-pity my friend. We have games to play and beers to taste'.

Drax laughs, 'Lucy, you're too good at this game'.

'What game?' asks Singe.

'Well, I'm going to give her these here beers to taste and she is going to guess- '

'Uh, excuse me Drax, I am going to KNOW...'

'Right yeah, sure', he laughs with his deep voice and his creasy smiley mug, 'she's going to *know*, which beer I have given her to taste'.

'Really?' Singe laughs.

'Yes really', says Lucy nodding and smiling.

'I don't believe it', he teases.

'Seriously, you should see this' says Drax pointing at her. 'She's too good. Man, she's supernatural'.

'And why not?' asks Lucy. 'I can't see so I might as well have golden tastebuds. Plus these beers are my babies, I BIRTHED them. Of course I can tell which is which'.

Singe laughs again, pulling up another crate. 'I am going to reserve my judgment'.

Good for you Singe. Congratulations.

And anyway, it's obvious that he's not reserving his judgment because he's shaking his head, scratching his brow and chuckling because he can't believe that she's going to taste what looks like seven different beers and get them all 100% right.

Drax hands her the first and then gives me and Singe a bottle as well. We sip in unison.

'Mmmm', says Drax.

I agree. It's fresh as a fresh thing but sinks into my tum with comforting warmth. I immediately take another long gulp and settle onto my stool more comfortably. Singe is equally chuffed with his beer and turns to me and grins. I mean he has a nice smile in a chiselled singed way but it is totally unnecessary. No need to smile at me mate.

I feel a very familiar prickly party urge coming on. I want to brush my gnashers, beer alone just isn't going to cut it.

'Lucy and Drax, can we brush our gnashers as well?'

'What?' says Drax laughing.

'We can't', says Lucy.

'Why not?'

'We don't have any. Rosée wouldn't have any of that kind of shit around, especially now she's pregnant'.

'That's a shame'.

'Yeah, I haven't brushed my gnashers in ages. But it's hard, I dream all sorts of horrible things. Don't think I want to go near it again'.

'What do you dream about?' I ask.

'I didn't realise blind people can see in their dreams', says Singe.

'I mean, I could see from birth, I just can't now. It means I can still have dreams. If I was born this way, it would be more auditory'.

'Right', says Singe.

She doesn't answer *my* fucking question.

'Now this', she says swigging, 'is, obviously, Daisy Donut'.

'Daisy Donut!' parps Singe with laughter.

'Yeah Daisy Donut'.

'What kind of name is that?'

'Clean and fresh as a daisy, heavy, reliable and tasty as a donut. And the rest of the best of the beers of course'.

Drax thumps his bottle on the table. 'Damn straight Lucy, you're fucking right'.

'I know', she shrugs, flicks her fringe out of her globes and takes a few gulps.

'What a name', says Singe, shaking his head incredulously. '*Donut?*'

Donut. It really is a great drink. I'm by no means a beer fiend because I tend to stick to bubbles, brown and clear and then I love a bit of the old brushing of the gnashers but this is good. I feel like making Daisy Donut a permanent fixture.

It doesn't take me long to swallow the rest of the beer and I realise it's because I'm fucking parched and the rest of them are really fucking slow. Drax is still drinking his as he starts to open the next beers, all in a darker brown bottle with an icy blue label stamped all over it. Lucy is swigging and there's foam all around her gob. Drax notices too.

'Aw Lucy, you have a moustache, queen'.

'Oh shit. Well I suppose we're all queer here. Give us a wipe Drax?' She waggles her tongue around and it's grotesque and froggy.

Drax steps forward producing a ready and prepared tissue from his pocket. 'Gammy yuck girl'.

'Yeah yeah yeah', she says pushing him away gently. 'Thanks'.

'Right, all finished?' Drax asks.

Singe slurps the rest of his bottle and places it down on the table and nods.

I burp a big belch.

'Hello,' laughs Lucy. Drax chugs the rest of his down whilst Singe looks at me slightly terrified.

I throw my head back and sigh deeply. I am full of beer beans and I want the next one. 'What's coming up?' I ask.

Drax hands us each the blue labelled bottles. I take a swig. It's sort of sharp, even fresher than the last one but not as smooth. This one would be amazing fun to get pissed on.

'WHOOO' says Singe. 'This one is sharp'.

'Much higher percentage' says Lucy. 'The highest you can go for a bottle'.

'Fabulous', says Drax.

'Which means, that this one is Kristalised'.

'You're right, of course', says Drax.

'Kristalised?' asks Singe.

'Yeah' says Lucy.

'But, you've spelt it wrong'.

'I don't care'.

'Dunked!' says Drax, laughing at Singe.

'But, you can't have it not spelt correctly'.

'I DON'T CARE'.

'But, you just can't!' says Singe, the wideness of his globes emphasised by his singed scalp.

'And why not?'

'Because, that's just not how you spell it. The letters are wrong and it doesn't make sense'.

'I can't see those silly signy letters anyway so why should I care?'

'The rest of us can-'

'Well they don't mean anything to me'.

'But they're all we have to even think about meaning!'

'Words and language change. Alright, they can be manipulated, twisted and bent out of all whack. What's the point in tying yourself down to a system of arbitrary markings that some of us can't see or understand in the first place, that we can't adapt and change? I'm surprised you don't understand that'.

'Yeah, I do understand that', says Singe hotly. 'But there's pointing out the ways in which language is fluid and changeable but then you can only express that through the structures we have. Use the system to take down the system and highlight its deficiencies'.

'Is that why you broke out of Strangeways?'

'That's different'.

'Doesn't sound very different to me. Shall I just go and call LAW FORCE?'

'But don't you have Braille? That's another sort of system of signs to help you create meaning?'

'Oh please. The UK got rid of all the supports and funds for written materials in Braille a long time ago. We get audio support only now'.

'I didn't know that'.

'Why would you? You're not considered a drain on

resources, a cost to cut'.

'Guys. Beer, games and fun remember?' says Drax. I totally agree with the return to beer thing because I really have no idea what these bods are going on about.

'Right', says Lucy. 'Truce?'

'Truce. But I still don't agree'.

'That's fine. I truly truly truly don't care'.

She's got an incredible temper for a bod who doesn't care.

'OK, so we have Kristalised', says Drax finishing his off. 'Mate, pass round those ones yeah?' he asks Singe, pointing to bottles with green and red labels.

Singe does so, taking off some lids as he goes. I take a sip and it's a light beer that every so often has a surprising firey pang. There's something fruity about it too.

'Tricky', says Lucy. 'And I have to say, bringing Kristalised into the game early on was a great way of confusing the old killer buds', says Lucy, swaying ever so slightly.

'You're welcome', says Drax. 'What are your contenders?' asks Drax.

'It's either, KJoed', says Lucy, scrunching her hair at the back of her head, 'or it's King Kong'.

'Those buds aren't on the wane are they?'

'NEVER', says Lucy, louder than we all anticipate. She grins afterwards. 'Whoops, soz'.

'Don't take all day about it', says Singe, who's powering through this one. 'Although, I'm really fucking enjoying this. Best one so far'.

'Noted', says Drax.

'Um...' says Lucy.

'Come on now Mother Beer'.

'Alright. KJoed, KJoed'.

'And you're right'.

'Fuck. I was worried about that one'.

'Really?'

'No'.

'Yeah fucking right', booms Drax.

'Nah, really though I was in a bit of a muddle. It happens to the best of us especially with beers that are kindred spirits. Pass us a seat please Drax? I'm getting jellies'.

Drax gets up and pulls up a stool with handles on either side and eases Lucy into it. It's amazing how much trust there is there between them. They are obviously two very different boddos but there's a kind of twinniness going on there that I haven't seen before and I don't understand. After all these beers, I'm beginning to feel merry.

'Whyyousogood?'

'What?' asks Drax.

I clear my choker. 'I mean, you two seem close'.

'Yeah and?' says Lucy wriggling into a more comfortable position. 'Drax get more of those beers out'.

'Alright alright'.

'I mean. Have you known each other long?' I ask.

Lucy looks upwards thinking. 'Well, I was here before him. I can't remember how long it's been since you've been here'.

'Coming up to three years', he says.

'Right. No, hang on, is it five or six?' asks Lucy.

'Feels like ten to fifteen with you flapping about'.

'Oh shut it, you're a fucking grandpa anyway'.

'Yeah'.

This has not answered my question and I don't want to pursue it because it's just confusing and I'll just end up getting fucking irritated.

'Drax is the jammiest git I've ever met', continues Lucy.

He laughs in return whilst passing round some more bottles. 'Yeah, I'm pretty jammy'.

'Why?'

'Put it this way', says Drax leaning on the bench 'you two aren't the only people running away from the shit State round here!'

I blink. 'I don't know what you've done but you seem OK about it'.

'Yeah, it's been years. Need to cut that stress loose after a while or it's just unhealthy'.

'What did you do?'

'Nothing rock and roll right. Literally, not a big deal at all, except to the UK and LAW FORCE. Out-stayed my student visa. I came over to be at the poly-versity. Did my studies and stuck about'.

Cheeky sod.

Singe perks up. 'Ooh what did you do at the poly-versity?'

Fucking poly-versity stuck up snob.

'I was an exchange student studying Maths'.

'Oh, that's impressive. I could never do Maths', says Singe, leaning forward.

'Well, it's not what a lot of people expected it to be. Lots of conceptual stuff. I actually preferred asking the philosophical questions instead of just doing sums and shit'.

'Like what?' asks Singe.

'Well, you know, asking what zero is for example? How do you quantify nothing?'

'Yeah man, that's cool. I mean, that's really interesting. 'Nothing' is articulated though signs, which I suppose includes numbers, so it must come from and mean 'something'. Nothing must be something. Is that what you concluded?'

'Can't remember. I don't care as much anymore anyway. I've been working with this bum ever since'.

Singe blinks and says nothing.

'Shut it', says Lucy taking a sip of the new beer. 'Hmmm, now this one is King Kong. Mellow and almost tropical with that malt'.

'Right', says Drax, clinking her bottle.

I take a sip too. I feel like Singe has sabotaged my question again with his gobby gob and chatting about all that difficult mind-bending shit so with fruity bubbly goodness fresh in my tum, I decide to pick up my babble from where I left off.

'But why did you stay if you knew it was illegal?'

'Well', Drax says, swallowing some beer hard. 'It wasn't so much of a big deal at the time, and it was a long time ago. I was in a relationship with a really great girl and I wanted to stay and get a job and we were great and then we weren't. Then I ended up at Magna and I was enjoying living here, paying my taxes, being part of the community, learning about brewing and Business, you know. But then LAW FORCE were created and Conscription was created and then who would be crazy enough to hand themselves in as an illegal foreign alien immigrant now? I'd be fucked and in that prison over there'.

What is it about this Clinking and Clanking brew shack? It's like all roads lead here. A fucking Hood's Hideout.

'I suppose that's fair enough', I say.

'You suppose? Girl you're in hiding, you're no better!'

This is true.

The next beer that comes along is slightly nutty but turns into a sweet bubbly blend. It's a bit of a mad one, never tasted it's like before.

'Harpoon!' shouts Lucy.

'I told you she was good', says Drax.

'I jusdon' believe it', slurs Singe.

'You better believe it buster because it's happening', says Lucy rocking backwards and forwards in her chair.

'And anyway', says Singe, 'what's the point in beer-tasting anyway, how is this a job?'

'You know, you've asked that question in a pretty Georg-y way'.

Singe shakes his head and smiles, 'Not true. Georg wouldn't have asked a question. He'd have stated it as a fact. Sorry though'.

Lucy contemplates and nods. 'You're right. He wouldn't have asked and if he had asked a question it would be rhetorical and followed by another question or statement that is equally ludicrously annoying'.

'He's not all bad you know, I agree with him on a lot of

things'.

'Yeah, but the guy is constantly flaming people, he never actually does anything to make a change or make a difference. Always on a fucking tilt', Drax says flicking a bottle top onto the floor.

'At least you did something to get put into Strangeways. You made some kind of impact', says Lucy.

'What has he told you?' Singe asks looking shifty.

'That you wrote some kind of radical blog that deconstructed the systematic oppression of LAW FORCE and the State', says Lucy. 'Sounded pretty cool actually'.

'Oh' says Singe.

Lucy glares in his direction. 'What do you mean 'oh?'' she asks. 'Was he wrong?'

'Well, um, yeah', says Singe, ripping the label of the nearest bottle to him.

'Go on', says Drax.

'Yeah, what *did* you do?' asks Lucy her arms draping over the handles of her chair.

'I, uh, it's not actually that impressive'.

'Go on', says Drax.

'Well, I was caught stealing'.

'Ooooh', says Lucy. 'What?'

'Something really expensive right?' asks Drax.

Singe scratches his ear. 'Not exactly', he says.

'Well?' I ask.

Get it over with already.

'It was, um, soup'.

No one says anything.

'Soup?' bursts Drax with laughter.

'What do you mean soup?' cackles Lucy.

Soup. How fucking ridiculous.

'I mean a tin of fucking soup', says Singe frowning.

'PAHAHAHAHAHA', bellows Lucy leaning on the bench and knocking some bottles flying.

'It's not that funny', says Singe.

'SOUP?' whoops Drax.

I laugh so hard I fart.

'Not a ze-TV or a camera?'

'No. A can of tomato soup'.

'What. Not even a luxury meaty soup? Tomato soup?'

'Yes, tomato soup'.

'Man, FYL', laughs Drax.

'Fuck... your... soup', gasps Lucy.

I look at Singe whilst I'm still laughing and his mug has completely clouded over. He looks pissed off. I think he might be getting upset.

'So what's so bad about stealing a tin of tomato soup?' I ask.

'I was charged with 'Resistance to Exchange'.

'Ah', says Drax, nodding and smiling sadly.

'What does that even mean?' Lucy demands.

'Spending money helps to uphold the financial system and cultural values of the UK. I went against that and so I was put in Strangeways'.

I'm confused. 'Bods nick and steal stuff all the time though', I say. 'I've stolen loads of stuff'.

'Yeah, but you never got caught', he says, slightly thumping his bottle on the bench. 'Strangeways is full of Poor Ones and people, or bods or whatever you call them, who have stolen little bits and bobs. And poor sods who get Unrecognised. There are tons of them'.

'Shit'.

'Yeah it is fucking shit', says Singe quietly, scratching his singed head. 'Thinking about, there are only two types of people in this world: poor sods and jammy gits. Jammy gits like you Drax. I'm definitely the former'. He's definitely getting upset now. 'And you know, LAW FORCE do all kinds of nasty things, I've had my whole head nearly burnt off, I'm full of trackers, I can't stay here very long and I bet it won't be long until I get put back in and then who knows when I'll get out again. I should probably have just stayed where I was and kept my gob shut...'

All of a sudden, the fact that he was put in prison for stealing a tin of tomato soup doesn't seem so funny. He might just be one step or scalp away from Malga. Singe is hunched over like he's got two big heavy weights sat on either shoulder, pushing him down and down, and he has big sad Bambi globes, twiddling his empty beer bottle with his hands. He must have been so shit-scared this entire time and riddled with those disgusting tracker things whatever they are. My Rick-knots scrunch in my belly and I kind of really feel sorry for this poor fuck. Not even his poly-versity education could save him, as much as he bangs on about it.

'Mate, I'm sorry', says Drax. 'When you've been hiding for so long, I mean, you, I... you get desensitised. You've been through a right shitshow'.

Singe shrugs. His globes are wet.

'Come on now, have another beer'.

Singe nods and scratches his globes. The mood isn't feeling exceptionally light but thank fuck there's more beer on the way.

'Yeah, make it a harder one Drax', says Lucy, 'this has all been too easy'.

Fuck I want the beers to come but I want this stupid fucking pointless game to stop. How is it a fucking game when one bod knows all the answers and no one else has a bloody clue? If there wasn't any beer involved it would be a waste of bloody time. Completely mis-sold IPA.

'Alright, alright', says Drax. 'Here's one that Georg wanted to get out. Did a huge order the other day. He's been working on some contract with some hip drinkie in the NQ that he's been going on about for ages'.

We all take a sip of the new bottle.

'Oh shit', says Drax.

Lucy almost spits hers out. 'What the fuck is THIS?'

'I know what you mean', winces Drax. 'I'm feeling pretty boulder about it too'.

I have no idea what boulder means but this tastes fucking rank. Like it's off and horrible and really really crap and wooden.

'Boulder?' says Lucy. 'It's beyond boulder, it's completely fucked. How many bottles were in that batch?'

'It's hard to say', says Drax, 'Georg took all of them'.

'Oh great', says Lucy, thumping her digits on the bench again. 'Rosée isn't going to go too ballistic'.

'Yeah', says Drax.

'Which one is it?'

'Calka-Lovelace'.

'Ro's favourite beer and Georg's fucked it up?'

'Um, yeah'.

'Great. Fucking brilliant'.

She pauses.

'How come I didn't taste this one in the first place? There's no way I'd have let this go'.

'Like I said, he wanted to get it out to this guy. Think he was doing mates rates and everything. I didn't know he'd delivered them until he came back'.

'Well, that's great. Now that they're going to think that one of our trademark beers is shit, they're definitely going to call back for more. For *fuck's sake* Georg, such a fucking... I don't know, hyper-hipster fascist'.

'I know'.

'You could have done more too Drax, you knob'.

'Hey, I didn't want to get in the way of the Georg Fun Train'.

'Yeah, but this reflects on all of us'.

'It's not my fault Luce'.

'Whatever. There's nothing we can do about it now'.

I look at Singe. His globes are still glazed over. I don't think wooden beer has helped to improve his mood.

All of a sudden, the door to the tasting session clicks open and in come Vida, Sam and Bun Bun. It's dark out there. Sam smiles at me and plonks a stool next door. He looks tired.

'We need to wrap up soon guys', says Vida, hands on her hips. 'Aaaand it looks like you've successfully drunk us out of stock'.

'Naaaah no way', laughs Drax.

'Soz Vida, I couldn't see how many we'd drunk', says Lucy.

'Cheeky sod', says Vida moving round the bench to squeeze her arm. 'You knew exactly what you were doing'.

'I don't know what you're talking about', says Lucy, taking a sip.

'Hey, Vida, just one more?' says Drax.

'Yeahhh Vidaaaa', whines Bun Bun.

'Alright. This one', she says, pointing to a bottle with a fetching houndstooth label. She takes Lucy's hand to it gently and helps her take a hearty swig. 'Lucy got this one wrong the other day'.

Lucy puts the bottle down and grabs the arms of her chair. 'Well that's not true'.

'Oh realllllly?' laughs Drax. 'Well, well...'

'Oh honestly', says Lucy shaking her head.

'You got one WRONG', says Bun Bun clucking like a chicken and flumping onto a stool next to Singe.

'SHUT it Georg', says Lucy. 'You and I need words'.

'I love words. Words words words'.

'Oh fuck off. You sent out a batch of shit C-L to that awful hip dive in the NQ and I'm pissed at you, and Rosée is going to rip your head off'.

'It wasn't bad was it?' he says, running his awful pointy digits across his smooth mug.

'It tasted like arse'.

'Well you should have checked it quicker. I was on a tight deadline'.

'So it's my fault. I'm not your fucking servant Georg. Magna doesn't revolve all around you'.

'No, but this was a QUICK ORDER. I thought you knew that'.

'I didn't'.

'Well, in that case guys', says Sam, reaching out and placing his hands on the table, 'next time we need to communicate better'.

'WE?'

'Sam I am too busy to-'

'Come on just give me some bloody beer', sighs Vida, grabbing a bottle of leftover Kristalised and swigging heartily. I like her style.

I take a sip and notice Bun Bun watching me out of the corner of me eye. Hell no fucker.

'What?' I snap.

'Oh nothing', he says hurriedly. 'You know', he says, poking Singe, 'the guy I did the deal with at the NQ place was in the hermeneutics class at the poly-versity'.

'No shit', say Singe, wiping beer from his gob. 'Who?'

'Ashton Cooke'.

'Oh cool! I haven't seen him in ages! How is he? He was always a great guy'.

'Yeah, we added him online a month or so ago and we re-connected big time. Which is WHY I don't think this bad batch will be a problemmmmm', he says loudly in the direction of Lucy's mug. 'I'll just visit in the morning and explain'.

'Fine-', starts Lucy.

'But anyway', Bun Bun says, turning back to Singe and cutting over her, 'he was in the hermeneutics class and then I also did aesthetics with him too'.

'Right. I think I chose metaphysics instead of aesthetics-'

'Yeah cool so anyway we kept in touch after graduation, then lost it a bit. Now he's coming into Employment after his years out so I thought we should definitely collaborate'.

'Cool', says Singe.

'That was a good group we used to be in wasn't it? I get out and see them as much as I can now. There's always some sort of drinks or dinner sitch going on. One of the old profs coordinates it'.

'Is there? I haven't really seen any of them since graduation'.

'Yeah, nothing special, just getting drunk and stuff'.

'Oh', Singe wrinkles his conk. 'Sounds fun'.

'It's the conversations I like the most though, they're still a great intellectual bunch. I like to keep up to date with what people are thinking and arguing about. It feels really collaborative. Do you ever see anyone?'

'No not really. Especially not recently'.

'Yeah, getting into Strangeways gets you out of the loop doesn't it? But seriously people are itching to meet you again. You should come along some time. It's been ages since grad. People are really interested in the fact you've been inside'.

'I don't know. I have got other things going on. Like trying to hide from LAW FORCE'.

'Shit yeah!' laughs Bun Bun loudly. 'I forgot, yeah, you have!'

No one else laughs. Because it isn't fucking funny.

'Well, I think your little group sounds like a closed shop', says Lucy snottily.

'What's that supposed to mean? Isn't every friendship group some form of closed shop or other?' asks Bun Bun. 'Isn't that the fundamental essential dynamic of friendship?'

'Well not always'.

'I think most friendships by the very fact that they occur in groups establish something exclusionary'.

'Not all the time. Most friendships I've known have been incredibly porous', says Lucy.

'I think people find safety in numbers and I don't think they like difference, be they left or right. Even if people don't look the same, the ideas and ideologies have to be exactly the same for the cohesiveness of the group. That's what creates solidarity'.

'I would say that it is the differences, culturally, socially, racially, in all the ways, that creates solidarity'.

'But then there is still commonality within the ideas'.

'I think, shock horror, you're being close-minded Georg...'

And off they fucking go again, Lucy winding him up and up and up and up.

Drax is watching intently, trying to get a word in edgeways every so often but is continuously batted down by both Lucy and Bun Bun, who is bloody well fixated all goggle globes at Lucy and it's so annoying and boring because I'm slightly drunk but more just tired, and that's OK because that can happen sometimes even though it feels like you've wasted all that beer you've drunk. All these bods can do is bang on and on and moan at one another. They should just say they don't like each other and move the fuck on. It's boring. I look at Sam and his globes are drooping. I don't know what time it is but I've had enough and I want to go to bed. I glance at Vida and she's onto her second bottle of a beer called Baker Street and she catches my glance expertly, rolling her globes at the argument that's going on. I yawn heavily and she nods.

I scrape my chair back noisily and everyone looks my way. Singe blinks with a quizzy look on his mug. I think he is nowhere near as bad as bloody Bun Bun who I am very glad I smacked earlier.

Vida gets up with me. 'Time to hit the hay I think', she says. 'And anyway this music is way too loud. Rosée is trying to sleep'.

Since when was there music playing? I didn't even fucking notice.

Sam smiles sleepily at me and gets up to follow. Seems like Vida and I aren't the only ones who want to leave these lot to their silly snobby squabbles. Vida nips my elbow and leads me out. I sway and stagger slightly but her cup of hand has the strength of a titanium Skeggy and she steers me to the door.

Once out, Sam breathes a huge sigh of relief.

'Have they been like that all night?' he asks.

'Only a bit'.

'Fuck'.

Vida laughs. 'You have the patience of a saint'.

Not fucking likely.

Sam raises his brows incredulously and Vida grins. 'Yeah alright. Go to bed both of you. Sam do you need anything?'

'Sleeping pills might be nice, Rosée's tossing around all through the night at the moment, it's exhausting'.

'Exhausting like a having a pound of human flesh strapped to your tum and stretching your womb and hurting your back and making you pee all the time?'

'OK. Point taken'.

'I don't want to be a dick, but don't be a dick', she says.

'Fine fine. Night Vida, night you,' he says patting me on the shoulder. He is a fucking good egg. I touch my egg. Was it good idea to drink so much after a bang? Probably not. Who cares. I needed those beers. I must remember to pinch some of that Daisy Donut to create my own little stash in my box. If I can't brush my fucking gnashers, a gallon of that will be the next best thing.

I thump up the stairs to my box. I whip off my jeans and don't bother removing my T-shirt. I'm ready to flump and sleep thank you very much. I'm too tired for even the quickest of wanks. My globes blur into paisley paisley overhead.

*

I wake up because there's a bod coming in and even though I'm all whooze from beery dreamless sleep, the Rick-knots immediately squirm into action and I clench my fists and bare my gnashers and get ready to snap and scratch at anybod who comes the fuck near me.

'Drax?' asks the voice.

'It's not Drax you fuck', I hiss.

'Ohsshit, sozzez'. The dim light from Clinking and Clanking and the box's little skylight shows the outline of a man who is scratching his scalp. Looks like Singe.

'Who's there?' he asks.

'Me'.

'Oh'.

'What do you want?'

'This isn' Drax'sroom?'

'No it's mine you fuck'.

'OK, OK, soz. Can I sleep here? Please?'

'Why?'

'Georg threwemup allover the room we're sharing. He's cleannininngg it up now b'Ijusneedtasleeeeep'.

That sounds like an utter shit state for old Singey. I'm not entirely convinced that his sleeping in here is going to be the best idea in the world but then again, he did ask relatively politely and my box is a Bun Bun-free zone.

'Fine', I say.

'Thanks, 'ppreciate it. I'mmsotired', he says, shutting the door of my box behind him and plunging us back into semi-darkness.

I can't see his silhouette for a few seconds until I see him heading towards my bed. He whips off his trousers and starts to clamber in.

'What the fuck are you doing?' I demand.

'I can'sleep on the floor'.

'Yes you can'.

'Pleazzzze? I really don'wanna sleep ontha floor. You have loadsa room'.

'That's not the point'.

'I'll turnamy back on you yeah? I don'do any of that sick ultra-shit'.

'You better fucking not or I'll rip your fucking thing off'.

'OK...'

He gets in. He turns his back forcefully on me. He kicks his legs up into his tum for good measure and to make it clear that he got the message. I carry on facing his direction and stare bright burning holes into the back of his skull. I can nut him from here with my head. Or do the classic spit and dash.

If his hands start roaming, I can peanut his digits until they twist and snap off. I will have him.

His breathing is not really happening because he can probably feel me all tense and rigid beside him and I don't care but then holding myself so strong is just a bit much so I start to really try and sink into the bed. He relaxes too. I get a whiff of something really nice.

'What is that?' I ask.

'Wha'swhat?'

'That smell'.

'Oh I wenin the shower after the drinnkzz'.

'Right'.

'Georg insistet ndthen by that time he'd throwwnup everywhere'.

'Oh'.

'Whyd'youask?'

'Nothing'.

He smells surprisingly good. Kind of fresh and soapy and clean. He doesn't smell like beer or sweet must or other things bods can smell of and shit. It's weird. I'm not really used to it.

I turn my gaze from the back of his angular sticky out skull to the skylight. There are no choppers and storms this evening. It's much more peaceful. Probably all buggered off to go after some other poor bunch of sods. Wonder where Mara is. I don't want her to be dead but she's probably dead. Wonder what happens to the bods of Poor Ones. She didn't have much left to rot poor thing. Probably in those fucking Arches somewhere.

I sigh and my Rick-knots squirm about. I wriggle to get them free and then turn my conk back to Singe and take a big sniff of his whiff to calm me down. It's kind of obvious. He shifts weight nervously.

'Are you OK, um cmmfortble?' he asks.

'Yes yes yes', I mumble quickly.

'OKummgreat'.

We're silent for a bit. I keep on my back and silently heave in his nice smellz as quietly as I can. I'm not sleepy anymore. I'm quite enjoying lying here smelling him. It's very relaxing. His back looks really muscular, if slightly on the skinny side, but I don't mind.

'Arya asleeeep?' he asks.

'No'. The constant fucking questions... I just want to sniff. Seeing as I can't brush my fucking gnashers I need to get as close to heady sniff sniff durgs as I can.

'Georg reall' pissemeoff this evening', says Singe.

I sigh. '*Why?*'

'Well, y'know. Makin'me feel fomo'.

'Right'.

I just want him to leave me his smell and his bod alone in peace.

'I mean, I know you carrn' makessomeone *feel* fomo. The AAAgency technicalilly lies with...'

He tails off.

'I can'remember'.

'Thank fuck'.

'Sorrrrry'.

'Whatever'.

'But the POINT is people, bodsss arreally selfish an Ifeel so leftouuuut'.

'So what?' Is this really such a surprise or really so unbelievable.

'Uh, theysoselfishhh'.

'I don't see what the problem is'.

'I just feellike I, I wasn' made for this time'.

'What time?'

'This time. NOW. This day and AAAge', he says waving his arms about in front of him.

'Why?'

'I should have been aroun'in a time when peepods actuallyreallyactually looked out for oneanovver. I'm so outtaf time'.

What a pointless thing to think.

'Well you're not', I say. 'You're fucking here'.

'I know I'm'ERE!' he huffs, scowling at me.

'Why say shit like that then?'

'Because it's the trooff'.

I roll my globes. 'Whatever'.

'Wha?'

'WHATEVER. This is boring, you're on a different fucking planet'.

'I   suppose   Time   can   be   conceiveeeddasa prettyplaneterenny...'

I slam a hand over his gob. Probably more forcefully than is necessary. Never mind.

'Stop'.

'Mphfuummpph' he muffles.

'OK'.

I remove my hand.

'Fuck', he says giving me a shifty side eye. 'You're jusabit...'

'What?'

'Melodramatuc...'

I wrinkle my conk. 'Speak for yourself. What is this?!' I say gesturing to him. 'What are YOU even doing? I'm fucking not melo-whatever'.

'Well then, why is everythin you do so...' he waves his hands around again.

'What?'

'Big an loud an violent an big'.

What is it about this poor fucking poly-versity fuck? Montmorency went to the same place and perfectly understands that a bit of a thump, a kick or a stomp with a heavy fat bovver is completely normal. Singe is so cotton wool he hasn't got a fucking clue. Can you imagine if he met Monk? She'd eat him alive.

'I still don't know why you're so surprised. You don't get out a lot do you'.

'Well', he says 'I do know about this daynage's violence and fuggery, how can'you avoid it ezpezially when it's instituionalizzed, but it's never reall'appened to meeee before allathis. I've never really come face to face with it'.

He looks at me.

'You're not fucking welcome you stuck up singey cunt'.

He blinks. It slips off him.

'Still', he continues, 'it's better than bein'selfish'.

'Um, OK'.

'But thathing is, I suppose we're all selfissh'.

'Yes. Absolutely'. It's both annoying and not annoying but it's true.

'Yeah, you have people who are toallyselfish. Then you have people who try to remain LOYAL to the toallyselfish people but then when everythin starts going well for the LOYAL people, like the systemstarts workin properygood for them, they selfishlily distance themselvesss from the totallyselfish in a way that is TOTALLY SELFISH too, y'know?'

'Um'.

'They have to get their way too, right?'

'Right'.

'I'm like that, I, I mean... I... always want to be a good person but I can'be because I want what I want. Because y'knowy'know, the sellafish people should have noticed those who were loyals to them more before they lost them'.

'Maybe', I say, 'but 'totally selfish people', those bods whatever they are, they're just trying to look after themselves'.

'But what about zocial responsibilities and'ope?' asks Singe desperately.

'Who cares? There's nothing we can do about it'. Malga flashes into my mind. We fight because there's nothing else we can do, but it doesn't get us anywhere. But we're still compelled to do it.

'Fighting is as good as nothing', I say.

'What?' says Singe frowning at me.

I can never say what's in my head out loud proper.

'Nothing', I say slamming my head into the pillow. 'Whatever'.

'I'm not of this timeeeee, not of this epoCHGHHHH', Singe continues, coughing loudly.

'Get fucking over it'.

'I shoul'be back. Or in the new liberraed rosyposyosy futurr'.

'Well I wouldn't want to be in any other time than this one', I say.

'Heeeehhhhhhhhh', he says taking a breath.

'Oh what NOW?' I snap, turning to glare at him.

'YEEEEEEECHHOOOOO'.

He sneezes loads of snot all over my mug and right in my gob. Panicked and in the midst of a natural reflex, I swallow the slinky filmy salty goblets in one horrifying gulp.

We both freeze.

'You are fucking disgusting', I whisper.

'I am sosoosorry'.

'Get out'.

'Yeahyeahyeah, tha's fair'. He wobbles out of bed and collapses in a heap onto the floor.

'Give me your T-shirt'.

'Oh sure'. He takes it off and I grab it and wipe my mug with it. It's fucking disgusting. I look at the T shirt and instantly regret it because I can see sticky gloopy snot and slobber all over it.

Should I go to Power Shower? Nah. Too tired.

Singe starts sighing big time. It's probably cold and hard on the floor but I don't care. He doesn't move.

I stare at the paisley for a while and feel like I might start drifting off, swept up in brown paisley goodness.

Staying here with these 'PEOPLE' is going to drive me mad. I've got to think beyond this Clinking and Clanking nuthouse.

'Are you asleep?' squeaks Singe.

'No', I snap. 'And never going to with your whining and shining about'.

'I understan', says Singe. 'Bu I wanna make it better. I wannassay sorryz'.

'Oh my fucking fuck…'

'Pleazzzzze'.

'Just get on with it'.

'I have a pome'.

'What?'

He sighs. 'A poem. I've been thinkin and writin poems a bit, you know in Strangeways and whils'ere in Magna, never reall'done it before, and there's this one tha'I think woul'work in thissitch and, y'know, maybe help you to understanme better?'

'I would really be OK with you just saying 'sorry''.

'Pleaaaaze?'

'Fuck's sake just do it'.

He jumps up off the floor and plants himself in front of me.

'OK.

Je rêve je me lève
Et je ris la toujours
Ma femme, elle pleure
Avec les yeux trop forts
Nous chansons et nous voyons
Le soleil et la lune
Et je dormi ; une souris'

He blinks at me with a very cautious smile.

'Whaddya fink?'

I mean. What do YOU think?

'Wh-what the fuck was that?' I stammer.

'I was just saying sorry, with a poem'.

'But how?' I burst into laughter. 'You didn't even say it! What were all those words?'

'Hey don't be unkin', I'm tryin 'ere. It was all metafforic', he says running a hand over his singed scalp.

I shriek and laugh. 'That's the stupidest apology I've ever heard!'

And anyway, what a fucking joke. This bod hasn't got a fucking clue.

I can't take it anymore.

I howl with laughter underneath my paisley moon, writhing around in the bed and my tum is hurting because I'm laughing so hard and he's standing there gawping at me before turning, flushed and embarrassed and devastated at my reaction and swings right on out of the box. The door slams shut behind him. I'm still rocking about, tears pricking my globes. What the hell was that? What the HELL was that? I have no idea why he thought that was a good idea. Poor silly fucking cotton wool Singe. Completely out of time and place. I wheeze and chuckle and chuckle as my leggies get into a complete fucking tangle with all my rolling and kicking about in the duvet and it turns out that laughing at silly old Singe is the only thing that has been close to getting rid of the crummy Rick-knots, better even than cleaning my gnashers, so I carry on and on and loud and on and eventually, I'm completely out of puff.

2.4

'I think we should fuck'.

'What?' he spits in surprise.

'Stop moaning and moping and let's fuck'.

'But you're, you're, you don't want to... you didn't want me in here'.

'Yeah well, I've changed my mind'.

You see. He smells just so good and he's singed and hot. He's a right whine and shine so to be perfectly honest, I want him to just shut up. No more noise. Just smell and bod. I've obviously still have my beer goggs on and I want to get down to this before they slip off completely.

I clamber on top of him and he's blinking up at me like a little lost cotton wool mutt and I am so much more in charge and in control and I like that. This is all about my terms.

'Well?' I demand.

'Sure', he nods.

'Come on are you sure?'

'What?'

'Are you sure? I'm sure.'

'Yeah, yeah definitely'. His globes are shining. I run my nails over his singed and scalped head. 'Just so you know, this isn't any Rick-shit', he says. 'I'm not about that'.

'OK', I say. I don't know how he knows about Rick but he does and he understands and that's very convenient but I also don't want to think about that right now.

My knots twist as he pushes me onto my back gently but with the right amount of force to get me all hot and bothered. Who doesn't like a little bit of consensual rough and tumble?

He mumbles something inane in my ear. I think it's, 'I've Yeahhhh I've been wanted wanting to hmmm to do do this this ever for since ages I first saw you', or a combination of something like that. Anyway, it makes perfect sense and I really don't believe him because it's obvious he thinks I'm a bit mad so probably wanted to run a million miles when he first saw me but I don't care. I'm not here for him, I want a really big orgasm.

I'm on my back, my digits digging and dipping into the mattress and it's getting exciting. He feels hard inside his pants and he's slowly winding himself up by pushing his thing up against my leg. He scuffles with the bottom of his T-shirt, ruffles it up and over his head and chucks it on the floor. I grab his buttocks and they're really soft and squishy and I smack and spread them for good measure. He moans and I love making him squirm. He softly shakes his head and grabs my wrists. He pushes them into the mattress, opening my chest wide making my nipples, hard with excitement, press through my T-shirt. The friction that the rubbing creates as well as the burns his hands are causing on my wrists feels so fucking good. He bends down and pushes my legs open with his thighs and he's got that hungry look in his globes. I look back and lengthen my choker onto the pillow. He knows what to do, lowering himself down and I can feel his full warmth and weight pressing down on me as he raises his chops to brush them against my choker. His thing continues to press against me but his hands stay at my wrists, twisting them down. He leaves a wide wet patch on my choker from where his chops and tongue have skimmed over, nipped and sucked at my skin. Slowly, he moves them from my choker to my ears, nibbling at my lobe before taking in my entire ear, his tongue tracing the curves of my cute little organ, so sensitive. His breath is warm and his hands are so strong and I can't move except to press up against his bod and it's getting really really fucking exciting. He leans to tug down his pants and use his thumb to gloss over my cunt and I breathe heavy and rasping. He's still playing with one of my ears before reaching down to tug gently at my nipples. 'This I'm is so going looking to forward feel to so being good inside you', he says. I keep my globes closed all the while taking little notice of his mumble jumble and it's all half-happening anyway in a muddled hot mess.

I know the orgasm is coming and I try to hold it off but I know that's only going to make the whole thing so much more powerful and the heat and the intense ragged sweetness runs through my bod as my clit goes up up up up up and ooooooover and I cry out, globes creasing in disbelief and my gob a giant zero as my breath is hot and broken as the waves come and the twitches and reflexes send sweet shocks all around my bod. It's so powerful and hard that my ears begin to ring.

After a while, I blink up at Singe and he's gawping and aghast, he doesn't quite know what to do with himself. His thing is no longer hard, but just hangs down limp and he's confused and frightened of what's just happened.

'Baby?' he asks. He looks confused. At a loss.

I burst into laughter. I'm still feeling weightless and trance-like yummies in all my limbs and I kind of don't want to snap out of it but he's just too funny. Normally I bark when I laugh but now I have a serene, graceful tickle of laughter that rings from my gob, coupled with an occasional soft hoot. His mug clouds over as I lie there chuckling still feeling cummy, dusty, flat and weightless and he backs out towards the door. His thing and his legs have disappeared and I just see a ghostly torso and black shadowed globes melting away. I stop laughing and lean up onto my elbows and everything goes cold. The paisley over the skylight shines bright and brown and the heat and the whooshes evaporate from my bod.

Lurking, it's lurking.

'Singe?'

Rick appears.

I scrabble back in the bed, knots scrunching and burning in my stomach.

I don't know what to do.

Why is he here?

How is he here?

He approaches the bed with his hammy fist raised and

reaching towards me.

I gnash my gnashers and try to lash out for a gob shot with my bovvers that have somehow ended up on my feet but they're too heavy they're too much, made out of heavy steel and they're attached to a shining shackle that has me completely bound to the bed.

I can't move.

Rick's yellow gnashers hum in the brown and he's grinning and reaching for me belly first his tongue lolling about.

I scream and scream and scream and then all my gnashers fall out all at once. No blood, no pain, just gnashers. Fucking everywhere.

I wake up with a husky yelp. The duvet has been kicked all the way to the end of the bed.

I'm alone. It's morning. I'm sweating like a pig. I have so many Rick-knots I might shit myself.

Fuck.

My thumper is pounding.

A stray chopper grates over head.

I peer at the floor.

Singe is gone.

I need Sam or Vida or somebod. I need to get out of here.

I collapse back onto the bed and sweat and sweat.

My cunt tingles.

Then comes the pain as womby cancels out my Rick-knots with a sharp twisting cramp. I wince as I roll myself up and heave over my knees. Fucking womb. This always happens. You think it's going to be a light easy breezy month then you get aroused once and it's like hell down there. Like it's a fucking punishment. I don't think I'm going to be sick but it's happened before. I get to my feet and stretch my arms up in the air. The whole box is dulled and brown thanks to the crappy canopy over the sky light and I am thoroughly sick of the dark so I rip it off and let the mushy grey light in.

I want to leave but I need painkillers and supplies now.

I pull up my jeans and secure my bovvers and head into Clinking and Clanking. It's still early and it's cold in there. All the vats are tapping and my breath comes out in moist dragon puffs. I start going down the stairs and I instantly start shivering. Fucking should have brought the fucking duvet with me. Luckily there's a bod about.

'Who's there?' I call.

Sam's head pops round the side of a vat. Excellent.

'Hey', he says, 'morning!'

'Are you measuring and stuff?' I ask, thumping down the rest of the stairs.

'Nah, I leave that to the professionals', he says smiling and brushing hair out of his globes. 'Got my paint on haven't I'.

I get to the bottom and drag my bovvers round to the vat he's standing behind. He's got loads of different palates in front of him and big metal bottles full of paint.

'I thought these could do with brightening up', he says jabbing at the metal with a paintbrush. 'Best way to spend a morning too, really fucking peaceful and therapeutic'.

I look up at the vat and on the side, Sam has painted a big, mad black dog thing with purple globes and an erect tail. It's scary but I like it.

'Smells good', I say. 'The paint...'

'Yeah they're new ones, extra strong and sticky so that they don't run off the metal. I was considering designing some prints to stick on but got up this morning and thought: fuck it. Paint'.

'Where did you get them from?'

'Georg knows a bod. The guy has his uses', he chuckles.

'I like black dogs', I say, thinking of Henry. 'I like the purple, for the globes'.

'Why?' he smiles.

'Just like it sees differently, different things'.

'I know what you mean', he says.

'Why did you do them purple?'

'Because I like purple and it looks a bit hazed and off its

mug'.

'Hmmm'.

'You know, beer, general fuckery'.

'The only way'.

'Right?' Sam says, smiling and looking at me.

I put my hand on the vat. I leave a clammy mark and quickly wipe and smear it away. I have a black smudgy stain on my hand. Sam doesn't notice.

'I want to paint on every vat', he continues. 'This place needs a bit of a lift, especially now that it's getting proper dark earlier now'.

Lunar goosebumps appear on my arms, catching his globes immediately.

'Shit, you must be fucking freezing!'

'Only a bit', I shrug.

He's already clobbered in a roasty toasty knit. 'It's cold this morning, coldest day of the year so far I would say. Let's get you a jumper'.

I nod.

He thwacks off his apron, wipes his paint hands on his hams and heads off. I follow.

'We've got a load of knits and fleeces left over from yesterday, the ones that didn't get trampled on', he says, marching to a cupboard and pulling down a big box.

'You haven't seen our runaway friend have you? He was wasted last night. Clanging about, he woke me up. And Rosée was actually having a good, quiet night'.

'Nah, I went to sleep', I say.

'Good, I'm glad one of us did. There was a right mess this morning. I had to clear it all up before Vida got up too, she'd have hit the fucking fan. Entitled bunch of shits'.

I shrug.

'They're probably cuddled up together in a pool of sick somewhere', he continues. 'It's not that I mind vom all that much, I've cleaned up Rosée loads of times but not for clueless man-bod-children. Ugh, never mind. Are you sure you slept OK?'

'Hmm. Bad dreams'.

'Oh really? What about?'

'Nothing much'. As if I was going to tell him the lot. 'My gnashers all fell out'.

'Classic'.

I scrunch up my conk. 'You've dreamt that?'

'Fuck yeah, with a pregnant Rosée and a baby not yet born, my gnashers fall out pretty much every night'.

'Right. Why?'

'Well, there's loads of potential meanings. Some bods say that it's because you're worried about money, you know, your gnashers becoming bitcoins or ze-coins or whatever. Then some say it's because you've got a big change coming in your life. I suppose both could be me!'

'Or maybe you're just worried about the actual thing', I say.

'What do you mean?'

'Well, there is no meaning. You're just shit scared of all your gnashers falling out'.

'Fuck', he says blinking at me. 'I never thought of that. Did anything else happen in your dream?'

'No', I lie.

'Shit. Well that must be it then', he says smiling and rifling through the box.

'Yeah'.

'I try and get a dreamless sleep by thinking about nothing'.

'What do you mean?' I ask.

'Well, I can't just think of blackness and dust and stuff. I think about the word itself, 'NOTHING''.

'Right'.

'I just imagine the word and the letters over and over again and then I start to miss letters off and then in the end all that's left is the O, like a rabbit hole, and I dive into it and hopefully into sleep'.

'Does it work?'

He folds his arms. 'I think so. Yes'.

'I might try that sometime'. I never think about sleeping I just sleep, but I think it must be difficult if you can't. This sounds like a good method for sleeps. Thinking about some kind of empty O hole to go through. Sam really is one of the only bods who has something original to say round here.

He carries on hustling and bustling about in his box. 'Look at me trying to get a meaning from a dream. Who do I think I am? I'm turning into Georg. Those bods make me forget myself.

He pauses before clutching about excitedly inside the box. 'Hey lucky you, there's a lovely jumper left behind that I think Vida knitted herself!'

As fucking if.

'That's the ugliest fucking jumper I have ever seen'.

There are literally no words for how yuck this jumper is. It is beyond.

'I'll take this', I say decisively. Bottle green thick cotton with a zip. Easy access, easy escape.

'Fair enough', Sam chuckles, 'I warn you though, somebod may have died in it'.

'I don't care'.

'OK. So what have you got planned for the rest of the day if Vida doesn't rope you into anything?'

'Nothing much'. Just running away.

'Sam?' I ask.

'Yeah'.

'Do you have any period bits and bobs? I need painkillers, pads or whatever you have to make it stop coming out like it is now. I can't remember where to find them'.

'Oh shit, yeah', he says, moving towards the utility space and the big cupboard under the sideboard. 'Help yourself'.

'Thanks'.

'Fresh pants too?'

'Absolutely'.

It's refreshing that there's a man other than Montmorency

who understands the normalcy of periods. It's all one and nothing to Sam. He just likes me and my lumpness. He's too sickly sweet and cute. He's going to get into trouble with that one day.

'Anything else, let me know. OK? Let me know', he says, smiling at me, his beanie hat on one side from all the muddling about he's been doing. I know he's not lying.

'OK, just checking: you haven't got anything for me like, you know, for brushing my gnashers?'

'Er, I have the standard flouride but none of the other shit, sorry'.

'Too bad'. Lucy and Drax were right then.

'I haven't brushed my gnashers in ages. Haven't even thought about', he says. 'I actually bloody miss it'.

Sort it out then.

'What are you doing now?' I ask.

'Going to get breakfast set up. I know there's all kinds of beef and tension around at the moment, but you know, we need to get on the same page, spend some time together. There's nothing like grub to get us all better'.

'Right'. Too good for his own good. I might not be around long enough for grubbies.

'Go and sort yourself out. If you fancy helping as well, that would be great'.

'Sure', I say. I need to come up with a plan to slip off, maybe whenever everyone's all over the place helping or whatnot. They won't miss me.

I grab the essential period necessaries.

I wander over to the nearest bathroom box.

Where do I even go after this? Montmorency's? LAW FORCE will hopefully have fucked off after another bod so I can get out and get to his pad, it'll all have blown over. No biggie. There I can spend the rest of my days doused in Memory Foam and brushing my gnashers whenever I need to. I can just flatten into the mattress like I always wanted. He won't care, I'm sure. Him and Monk might even join in.

I wonder if they're worried? I wonder if they miss me? And anyway if they're not I bet they won't find it half as fun to fuck shit up without me around. I'm sure they wouldn't find it as fun.

I head in the direction of the downstairs bathroom box and squeeze into it with all the supplies clutched to my chest.

'Oooh it's you!' says a rosy voice.

I spin around and Rosée is naked in the bath, her big bump bursting forth from the mass of bubbles that are completely masking the surface.

I almost drop everything. I thought I would have turned my mug in surprise at her nakedness but I can't help but stare at the big old bump that has a dark line running down the middle and marks where her tum has stretched and yawned to make way for bab. She waves at me and has her mermaid hair piled and knotted up on top of her head in a frantic Monkish fashion but with more grace, the strawberry shade shining with natural zest. Her mug is dewy from the steam and she beams at me and beckons me in. 'Come on in', she says quietly but full of calm joy.

I sort of hover and don't know how comfortable I feel about going to the loo in front of a bod who is so serene and clean but in the end I stop giving a fuck, stomp over to the toilet, pull down my trousers and plonk myself down. She chuckles as I start to piss and fumble about with the painkillers.

'Do you need some water?' she asks, pointing to the door.

'Nope'. I chuck them into my gob and dry swallow them in front of her, cranking my choker back so that I have maximum gulping capacity and down down down they do.

She raises her brows and laughs, 'You surprise me', she says, 'I guess that's why I like you!'

OK.

'I'm so glad you came in because it means we can share a moment of peace and just let our bods be and do their thing. Nothing chills me out quite like a good old bath'.

It's hard to think of your bod in a romantic let-it-all-go kind of way when you peek through your legs whilst you're sat on the bog and see clumps and lumps of blood and clots and a little bit of shit that came out on the sneak.

I look up at her bump again. She is something I have never seen before. Utterly carefree. In this free-standing bath on this cobbled floor in this steamy box. In this Clinking and Clanking. She is happy because she has bump and she is happy with her set-up and she is just happy. In general.

'Does it hurt?'

'What?'

'Having a bump?'

'Well it's heavy, and my feet hurt and my back hurts but apart from that, it's really OK'.

'Right'.

She shifts weight and sploshes suds about.

'Hmm waves', she says, as the water breaks around her bump and laps the sides of the bath.

I start undoing a tampon wrapper. I crouch down like a crinkled old pooch and shove it up. I pull up my trousers and make my way towards the door.

'No, don't go', she calls after me. 'Not yet, just stay with me for a bit'.

I brush my conk. 'OK', I say.

I walk back to the loo, slam down the lid and sit on it with my natural slouch.

'I think everything happens in waves', she says.

'What?'

'I think everything happens in waves'.

'Right'.

'You know, you asked me about pain. I don't feel pain all the time, it sort of ebbs and flows. Like waves'.

'OK'.

?????

'Some days it's worse than others but I feel alright about it because I know the next day will be better'.

'Yeah'.

'It's how I feel about the birth, you know, trying to make myself less nervous about it', she says, running her digits over her legs. 'If I just think about it as a wave, I know that beyond all the hurt and pain there will be peace on the other side'.

I don't know what to say so I nod. Even though I heard babs can be right noisy little shits.

She's restless in my silence and asks with a determined look on her mug, 'What do you think?'

I don't know what I fucking think. It all sounds so wishy washy. There's always some big fucking opinion about not very much that has to be expressed here isn't there.

'I've always sort of enjoyed pain', I try. 'The stabby kind of pain, not the period shit'.

She nods, 'That's interesting'.

'Cramps just want to make you curl up and stretch out your womby, they do nothing. But stabby pain, it pumps me. Makes me want to give something a smack and then you can easily do away with it'.

'That is so curious'.

'What?'

'How violent you are. I mean, it's in everything you do and say'.

Oh for fuck's sake. This. Again. Anger begins to pulse around me and she's winding me fucking up. Singe was drunk but she's just asked me for my fucking opinion and now I'm getting stitched up.

'Well if you don't fucking like it, I'll fuck off then you cunt', I say jumping to my feet.

'No, it's OK, I mean, sorry', she says waving her digits.

'I'm not here to make you feel better. I'm not here for you or me or anybod at all. I'm going to fucking leave', I say.

'Please don't leave', she says, 'I want us to be friends, I really do'.

'Well why did you say that?'

'I don't know, it's just violence isn't so much a part of my reality'.

'Are you kidding?'

'No'.

'Have you even spoken to any of those Poor Ones you invite round reggy?'

'Well of course, they suffer so much at the hands of the system'.

I think about Mara. 'It's all violence', I say. 'All violence'.

'Sure but it's a structural oppressive violence that forces them on the streets and in the Arches'.

'No it's bovvers and bats and fists and knives and THINGS'.

'I suppose there is LAW FORCE-'

'No it's not just them, it's everyone else, all of us. We're all at it. You're at it. I mean, come on. You must have punched a bod in the gob at least once'.

'I haven't', she says proudly.

'Never felt the urge?'

'Of course but there's a difference between wanting to do something and actually doing it. I guess you could call me old fashioned'.

I could call her a lot more than that.

'Yeah well, pretty much everyone apart from you poly-versity lot in here don't have the freedom of that choice'.

'But you see', she says, 'it doesn't have to be that way'.

'Yes it does'.

'No it doesn't, it's all waves'.

'I don't know what you're fucking talking about'.

'Now I think about it, there's always waves in everything. In art, culture, politics, there's always waves and this system we live in, it won't last forever'. She delicately lifts a bubbly digit and smiles as it pops in her mug.

'There is no other way', I say.

'I wish you could see, like with the Poor Ones', she says, lowering her digit back into the bath. 'We're at the crest of something, something big. It can't carry on like this forever.

The wave will break and the truth is, change will happen. We have to be ready to seize it'.

'You are so fucking high and mighty. You're a fucking snob. Like the rest, like, like Bun Bun'.

'Bun Bun...?'

'That's not the truth', I shout, and I don't know why but she's really upsetting me. 'You're nothing like Vida, she gets it'.

'Nana? She's a tough rough old boot, She's lived though something totally different. I love her but I take a lot of what she says with a pinch of salt. She's always got some kind of grudge on the go'.

'She's RIGHT'.

'I don't know about that. Sometimes, but not all the time'.

'Well she is and she understands'.

'Oh no, don't, don't cry, oh please, I didn't mean-'

'I'M NOT CRYING' I say, tears pinching my sockets.

I get up and kick the wall.

'It's not the truth', I say under my breath, heaving myself back to calm while she sits there waxing fucking divine and lyrical in the bath. 'It's not not not the truth'.

'You know', she says, 'there's no such thing as objective truth. I don't want you to live your life thinking that's the case. You're just going to be disappointed again and again'.

'Shut UP', I bellow.

'I only-'

'You make me feel like I'm stupid, like I'm mad'.

'I'm so sorry', she says. 'Really, I don't want to be like them, like Georg. Shit'. Now she's started welling up. 'I try and stop myself, I just, I want to help, I just need it all to make sense'.

'UGH I DON'T CARE'.

Suddenly it happens and we both catch it. The bab kicks her tum and it's quickly followed by little digits pressing up.

I've never seen anything like it. The digits keep pressing Rosée's skin and then suddenly, they disappear. We both watch the bump to see if anything else happens but it doesn't. She brushes away her tears and laughs.

'Did you see...?'

'Yeah, yeah', I say. 'Little bab'.

'Knows how to kick about already, huh' she smiles.

'Good kicker'.

'Yeah'.

'Did it hurt?'

'No. Bit of a surprise, but no'.

'Ready for some bovvers, maybe'.

'I don't know. I worry. I worry about this one coming into a world that is so dangerous'.

'Well', I say, 'there's nothing you can do about it. Nobod else is going to care'.

'Yeah'.

'Little one just has to be prepared. Has to be fucking ready for all the shit'.

'But I just want baby to know love'.

'That's the most loving thing you can do I think'.

'Really?'

'I don't know. I don't really know anything about love. I don't really believe it exists'.

'It does, oh it really does', she says nodding her bun about. 'I love bump and Sam and Nana more than anything. It's where I get my strength from. It makes me fierce. That's why I get so irate with Georg'.

'This is it. You are violent too you know. No punching. Just violent with your ideas'.

'What?' she folds her arms.

'Yeah, you sort of just put your bovver down all the time like you're in charge. There's no going against you'.

'No, no, no. But... yes. But it's not like I mean or want to force them on anyone, I just do. I expect people to either think the same way or do the same with their ideas I suppose'.

'Right'.

'But then they don't'.

'It's the same thing when I smack a bod in the gob. I find it weird when I don't get a whopper back. But then with you lot and your gabbing, it's like I'm getting punches in the mug and I can't hit back. It's tiring and unfair'.

'Oh'. She licks her chop awks.

'I'm just telling you what I think when I experience shit. Just saying'.

'Right'.

I don't think Rosée and I will ever be on the same page, which is a shame because I kind of wanted to like her straight away when I first saw her because she really did seem to be my type of basic bad bitch. That's not to say she isn't the coolest pregnant person I have ever seen, because she is, but unlike Montmorency or Monk there's not enough release there. Too much pondering and poncing and prophesising, however much she supposedly hates herself for it. And I can tell she does. I can tell she wants to shake that away and stop it but she should just give up because she can't change. No one ever does. At least she has Sam who won't just put up with it but loves her for it. I'm out.

She smiles because she knows it too. We'll just slip casually but respectfully from the personal into the inane. You need bods for that too you know.

She leans back in the bath.

'So anyway. What happened last night? After I went to bed?'

'What do you mean?'

'Anything exciting? I was sick as a dog and covered in my own piss. That's why I so badly wanted a bath this morning'.

'Um, nothing really'.

'Did you guys get wasted?'

'I was merry but not out of my mind. Tired mostly. The others though-'

'Lucy always gets rowdy. I love her'.

'Yeah, she and Georg were at each other's chokers pretty much the entire time'.

'I could hear. Sounded hilarious. I wish I hadn't missed it but I was so, so tired'.

'It was stressful'.

'I think it's so funny the way she winds him up'.

'I just wanted to sleep'.

'Did you see what happened to our fugitive friend?'

'No'.

'Well I'll tell you. He had a green mug this morning when I saw him. He was up super duper early before anyone else, even Nana. I had cravings and I bumped into him in the kitchen. Cramming his pockets'.

'Oh right'.

'Basically, he's gone'.

'Really, already?'

'Yeah, he was on his way. I told him to take the old auto. To be honest, I'm glad. It was getting close to being dangerous having him around'.

'Was he OK?'

'Yeah, looked like he hadn't slept at all. But I bet the trackers combined with the alcohol were making him really ill. I think he was glad to go to be honest'.

'Yeah'.

'He's a sad boy. I feel sorry for him'.

'He was pissed as a fart'.

'Was he?'

'Yeah, he was slurring all the words, getting into some heavy chats with Lucy and Drax'.

'Oh I'm SO annoyed I missed it. It's not as exciting as Lucy and Georg getting at it but still, I'm sure it made for interesting listening'.

'Like I said, I was just tired'.

'Then what happened?'

'Well it was kind of funny. I went off to bed at the same time as Vida and Sam and then he bloody came into my box making a racket'.

'What a mess!' she laughs.

'Well I let him get into bed-'

'Oh my god did you fuck?'

'No, NO. Just no'.

'Are you sure?' she says flicking water at me.

'YES', I say, scowling.

'OK, OK, just checking'.

'He was moaning and stuff and it was really cold and Georg had been sick all over the place or something in their box so I thought, whatever'.

'Right'.

'Plus if he had tried anything with me he knew the score'.

'A bovver to the nut?' she chuckles.

'Or I'd just pull off his thing. Something like that'.

'Hm', she says, her globes widening, before nodding and saying nothing else.

'Then', I continue, 'he was chatting all sorts of strange bollocks and it was getting annoying because I just wanted to go to sleep and then out of nowhere he just sneezed in my mug'.

'Oh fuck', she rasps, clutching at her choker as if to retch slightly.

'Yeah, right into my gob. It was fucking rank'.

'That's nasty'.

'That's not even the worst bit. He then decided to apologise but went off on one with this weird rhymey poem shit and I didn't have a fucking clue what he was saying and then was like 'we good?''

'So what did you say?'

'I just burst into laughter and he ran off'.

'Oh no'.

'Yeah'.

'Poor thing'.

'Whatever. He was ridiculous'.

'Wait', she says sitting bolt upright splashing water about.

'Snot actually went into your gob?'

'I don't particularly want to go over the nitty gritty, it was horrible'.

'Sorry, fuck, yeah but that's, that's not good'.

'You're telling me, it was completely slimy and disgusting'.

'Yeah but the trackers...'

I freeze.

'What do you mean?' I ask.

'He, his fluids, he was full of trackers'.

'His blood, surely, not his fucking snot?'

'I don't know. I'm fairly sure it means all fluids'.

'Yeah but, blood or even sperm would make sense, but spit and snot?'

'I really hope not. I really fucking hope not. Pass me that towel', she says, pointing to a crumple on the floor by the toilet. 'We need to speak to Nana, she'll know'.

'What will happen if his snot did have trackers in it?'

'They'll come and find you. The 48 hour window is closing, it's probably already gone. LAW FORCE will come'.

My tum drops and my Rick-knots churn. There's no way. No way. This is just so unfair. If there was ever a time to brush my gnashers and fade away this would be it.

I chuck Rosée the towel and she stands up and she drips bubbles and suds everywhere.

'Pass me that robe', she asks nodding to another crumple.

I fling it to her.

She starts to wobble getting out of the bath so I lean over and give her my shoulder and arm to lean on. I don't want Rosée or little Kicker in there to slip.

She smiles at me. 'Thanks', she says. 'Can't even see my fucking feet these days'.

She leads me to the door of the bathroom box, opens it up and immediately we're hit by a blast of cold air. Rosée coughs as steam escapes around us and we head back towards Clinking and Clanking.

'Nana? Sam?' she calls.

Sam pops his head around one of the vats. 'What's up?'

'I think we have a problem'.

'Why, what's happened'.

'I think she's full of trackers'.

Sam looks at me. 'What, why?'

'Tell him', she says elbowing me.

'Oh because that stupid runaway freak sneezed in my gob'.

Sam pauses for a second. He starts pissing himself laughing.

'Sam, it's not funny', says Rosée.

'That is fucking hilarious'.

'Well yeah, but do you think they'll come for her?'

'No don't be silly, they have to be injected'.

'Are you sure?'

'Bods spit and slobber and cough all the time. We'd all be in bloody Strangeways if that happened'.

'I know but I'm just not sure...'

'Morning everyone'.

It's Vida. She catches Rosée's worried mug.

'Is everything alright darling? You? The baby?'

'I'm fine. I'm just worried LAW FORCE are going to come after her'.

'Why?'

'Scalp sneezed in her gob', says Sam calmly before creasing with laughter again.

'He sneezed in your gob?' says Vida, looking at me and then grinning broadly with flashing globes.

'Alright, it's not that funny', I say.

Vida catches Sam's globes and they both start whooping and wailing with giggles.

'Oh for fuck's sake, you're such children', says Rosée crossly. She folds her dressing gown arms. 'This could be really serious, I don't think it's a laughing matter'.

'I bet it wasn't for you', says Vida, looking at me.

'What did the snot taste like?' asks Sam.

'Ketchup'.

'REALLY?'

'No it FUCKING didn't. I don't want to think about it

anymore it's making me sick'.

'Look', says Vida. 'We just need to think about this. They would already be here. Surely, they'd already be here'.

Rosée nods slowly. 'I suppose you're right'.

Bun Bun comes into Clinking and Clanking looking ashen.

'Has he gone?' he asks.

'Morning Georg', says Sam.

'Yes', says Rosée. 'But we still have a problem'.

'He could have at least said goodbye'.

'It was kind of a rushed thing'.

'Anyway. I feel fucking dreadful. What are you lot all doing out here? Is there any coffee on? I feel sick as fuck'.

'Well, this one', Rosée says looking at me, 'might have trackers in her'.

'From, him?'

'Yeah'.

'Oh my days did he fuck you?' he says wrinkling his conk at me disgustedly because he's a judgemental sack of shit.

'Absolutely fucking not', I snap. 'He was so fucking drunk he couldn't have got his thing up even if he wanted to'.

'All right, it was just a question'.

'Oh stop Georg', says Vida.

'He sneezed in her mouth basically-' starts Rosée.

'He WHAT'.

'Oh for FUCK'S SAKE', I roar.

'The point is', says Sam, 'she may or may not have trackers inside her, which means LAW FORCE may or may not be on their way to lock her up in Strangeways'.

'Shouldn't she leave as well?' says Bun Bun tartly.

'No, absolutely not', says Sam.

'I agree', says Vida. 'We brought you in here to help you, I'm not casting you off'.

I shake my head. Maybe I should just leave when they all get too bored with thinking and talking about me. It's what I've wanted to do all along anyway. This is almost the perfect excuse to get out of their hair.

'It's OK. I can just-'

Rosée butts in, 'Nope. It's already settled'.

'Guys?'

It's Lucy at the top of the stairs. Drax is with her.

'What's the plan for today?' she calls.

'Not much. We carry on as usual', says Rosée. 'We still need to get this place cleaned up and then we need to do a whole lot of brewing'.

'I've got to contact Ashton about that new contract', says Bun Bun.

'If he even gets back to us...' mutters Lucy.

'What about all the Poor Ones outside?' asks Drax.

'What Poor Ones?'

'There's loads of them, outside'.

'How?' asks Georg. 'I locked the gates last night'.

'Oh for goodness sake Georg', groans Rosée.

'I did!'

'Are you sure?' asks Vida.

'Yes', he says sulkily.

'I mean, it's OK', says Vida.

'It's not ideal', says Rosée.

'Yes', says Vida 'but we can get organised quickly. We still have loads of new stuff. We just need to quickly box everything and then we can be of help'.

'OK', says Rosée, 'I want Lucy and Drax helping me with brewing and tasting, the rest of you can help the Poor Ones. You', she says looking at me, 'have to stay inside, just for today. They're already looking for you, we're fairly sure they don't know where you are. But just to be on the safe side, I think it's best if you stay indoors'.

'OK'.

'I can even give you a brewing 101'.

This is a life skill I could definitely do with learning. But no. Stupid idea. I need to run. It's not worth it. I'll leg it when they've all split up.

'All agreed?' Rosée asks.

They nod.

'Right, I'm going to actually put some clothes on'.

Bun Bun moves towards the front doors of Clinking and Clanking. I hover around near the vats whilst everyone else starts to head in their Rosée-assigned direction.

Bun Bun unbolts the huge door. Maybe Mara will be back. I know I need to get a move on towards Montmorency's but I could just pop out, just for one minute before, on the way, to see if anybod has seen her, or to see whether or not she's back with that Armie for some more stuffs. Sam could help her when I push on. He wouldn't rat on an old rat.

Bun Bun pulls the door open slightly and immediately slams it shut again.

'Fuck', he says, staring at the door he's just shut.

'What?' calls Vida.

'There's loads of them'.

'Oh come on now Georg', says Vida. 'Don't be a big bab. You've done this before. They're BODS, not animals'.

'No, it's-'

All of a sudden he's drowned out by an enormous chopper that swoops low and hovers over Clinking and Clanking. He looks at me.

Fuck.

'What is it?' asks Sam.

'LAW FORCE'.

We can't hear him over the racket. But his gob says it anyway.

We all look at one another. An enormous hammering begins on the door. We don't move.

Bun Bun runs towards me. I think he's going to hit me or drag me out to them or something so I immediately clench my fists and start to bare my gnashers. He grabs my arms. He thrusts his mug in mine with a sour panicked snarl and hisses right at me. 'This isn't for fucking you. If they come anywhere near her and her bump because of fucking *you*-'

'Because of YOUR fucking mate', I snap back.

'Whatever. This isn't about you'.

'I don't care', I say shoving him off.

'Rosée, Vida, what do we do?' he asks. 'Where do we hide her?

Vida joins him, 'I'll take her up to the top'.

'I'll keep them back', shouts Drax, running down the stairs and joining Sam.

'SAM!' screams Rosée as the hammering gets louder.

With a crash and a crunch huge armed LAW FORCE guards break into Clinking and Clanking. They're followed by a stream of autogrammers who are live-snapping at everything they see with flashes and spats of light.

I have a pheromonomenal siren call or whatever. LAW FORCE beeline for me. It's like they've already sniffed me out and there's no obstacle too big to get in their way. With their big black visors and their ultra-robotic terminator thing going on, they are strong and they're going to hurt me and I think I'm going to shit myself.

There's no time to think. Sam runs at them and is instantly overtaken by Bun Bun who runs head first into a wall of LAW FORCE. I press up against the back of the nearest vat and begin to try and squeeze through to the other side. LAW FORCE whack Sam and Bun Bun out of the way easily in their monstrous automatic manner. Blood and gnashers fly everywhere.

I try to wriggle into the tiny gap so that I can dart away but they're too quick. One of them gets a hold of my bicep and hoiks me up with a big big arm and my stomach drops because I've been flung weightlessly into the air and smack into him. I try to kick about with my bovvers and get my elbows free so that I can try and nut him but it's too late because they're pinned to my sides. My bovvers flail about and I'm hanging off the ground because he's holding me up and I'm getting nowhere near to hitting him.

They pull me out towards the door of Clinking and Clanking. As LAW FORCE storms through, we pass Bun

Bun who is lying in a bloody purple mess on the floor.

We get to the top of the steps outside and autogrammers have framed the entire courtyard. The chopper overhead's live casting everything. This LAW FORCE gobshite hauling me along is being really fucking rough so I start to yell and scream, waving my head about like a mad thing and spitting and gnashing at all the autogrammers.

Come and get some of this then you fucks, you fucking fucks. No Molly, Dolly or Polly not me. Behold my gums and flared conk and yellow gnashers you cunt cunt cunts.

Down the stairs and across the courtyard.

Sam is trying to follow. His globes are narrowed with determination and he has no gnashers and he's reaching towards us with his arms but is immediately swiped away again by LAW FORCE with a crunch. Rosée is crying and screaming his name. LAW FORCE punch her in the mug and she falls back and onto bump, her little Kicker.

I howl with rage. I kick with extra force and manage to nick a LAW FORCE visor standing in front of me, who's been there pushing a path for my brute to get to a big black van. He does a double take and then gets a big heavy hand around my choker. He brings his mug right up close to mine and all I can see is my own haggard reflection glaring back at me. He dweeble weebles something electronic to another LAW FORCE fuck so that I can't understand what they're saying. Then another one rounds on me with a spit-hood.

I kick again. More frantically. More wildly, more out of fear than out of misplaced bravery. My Rick-knots twist and turn.

I don't want that thing shoved on my head.

I try to shake off the digits round my choker but it stays firmly in place and gives a squeeze for good measure.

He forces my gob open with his fat Buzz hands, stretching it until my jaw creaks and cracks and it really fucking hurts and it's as wide as it will go. Then I see the big soft plastic dough stuff. The lump is far bigger than my gob. My globes crease and I use my tonsils to bellow forth NO NO NO NO but it only comes out as GZAHHHAAHHHHHHHHHHH. They shove it in. It props my gob open as my gnashers sink into the gunk. I peer down and I can see it protruding out in front of me.

I start to feel slightly off my mug already. They clip it into place using two thick plastic straps onto the LAW FORCE's chest that I'm strapped to and I can no longer move my head or make a sound.

Whimper. I whimper. Spit-slime squeezes out of the corners of my gob.

They seamlessly scoop my head into the spit-hood.

It's too tight and my mug is scrunched up and squashed against it, my skin popping and bursting through the mesh. Some gargoyle minger I am for my close-up.

I'm chucked into the back of the black van still attached to this LAW FORCE brute.

They all weeble dweeble.

My vision starts to slip and stir.

The doors close on Clinking and Clanking where all the LAW FORCE hell dogs are still on the loose.

I can't see the people-mad beer bods. They're gone.

My egg hurts again.

The Rick-knots find their way all round the rest of my limbies.

I've been truly and utterly ganked.

3.1

I'm in an old fashioned hospitalish bed and I can't open my gob because there's a big old metal brace thing round my chops. Fucking LAW FORCE fuckwits yanked me into that spit hood too hard and my jaw nearly fell off so I had it crunched back into place and now I can hardly open my gob. Which they're probably really happy about because now I can't get to them with my gnashers and I don't feel up to nutting anybod. I'm on some very powerful pillies to block out the pain and it's a good thing too. I hate this kind of achey pain. Totally debilitating. The durgs feel niiiiiice. Even though they're feeding me with a drip and now I feel like a fucking stabbed and pricked thing.

I have a pretty good idea of where I am but it's OK for now because I have my own private box. I think they considered me too dangerous to be near the rest. Whatever. If it means I'm left on my fucking one for five minutes I'm happy. Anyway Singe said that this place is full of accidental lowlifes and Unrecognised bods. It can't be that bad. Plus they gave me a mooncup.

I rest back on the pillow as much as I am able. I'm in some kind of weird paper dress thing and my ankles are shackled to the bedstead.

I know right. New day, new shackle. It's like it never stopped.

There is a big bay window behind me and all the light is a kind of rosy yellow. This is the thing. I would have expected this place to look more obviously high-tech and modern like any of the UK's new shiny official buildings but it seems that they've tried to maintain the ancient Victorian rest and recline feeling to this hospital place as much as possible. Nice windows, nice carvings and borders around the ceiling. It's the sheer gun metal grey door that undermines the oh-isn't-this-place-LOVELY thing.

Ze- has evidently branched out beyond ze-phones and ze-emails into security tech and it has excelled at this particular prison door marvel. From what I've managed to peek it's state-of-the-art, palm reading technology with these special magic second skin glove thingys, except it's not just confined to some poxy little ze-pad on the side, it's the whole the door. All you have to do is slap your hand in the appropriate glove anywhere on the door and push and it will open. If your glove isn't registered then you're not getting in or out. I know because I tried with my sticky palm.

When they first brought me in I was dumped on the bed and I could wander around a bit even though I was still slightly druggy and then a medic in a white boilersuit came too close for comfort so I nutted he/she/it in the choker with my elbow and then they bashed me on the head, put a brace on my mug and shackled me to the bed.

Bloody shackling. Such a fucking mare. Rich, LAW FORCE, they're all fucking obsessed with it. At least when I wanted to run away from Clinking and Clanking I could because they didn't make me shackle up but then I didn't run away anyway and now I'm shackled up again like a fucking idiot.

I wonder what's happened to the others. Looks like they all ended up in a puddle. Sam, Vida...

A medic in black barges in with a hand slapped against the door. Not seen this one before.

I can tell it's a she though because I can see she's got two mounds like mine underneath her black Uniform. She's got no visible hair, she's got a mask on her mug and her globes are just slits and it's kind of creepy. I scowl at her.

She puts some anti-bacti on her hands and then starts fiddling and prodding with my brace, tightening it so that my jaw carries on locking into place. I scowl at her even harder because she's being rough on purpose but she is a silent force and she doesn't give a fucking shit so I'm wrenched about for about half a minute before she lets go.

She leaves. I want to spit after her but I can't because of my fucking brace.

I stare at the door.

She barges in again and this time she's followed by some minions in white jumpsuits. I love the utilitarian look they're going for but I immediately stop caring because I see that they've got an electric wireless comb. I try to scramble out of their reach. They pin down my arms and legs and I can't move my head because she's done my brace up so fucking tight that any movement will just cause even more severe pain of my own making.

One of them grabs my shoulders and sits me up so that I'm as straight as I can be forced to be.

I can hear a loud humming sound and all of a sudden I feel a hot searing pain. The hottest burning thing I have ever felt and it's too too much.

They're doing it. These mad fuckers are burning the hair from my head.

The smell. Ugh the fucking smell.

It's eggy and gassy like there's fart oozing out of my skull and it's rank and I feel like I might vom and spew everywhere both from the stench of burning hair but also because the electric comb is on its most powerful setting and it's so fucking hot against my head and I can feel sweat trickling down behind my ears and the electric humming heat is burning so so hot and I can see all my dried up burnt hair falling like ashes around me.

Sweat sweat sweat and smoking singey dead hair.

They not stopping with just my hair.

They brush and knead my skull with it so that the stubbles left on top are blackened and burnt and I get a few blistering gashes for good measure.

I want to shriek and scream because it hurts, it really fucking hurts and I want to squeal and retch with every turn of that hot hot hot thing but I can't even open my gob.

YYYEEEEERRRRRGGGGGGHHHHHHUUUUWWW

WHHHHHHH is all I can get out.

My choker gurgles and gargles and yelps and I can feel thick snot coming out my conk because my squashed cries are forced out in the only available groggy opening.

The medic in black gives my head one last seething fucking burn and then one of them in white takes it away. They all let go of me and I crash back onto the bed.

The one in black stays staring at me whilst the others leave.

I gingerly touch my head but immediately inhale with a sharp sheeeeeeeeeeesh because it really hurts and it feels like there are all sorts of squishy sticky sores and blisters up there so instead I start hugging my elbows.

I want to curl up into a ball. I want to curl up into a ball and die.

I don't look at her.

I knew I should have left Clinking and Clanking before the fuckers got to me.

I don't look at the medic. I'm too shocked and her gaze is so malicious and penetrating. I want to scowl again, I want to push my tongue up to the front of my gob and waggle it about and be obscene. But I don't. I can't. I can't move my gob so I just blink at my digits. I don't look at her.

She moves towards me slowly and I recoil. She starts to loosen the brace so that I can move my gob about again. Not that I want to because it hurts so fucking much.

She then takes out a silver tube of cream that literally smells like vom and starts slapping my head with it. I still can't bring myself to scowl at her. I just look at my digits.

It's not even like I really fucking liked my hair, you know like those bods who obviously do and swish and bounce about with their tresses all over the bloody shop, trying to be like Leah, Teah or Feah, trying to get snapped by some Autogrammer fuck but it's not like I wanted it singed right from my fucking head. It's all lying about pathetically around me. Dead.

She pockets the silver tube. She still says nothing. She rots behind her mask the cunt. I close my globes.

She leaves.

I don't touch my head.

I put my digits into my pants and try to have a wank, just to make myself feel better and I don't care if there's a ze-cam in here watching. I need my little self-comfort.

I... I can't.

My hand is shaking too much.

I clenched it too hard when they were... Never clenched that hard before.

Shaking. Too much shaking.

I ... just...

Nope.

Fffuck.

Give up.

Can't.

Lie there.

No warm paisley brown.

Just gorgeous curling curving fascist flowers.

****

I start awake because I'm throwing up and seeing stars.

My gob is only half open and it dribbles all over my front smelling completely shite.

I glance up in front.

'YEEEEEEEEEEEEEEEEEEEEKKKKUHHH', I squeal.

There's a fucking medic just standing there watching me. Dressed in black, mask on. Pale slither moon of a mug literally ringing in the dark.

Is this Rick-shit?

I start shaking straight away with vom going everywhere.

This is sick-shit.

The medic in black reaches forward and starts clearing me up, dabs my chops with a wet cloth and is careful not to touch my brace in case my jaw cracks.

I can't see its globes. They're just black empties.

When it finishes, I'm clear and staring at it.

The moon is breaking in from the grilled window behind me. The whole box is electric blue.

It stares at me.

It slowly reaches towards its mask and brings it down. It looks like a he and he has a yawning scarred switchblade smile. I can't see his gnashers.

The Rick-knots pound against the wall of my tum. He's just cleaned me up but he is within his power to clean me up. Proper.

He leans forward and I'm stuck to my spot.

I can see all the flicks and nicks and gashes that score his mug. They're glistening with sweat and spit after being trapped behind that mask.

I think I'm going to pass out again. I'm seeing stars.

'Sleep', he hisses.

****

I don't know what's going on.

I don't know how long I've been here.

I wake up and I'm still in my bed but now I'm wearing a red boilersuit.

Bods have been in here doing stuff with me when I don't know about it the sneaky fucks.

Looks like they're going to want me to get up and out and about.

I still have my brace on.

I look at my arm and a drip has been in or some kind of other doss needle because there's a perfect round bruise in the crook. Feeding me whilst I was passed out. That's what made me sick. Must have been.

A medic in white pushes its way in and I immediately recoil because I don't want to see any more gobby grotesques with masks.

It walks to my arm and starts dabbing cream on it.

I watch it do it.

It looks at me watching.

'For convenience', it says in a hushed authoritative voice.

'Hmmm' I say.

It grabs my digits and shoves them into cuffs.

'Up', it says pointing to the door.

I carry on sitting there.

'Come on'.

I scowl back and kick and clang my leg about making it perfectly obvious you stupid flack fuck that I'm still shackled to the fucking bed.

The medic is pissed. It roughly unshackles me bleeeeeeeeeeeeeeeep and pulls me up. I slap on a smug told-you-so smile because it's not my fault it fucking forgot.

I walk towards the door and receive a big stinging slapping thump on my back.

I stumble forward and look back trying to bare my gnashers but just end up sending waves of pain all round my mug.

My beautiful bovvers. They're gone. I'm wearing shitty little plimsoll things for kiddies. No clumping no stomping no weighty weight weight just these flimsy dainty little rubber things. No impression. My bovvers beautiful lost lost lost.

The medic pushes past me and slaps a gloved hand against the door. It smoothly opens with some slight clicking with all the little locks breaking free. Really is a dream door.

I leave the box and in front of me is a corridor in the same clean cream colour.

This is an empty place. Where are all the bods that Singe was talking about? All those bods who have been crammed into this joint?

The medic leads me down the corridor and there are boxes lining it and the place is quiet. It feels like an old school or an old manor house that's been converted into prisonicles.

The doors we walk past are other ze-doors. My plims don't make a sound and it's really upsetting. It's like I'm not even there.

We get to the main door leading to this corridor and we go through it. On the door is a ze-pad. It has a screen lock on and three words standing out in bold.

'Threat to Society'.

Is that a fucking joke?

The medic swipes its finger across and we're freeish.

The staircase we've started walking down is beaut. Really old, big thick, substantial steps. Iron railing with some more of those floating flicky fucking flowers. The window facing the stair case and all the way down is big and bright with large rectangular panes. There are some diamond shaped panes that are seared in. They're rich ruby red sort of irregular and all over the place. The light that breaks through them is really pretty. More cream on the walls.

We go down about two flights and then we're on the ground floor.

The carpet is mossy green and the way is panelled with dark wood. Montmorency would love it.

A door and a screen and a door and a screen and a door and a screen.

Fucking high-sec here.

We get to the last door and it's big and heavy and cream. We go through it and there are some stone steps like at Clinking and Clanking and then high walls all around that lead to a courtyard.

It's empty.

There's a stone circle shape and grass in the middle.

The medic stops and I stop.

'Go on then', it says.

I go on without it.

'Eyes low', it calls after me.

I keep my globes on my plims, even though craning my choker is uncomfortable with the old brace.

I walk around the circle going nowhere.

The floor is tarmac and the buildings all around are reddy brown like Clinking and Clanking and Rich's smoky ex-gaff.

I turn back and the medic is gone. Doesn't mean I'm not being watched but they know I'm not going to pull anything.

Off I go.

Why am I the only one here playing dizzy dinosaurs?

Where are all them bods that Singe was chatting about?

I walk round and round and round.

Bored.

Is this what it's like to be dead?

There's a tree on the far right hand side.

I know I hated that tree at the warehouse but I really want to go and have a look at this one.

They're watching me but what's the harm in looking at a tree?

Why would they put a tree there if they didn't want bods to look at it or something?

I have never wanted to go and look at a tree so much.

Round and round and round my O.

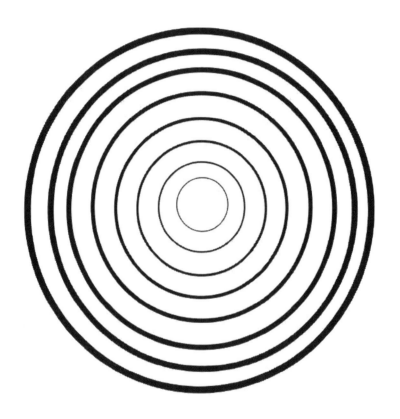

Kind of want to dive into it, like Sam said.

Dive   into   deep,   juicy   sleep.

Sam…

That's it. Tree time.

I tip toe over to the tree.

I can't tell if it's always been here or if they had it dug out and plonked here for the whole old schoolish effect.

I circle it and it smells earthy and sweet. Its branches dip long and low, like big giant digits reaching to sweep the ground. I can't look up properly to its top because it hurts my jaw.

Behind the tree is a gap and then a fence with horizontal wire lines.

Seems odd. Everything is bricky and secure here so why would there be a simple fence.

Oh wait. It's fucking buzzing.

I slowly reach down with my cuffed paws and grab a twiggy leaf thing that's on the ground.

I raise it to the fence.

'YEEEEEEOOOWWWWW', I shriek as it immediately gives me a shock and I'm thrust back and land on my bum.

Fucking stupid fucking CUNT.

My muscleys are all tight and hurting. The twig's just lying there, it's not even crackled or anything.

I bet one of the zombs saw the whole thing and is finding this hilarious.

I reach across panting and snap the twig in half and start pounding it into the ground with my pathetic plim.

Serves you fucking right. Why should I be the one getting a fucking shock?

I can see through the fence though.

On the other side, I see loads of bods. Loads of bods and they're all scattered around all over the place. Some of them are wandering around another stone circle like mine, but then others are sitting around or scampering about doing other things.

On the other side of their circle is the round central hub of the prison. They must all be shoved in there.

That's unfair. Why should I be left on my tod?

There's a bod pretty close up to the railing.

I think it's a she. It's hard when everyone's been singed. She's sat by a pond.

How come they get a fucking pond?

There's a big see-through barrier all around it, like on the trammsmuter loading docks. Probably so that bods don't end up trying to drown themselves.

She's got a stick in her hand. Oh wait, no it's a net. There's a net at the end.

So the net is in a purpose built hole poking through the see-through barrier. She's fishing lucky fucking sod.

I catch her globe almost immediately. Probably because I'm wearing red and all her bods are in purple.

She looks behind her. She looks slightly nervous.

I look behind me. Still just me.

I raise my hand.

She does nothing.

I really want to know why she's in purple, why there are loads of bods in purple over there and why I'm on my one.

She gets up but then moves slowly backwards, like she thinks I'm going to blow up or something.

'Wharrayoudoin?' I manage to squeeze out of my knackered jaw. I try to be as quiet as possible.

'What?' she gobs back.

'Wharrayoudoin?'

To be honest, I can see why she's a bit nervous. I am clad in danger red with a fucking metal wire wrapped round me and I can't even speak. What a mess.

'Um...' she says. Still walking backwards.

'Fishin?'

'Um. Yeah...' she tails off.

She stops walking backwards. Even though I look like a shitshow, I don't think she was expecting me to ask about fishing. She looks carefully at my mug.

'Pond dippin', she says. She wants to be quiet too.

'Fissssh?'

'Nope, jus' weird bug things'.

'Wrhyy? Whatssapoint?'

'It's my activiteh, gets meh aweh from all the othuhs'.

'Luckyfuckinsod'.

She peers at my mug.

'Oh mah god', she hisses. She darts forward towards the fence.

'Sorrrwee', I say, edging back. Maybe I shouldn't have fucking sweared. Now that I have a bod who can answer my Qs I probably shouldn't start chatting like a shit-gob.

'Oh mahh god', she says again.

Maybe it's because my mug is a mess and I look like a rag and my gob is tightly shut with metal.

'Iknoww fuckinmedix mygobissmahshed'.

'It's YOU', she says.

Fuck. She Recognises me. Probably because my ghostly mug has been swooping about for the past few days. Fucking UK.

'Uhhwhat?' I say.

'I didn' realise they'd got yer'.

'Wellyeahh'.

'Yeh don' Recognise meh do yer?' she says with a low humourless chuckle.

'Um yeah'.

'It's ME, yer twonk, Marissuh'.

I blink at her.

Holy fucking shit. It's Marissa.

She has bloody good sight to Recognise me from all the way over there.

Almond globes, excellent bone structure, seething badass. It's fucking Marissa.

Except her beautiful braids are all gone. Just a blackened crusty head.

She sees me looking at her head and rubs it nervously.

She also has split chops that're just about to start healing up and a bruised choker.

'Marrisuhh!' I grit out through my silly stuck gob.

'Fuck dude', she says. 'What the fuck is that thin on yer 'ead and how did yeh end up in TTS?'

'Wharthe fuck is TTS?'

'Threat to Societeh. Yer a Red Suit. The mos' dangerous categoreh'.

Threat to Society. Fucking boo.

'Well theyhaven' even askemeeanythinyet', I scoff.

She nods grimly. 'Theh can do that'.

I shrug.

'Bang you uhp and not even tell yeh whyuh'.

'I haveaprettehgoodidee'.

'Wha'?'

'Don'wannasayy theylistennin'.

'Oh, righ'. Let's just try and be careful then'.

'Rich and Ryan'.

'Yeah?'

'Yeah'.

'Oh'. She says.

'Yeah'.

'The, um, whoosh?' she says, wiggling her digits.

'Yeah'.

'Good for you. So it WAS yer mug uhp and abou' in the sky'.

'Yeah. Whahappenetoyou? Cannayoutalkabouit?'

'Yeah, it's fine', she says scratching her head. 'Theh made meh wait for a while when they first brough' us in but then I had mah interview and Charges. My Reformation programme is in full swing'.

'Go onn'.

'So we got out, didn' realise yer weren' with us for a while, sorreh about that. Rachel decided to run aweh down the hill but me and Lauren were stupid and decided to hide and then we were surrounded by all these Autogrammuhs and journos who brough' LAW FORCE with them and we were shoved into a van and brough' in here'.

'Whadid they chargeyou with?'

'Unrecognition'.

'Shit'. Probbably because all of our Uniforms were left lying around.

'To be honest, it could have been worse'.

'Why?'

'Well there are loads of bods in here for Unrecognition. It just makes meh think that the whole thing is stupid, Clothin' Recognition and Uniforms. Bods break stuhff or leave thingys lyin aroun' all the time. There are too many Unrecogniseds in here, it's a joke'.

I always really liked my Uniform. I don't know why bods find it so hard to stick to one thing. But Marissa's probably right. There are a heck of a lot of purple bods over there.

'Areya OK? LAW FORCEnstuff?'

'Ugh. It's shit. Ah say it could have been worse than Unrecognition but that lot, they're a bunch of twats'.

'What happened?'

'So Lauren was all teareh and scared and cute and Ah was just trying to hold mahself togethuh and stay coooool. They ended uhp lettin Lauren FREE because she agreed to become an Autogrammuh and have her Unrecognition written off'.

'Shit'.

'Did Ah even get a fucking option? Nope. First chance they got they chopped off mah hair and stuck meh in a boilersuit'.

'That's soounfair'.

'It just pisses meh off. Ah didn't get aneh chance to stick up for mahself, tell them that the reason Ah was out there in an Unrecognisable state was because a bunch of fuckin snide jobbos were literalleh goin to chop us'.

'Yeah'.

'And Lauren, well. She took the first chance she could to piss off and Ah can' say Ah blame her, but she didn' try and stick uhp for meh at all. Just got so overexcited about becomin a profesh Autogrammuh, didn' give two hoots abou' meh. She was out in a couple of hours. They made meh wait about all night. Ah might nevuh get out of here for all she knows'.

'When dooya getout?'

'A few months Ah think'.

'N'badd'.

'We'll see. Ah don't trust them'.

'Me'neither'.

'Ah hope this doesn' damage meh becomin an Employuh', she says. She doesn't sound hopeful.

'Yeah', I say.

Poor Marissa. With this Unrecognition Charge, her life is going to be even more crap. She already has a fucking hard time of it and now she's been stuffed in Strangeways. Employers aren't going to want to touch her, poor sod, let alone vote for her to become one. I don't think she'll ever become an Employer now.

'And anyweh', she continues, 'they can' keep us all bunched uhp like this. It's not just Unrecogniseds you know'.

'Imet a bod whoawas 'ResistancetaExchange'...'

'Did yer?'

'Yeah he-'

'Wait, shut yer gob'.

'Yeah'.

'What have yer got goin on in there?' she says, nodding behind me.

'Ugh, jusastone circle, walkaround'.

'Sounds borin'.

'Yeah'.

'Ah suppose all yer can do is think. Maybeh that's the whole point. Yous lot more than anehbod will be made to think about what yer've done, who yah are. And not talk to anehbod about it'.

I've done none of those things. Wallowed in the O O O and fantasised about a tree but I don't think that's the same thing. Whatever. I'm a bad prisoner or Reformer or whatever I am.

'So wha'thefuck is tha'pon allabout?'

'We have loads of things this side. Theh've tried to make it into some kind of fun park, there's pond dippin and there's a pettin corner and hay mazes and tunnels. All bods are assigned to an Activiteh as part of theh Reformation programme and Ah don't realleh know why. It's freakeh. Theh make us pleh'.

'I can't play'.

'Of course not'.

'Wha?'

'Yer know, Ah haven't even seen a Red Suit before. Yous lot are kept so far apart from us lot. Yous must have tons of space'.

'Squiet'.

'Yeah well suck it uhp, Ah sleep in a single box with FOUR othuh bods. It's a bit of a squish'.

'Really?'

'Yeah. You know that bod who managed to get out?'

'Yeah'.

'Has it been a big deal out there?'

'Pretty big. I wasn't keepinnup to date withallaThe Money News and holograms. But Strangewayswas crawlin'.

'Ah'm not surprised. It was huge in here. Huge. LAW FORCE realleh put their foot down. Ah was only just brough' in and they didn' let us eat for a deh and we had to spend pretty much all deh locked in the cells'.

'Fuck'.

'Theh were seriousleh pissed. We had to shit in front of each other as well because theh wouldn't allow us to go to the bogs. It was disgustin. The whole thing. Ah didn' evun know mah cell mates. Not that Ah would have wanted to shit in front of bods Ah *did* know but it would probableh make it easyuh'.

'Tha'shorrible'.

'Yeah. Ah wouldn' be surprised if more shit doesn' go off if they don' sort it ou"'.

'Do'you havathe medix over there?'

'Medics?'

'Yeah maske'bods in blacknwhite'.

'No. Just the LAW FORCE guards. But theh're just thugs. Ah'm not realleh scared of them anymore. Theh're stronger than us and that's just abou' it'.

'No medix?' No ghoulish switchy weirdos for them then. That's weird. No wonder they all feel comfortable rebelling and running away.

I look back and there's nothing and no one there. Just the big concrete circle idling. Too quiet. These bods don't announce their presence but they will be close by. I shudder.

'The break out, it was embarrassin for them', Marissa continues, really hushed now. 'Bods are still thinkin now that they could-'

'Stop', I say. 'Don'say anything more. The medix'ere, I think they're listenin'.

'Riiight, sure. But wha' medics?'

I look behind me again.

They probably know I'm talking to Marissa. If I'm supposedly that dangerous, why are they letting me chat? There's no way they don't know what I'm up to.

They might do something to her just because she's been chatting to me.

'Mm gonnago'.

'Yeah, OK. Me too'.

'I hopeeyou're OK, get out soonaneverythin'.

'Ah am, no worries. Don' let them get to yer. Good luck. Stay spunkeh'.

'Yeah'.

We both turn at the same time. She picks up her net and starts swishing it about in the water. I scuff my way round the tree and pad my plims back to the stone circle.

I don't know if I'll see her again. I feel sick. My Rick-knots twinge.

She and the rest of them bods didn't realise they'd left me

behind. Bit snide. But what do I care? I suppose the honey-oil flames were worth it.

There's a zombie medic there. One of the ones in black. My thumper comes up into my gob.

Shit. Switchblade.

I don't know what to do. There's nowhere to run.

I stand still. I look at the ground. The Rick-knots churn in my tum. Everything about this place and this shitshow I am in is making my guts squirm overtime and if I'm not careful I will probably shit myself.

It walks right up to me.

'Follow. Now', it says in a really cold voice.

We go back up the stone steps into the Cream Castle and then along the mossy floor. This place is literally like something out of Downstone Bubby. Instead of heading upstairs towards my bedroom box though, the medic leads me down some dark stairs into a basement floor.

The corridor is still cream but there are no windows, no natural lights.

My Rick-knots are on high alert squirm and my thumper is hammering in my choker. This must be it. I'm going to get some kind of chop. This is going to turn into something shit and rotten. If only I didn't have this fucking brace on. I might be able to nut myself out of this mess.

The medic leads me down the hallway and we stop outside a big black door.

It opens it up.

I'm slightly taken aback to see a very normal looking oldish white man sat behind a mahogany table. He's wearing a snappy suit, he's got a neat side parting and is writing with a gold pen. There are no windows and the box is very dim but it's normal enough.

He looks up and says, 'Ah, good'.

The medic pushes me in with a cold prod and the door is shut behind me.

'Our newest visitor', he says.

He looks happy to see me, kind of like a frog. Not exactly a fucking visitor am I? Cunt. He looks like he'd own a pretty-car, with that haircut and flashy pen. As he finishes scribbling, a mahoosive watch jingles on his wrist.

At least that fucking zombie has gone. I feel much more at home with this arse-wipe whose mug, stumpy digits and pulse I can actually see. This one is familiar territory.

'I am the Prison Manager, it's great to meet you. Please, take a seat'.

I don't say anything. I plonk myself on the red leather chair. I try to look at him with a look of severe disrespect as if he stinks of shit because that's probably all that's going to come out of his gob anyway.

The seat is sort of wonky and unstable and I nearly slip off. He gives a hearty chuckle.

'Steady on! Ah, you've got to love my comedy chair. Lots of people have trouble with it!'

I barely twitch my gob.

This is it. It must be question time. I need some kind of tactic like in all the old filmos. Dumb? Play dumb. Dumb and dead as a dead thing, answering questions with questions and statements with questions and all the dumb and silence for as long as I can. Or angry? Maybe I should make so much noise that he doesn't have a fucking clue what's going on and then there's nothing for it but to send me back to my box.

I don't know. Got no gut feeling. Just Rick-knots.

'So let's go through your records-'

'Wharecords?'

'The ones that have been collated'.

'Evidence?'

'That's one word for it, a euphemism if you like', he says raising his brows.

'I haven'doneeanything'.

'No, you don't need to worry. We're just going to establish exactly what happened on the night of the fire'.

My knots churn. Fuck.

'Wha'fire?'

He chuckles. 'Nice try missy but if you've done what I expect you have done, you're going to be in deep trouble. Or, as I suppose people of your ilk, 'bods' isn't it, would say, 'shit''.

OK. The voice is calm and slightly snotty. He looks like Business and he means business.

'Do I neeealawyer?' I ask.

'Lawyers are not necessary', he says shaking his head and grinning. 'Courts and trials... it's too much bureaucracy, too much noise and not enough action. This country has moved beyond bureaucracy, which is why we have LAW FORCE. Why do you need a lawyer if LAW FORCE are doing their job perfectly? It's common sense'.

Common sense. That blast from the past.

'How do I knowatha LAW FORCE haven'fucked up'ig time?'

'I don't think your language is adhering to the protocols we have in place'.

'You jus'said 'shit''.

'Whilst you are sat in that chair in that colour you are wearing, you are to adhere to our protocols and codes of conduct. It's not too much to ask considering how, let's say, challenging a situation you find yourself in'.

'You haven't accusame fffanythin' yet'.

'Accuse? Accuse? Come come, that's very hyperbolic and emotional of you', he says leaning on his elbows and waving about his hands. 'We are compelled by the various visual and audio sources we have collated that you have challenged various societal status quos. These are in place to protect the UK, our traditions and our values. Therefore we are going to establish what occurred and arrange a Reformation programme accordingly, and to make sure no further indiscretions, and subsequent safety violations, manifest'. He pauses. 'Understood?'

I don't say anything. Reeeeeeeeksabullshit. He sounds

nice, sensible and normal but it doesn't feel quite right.

'In addition, before we really get to the nitty gritty money-in-the-bank questions, I have to say that your actions have been, well, *again*, challenging to say the least for my colleagues who are trying to do their jobs here, an honest day's work'.

'Colleagues?'

'Yes. The healthcare professionals'.

The healthcare professionals?

'Demente'crazy ghoss-shits wanderin'round?'

'They are invaluable colleagues in the new Reformed Strangeways. Please don't do them a disservice by referring to them in unsavoury colloquial diminutives'.

Diminuwhat?

The fuck...

'Are we agreed?'

'They'renot even-'

'Our', he says, raising his hand and jingling his watch, 'healthcare professionals have been given extensive, vigorous training, watertight operational matrices, the likes of which makes them extremely apt, qualified and experienced enough to deal with today's difficult delinquents'.

Right. Difficult delinquents. I am a difficult delinquent. Seems fitting. But I don't think he's going to like me much for it. Can't say that I completely care what he thinks, but I don't think it's going to get me out of here very quickly.

'I have received reports that you have shown a most aggressive disposition which, in addition to your suspected challenging behaviours, has meant you are what we might call a Threat to Society'.

'Can I jus'say that they have pushedame 'round like absolute fuck. Majaw, tha'spithood, this fuckinbrace, dripsinnamysleep...'

'These are all measures my colleagues have had to pursue because of the sort of behaviour you have displayed'.

'Itwa too extreeeme'.

'I believe extreme measures have to be taken in extreme

cases'.

'Howama extreme?'

'Well, let's take a look shall we?'

I scowl at him.

He holds my gaze before flicking his fat digit through a ze-pad full of Autogram snaps and notes. I can't say I'm surprised, I bet they've got all sorts on me. Not fair to use it against me though when nobod's asked me anything yet.

'Now. We have a lot of infographics about you, but I want this information straight from the horse's mouth. I want to test your compliance shall we say'. He pauses. 'And we will know if you're not complying'.

Jeez. And bods say I'm melodramatic.

'Now', he continues, 'how long have you been Conscripted to this area?'

'Can'remember'.

'Right. Did you attend the poly-versity?'

'No'.

'So you left the Academy and went straight into Conscription?'

'Yes'.

'Right. And who were you Conscripted to?'

'Rich'.

'Rich?'.

'Yeah'.

'So Rich was your Employer and what was the area of industry in which you worked?'

'Fashion who'sale'.

'I have always been slightly wary of fashion'.

He doesn't continue.

'Why?' I ask.

'It doesn't exactly walk hand-in-hand with our policy of Unrecognition'.

'Right'. This is very true.

'But we need to give our Concripts a sense of freedom, even when that freedom is still dictated and framed by rules and regulations in available media'.

'Why?'

'Well, even though weekend fashion is allowed, fashion still doesn't mean total freedom. We believe it's enough to make our Conscripts think that they are making their own choices. But they are *safe* choices, carefully laid out by the national fashion industry. That's enough don't you think?'

He chuckles. It is very phlemgy and I don't want him to do it again.

'OK'.

'You understand, it's something of a tightrope. We can't be allowing people, young people like yourself, to get any non-regulatory ideas. You 'bods' need a tight leash'.

'Whyaareya tellin me this?'

'I'm just ensuring that we're on the same page, that we understand one another. We do understand one another?'

'Dunno'. I really don't.

'What was your Conscription Contribution?'

'Content'. So contentful with my content. My stinking oozing content.

'That's a writing position if I'm not mistaken?'

'Yeah'. I wouldn't go that far. It's a mechanical churning empty thing.

'So would you describe yourself as a writer? As a conveyor of ideas?'

'If tryna sell bods shit isathe same thin'then yeah'.

'Would you describe yourself as idealistic?'

'No'.

'Would you describe yourself as a team player, a contributor, someone who wants to build something of tangible goodness?'

'Um. No'.

'No?'

'Nah'.

'Indeed'.

I rub my conk. My jaw is throbbing. This fucking brace is

driving me mad.

'So what do you do with yourself?'

'Conscription, sleep, see'a'ma friens'.

'Would you say you have good friends?'

I think of Montmorency and Monk. They are fun and they are good. I'm not particularly close to anybod but they're the closest I've got. Would I count Vida and Sam as new friends? Perhaps. Fuck knows what happened to them. And maybe none of them will care when it really matters.

'Yes'.

'What do you like to get up to of an evening?'

'Drinks'.

'Anywhere in particular?'

'Town'.

'Around the poly-versity?'

'Yeah Isssuppose'.

'Big Hands?' He asks flashing me his palms.

I don't say anything. How does he know about Big Hands? Sure, it's a famous joint but slightly too close to home.

'Well?'

'Suppose'.

'Been there recently?'

'Wellum, yeah, probs'.

'Interesting'.

'Is tha'it? Wha's that gotta do witanything? How is gointa 'ig Hands a crime?'

'I didn't say it was'.

'I don'understan''.

'What I'm interested in is who you are spending your time with'.

'Why don'you talk ta'them then? Whyama here?'

'There really is no need to get so defensive'.

'Well if this isn'bout me then wha'sthe poin?'

'You're lack of loyalty to your friends is surprising, and a potential cause for concern. It makes me question your loyalty in the bigger sense of things, for the greater of goods'.

'Wha?'

'Who else, what else would you betray?'

''ang on. You don' wanname hangin ou with some bods but attathe same time yadoo?' You can't win with this cunt.

'Like I said, I'm just working out who you are, how you slot into the current events and if you will comply'.

'Wha'exactly are theeese'urrent even's?'

'There have been two very strange, *very* strange occurrences in the past few days and interestingly you have been involved with both'.

Have I? I yank my brace and it fucking hurts. The fire yes but what else could he possibly be blithering on about?

'Would you say that you're a sexually loose character?'

Ummmmmmmmmmmmm.

'Like wha?'

'Well, like you have a lot of sex with other people, both men and women who you may or may not know'.

'None of yourabeezwax'.

'I'm afraid it is', he grins, gurning at me like a fucking Rick-creep. 'Please answer the question. Comply'.

I throw my head back and stop when my jaw hurts. Come on then you fuck. 'Not comparedtamost bods. Iyalike the do-it-yourself way'.

'So you like to masturbate?'

'Yeah'.

'Interesting. And do you regularly engage in strenuous sexual activity with men and women?'

'Sometimes'.

'Men and women?'

'Yeah. Mos' bods do nowadays'.

'Hmm yes'. He pauses and frowns. 'It is not illegal, but it is still, I have to inform you, unacceptable, intolerable'.

'Why?'

'Because it negates tradition and challenges roles and morals that the UK has carefully crafted for itself in our history. Roles and morals that you and you boddish Big Hands lot are flinging apart'. He is still frowning his heavy frown of judgment.

I shift and wobble on his stupid chair.

'What lot?'

'Do you recognise this person?'

He jabs his ze-pad and a hologram image of Malga flashes up.

My tum flips and my knots clench.

'No'.

'Don't lie'. He leans forwards and glares at me. That sweet sugary froggish smile has been wiped clean off his mug.

'Immanot'.

I only met him once. I'm practically telling the truth.

He clenches his fists together. 'I want to make you aware that anyone caught lying will undergo due medical process. We will be keeping a constant track of your heart rate, pulse and monitoring everything that takes place in that 'bod' of yours to get you on the right Reformation programme'.

'OK'. Sounds desperado.

'If you are lying, then I can only assume that you are not willing to comply. That you are trying to subvert your correct and proper course of Reformation. This is not acceptable. I don't mind if we dance around this for a while, but you will be Reformed, and this piece of information is key in helping to decide your official Charges and the ultimate structure your Reformation will take'.

I don't have a choice really because, let's fucking go there, I'm a Blunter not a Dancer, just like Lucy said. I've never really been able to lie and dance and gloss. All those old cinematics with prisoners bluffing and dancing and twisting with the law. I can't do it. I can withhold information for a while perhaps but I can't dance that dance. I'm too much of a bovver. I don't know. I have a bad feeling about this whole sitch. I don't even know if I want to be Reformed. I don't know what that even means.

'Now. Do you Recognise him, this person?'

'Wellyeah, all bods knows wha' he looksalike. Firs bod, um, person Unrecognise''.

'Hmm yes. A slight urban myth that. He was the first Reformer with whom we openly divulged the Unrecognition policy to members of the public. But many more were involved before and during that process. So why did you lie?'

'You lot don'talike him much'.

'That's true', he says grinning. 'Daniel Lawson did his time, undertook the Reformations that we proposed, even though he resisted quite heavily. The only problem is now he is hard, too hard to keep track of. The technology is still only being developed. Virginal I like to think'.

'Um, righ''.

Malga's called Daniel Lawson?

'It leads us to conclude that he is up to something. We have reason to believe that he was in Big Hands a few days ago'.

I know he can probably sense my pulse throbbing and my gut churning but I try to keep as cool as possible.

'Um, righ'', I say again.

'What do you make of that?'

'How doya know he was in 'ig Hands?'

'We have our sources. And technology'.

'In 'ig Hands?'

He leans back and he's got a big Rich belly protruding in front of him. 'As if we would let you and all your little friends congregate in dingy little hovels without us knowing exactly what is going on'.

'It's notalike much happens there. Jus' 'ubbles, 'rown and clear'.

'Yes and a whole lot else besides'.

'Hmm?'

'Don't you 'brush your teeth'. Regularly?'

'Sometimes'.

'Well, in that case I would perhaps question your

efficiency in a Capital sense'.

'I wouldn' know'.

'Wouldn't you?'

'No'.

'And that night?'

'Wha night?'

'You didn't meet Daniel with your friends, you didn't engage in questionable deviance with him, you didn't have solicitous coded conversations'.

Errrrrrrrr.

'No'.

'Don't lie'.

'Immanot'.

Well the first bit is true but there was nothing questionable about our convo. Malga is definitely the most erotic bod I have ever seen. Indulgent, yes, deviant, definitely, but in the best possible sense, not the way he's twisting it.

'Are you familiar with his politics?'

'I know bodsa more familiar with it'.

'But you are still aware that he was and still is widely critical of the UK'.

'Yes'.

'OK, good'.

'Wha' doesatha' prove?'

'Nothing'.

He presses a tab on his ze-pad.

I sit there looking at him. He has an old conk with crusty snot round his nostrillos. His wide gob becomes even more uncannily froggish the longer you look at it.

'Now, do you Recognise this person?'

Up flashes a hologram of Singe.

'No'. I try to shake my head for added effect but the brace makes it painful so I stop. There is no way in hell that he's putting me in the same box as Singe.

'Are you quite sure?'

'Wasn'ee the bod who ranaway?'

'I wouldn't say runaway, I would say he subverted the course of law and chose to relinquish his responsibility, his Reforms and renounce those who were there to help him, like a coward. An utter coward'.

'Isn'that the same-athing asawhat I said?'

'Absolutely not'.

'Why?'

'That is none of your concern'.

'OK'.

'So you are sure you don't Recognise him'.

'Yeah'.

'Final answer?'

'Yeah'.

'So it won't concern you to know that this person was found dead at the Devil's Arse?'

I choke with laughter.

Devil's Arse?

''Scuse me?'

'The Devil's Arse. It's a notable cave, near a little village in the Peak District. Castleton I think it's called. I'm told Her Majesty Queen Victoria visited once'.

'Oh'.

'Indeed. This boy was found near the mouth of the cave, it looked like he'd taken a tumble from the top. We were pretty close behind him but still not exactly sure of his whereabouts, but it seems he took another cowardly decision to cut the chase short. Or his car couldn't see though the mist and he went flying by accident. Either way, I don't care. His remains were found in the ravine near the mouth of the Arse'.

Poor old sorry silly Singe.

Imagine dying at the gob of the Devil's Arse. I didn't know the bod that well, apart from the fact he was a cotton wool whinger, but, you know, I did have a sex dream about him. He may have been just a prop in that dream really but a sex dream is a sex dream. And he was a feature in mine.

'So you are 100% sure that you do not know who this

person is?' the PM says, peering at me and zapping the hologram off his ze-pad.

'I don'know who that bod'is'. If I admit to knowing him then I'm not only thrown in with him and his stupid shenans but it could also send this old bonk to Vida, Sam and Rosée and the others. He'll know for certain that he was harboured at Clinking and Clanking. I can't do that. Plus he might bite, he might believe me.

'Then how come we found a multitude of his trackers in your system?'

Oh yeah.

Fuck.

'Whaddaya mean?'

'We found a multitude of his, *his*, very own trackers, certified by the medical professionals you are by now well acquainted with, in *you*. Would you care to offer an explanation?'

I flush hot. He must think we've fucked or something.

'I don'understand howwaya checkemy system?'

'It was a standard medical examination. Unfortunately you were under anaesthetic as a result of the damage done to your jaw'.

'Soya didn'wait fa me to wakeup you jus'did it anyway?'

'It was a standard procedure. There is a very strict set of guidelines that dictates a *very* strict timeline for new Reformers to be examined and assessed before it is decided by management how to proceed with the Reformation course. You chose to misbehave and disrupt the procedure so we had to push on despite your lack of consciousness'.

'Bu'what abou'consen'?'

'Consent?'

'Yeah consen''.

'I don't follow'.

'Well, yacan'just poke about ma bod when I haven'said thatayou could'.

'Ah I see', he says inter-locking his digits and leaning

forward. 'You think we should have asked your permission before following our strict governmental guidelines'.

'Yeah'.

'The guidelines that are supposed to keep us all safe and secure within the confines of the law?'

'Yeah'.

'You see, that's just not how it works'.

'It'sanot that 'ard to understan, you jus'askame ma permiss-'

'NO, *you* don't understand', he says, pointing and scoffing manically. He really doesn't like his understanding questioned. 'That 'consent' method and any other form of consensual contract, particularly in the case of prospective Reformers like you, is officially and legally outdated. You should know that'.

'Why?'

He sneers. 'Because it was a collective UK decision that if people, be they Employers or Conscripts, have nothing to hide; that if they are positive and certain that they have done nothing wrong, then they should be willing to contribute and open themselves to analysis without being formally asked to comply. It's common sense. It really is'.

'Commonasense?'

'Indeed. And as aforementioned, this is particularly apt in your very special case because it is posited by this establishment that consent is absolutely and unequivocally forfeited when you surrender to the law'.

'Bu', bu'-'

'But nothing', he says quietly and firmly. 'You are here at our discretion so you must play to our rules'.

'But, you don'even know if I've adone anythin!'

'I beg your pardon?'

'At the pointawhere you brough'me in, you hadn'even askame a question. It's only now that Ima even bein askathings and I'm still innocen until Ima proven guilty'.

'We already know too much. Your case is a foregone conclusion. Our actions were justly apt and we will stand by them'.

'You c-can'-'

'Yes we can. You shouldn't have got yourself into this little predicament in the first place and then none of this would be happening. And quite honestly, your knowledge of the due legal process in the UK is severely lacking'.

He can't have anything. He'd have told me. I'm not even dancing with him and he must know that.

'OK then. Wha'have I done?'

'You may mock, but you don't know the depths on what we have on you yet'.

'Yeah yeah', I say rolling my globes because this bod is full of shit. Or that's what I want him to think I think.

He clenches his digits tight. 'Finding you because of the trackers in your system and then finding said trackers is pretty incriminating don't you think?'

Well, I suppose he does have a fucking point there.

'Idunno. Idon'think it should'ave got to that point inathe firssplace'.

'OK...?'

'Because you didn'aska permission'.

'I am telling you that you have lost those sorts of rights when you made bad choices. It's common sense'.

Common sense. Again and again.

What is this common sense? I used to think I had it but now it doesn't sound pretty fucking common at all. We're not on the same fucking page. Sounds like he's got a totally fucking different idea to me of what is right and wrong but he's making his opinion sound obvious and acceptable by calling it 'common sense'. How can I disagree with 'common sense'? I don't share his 'common sense'. I want him to shove his fucking common sense right up his hairy fucking arse and make him choke to death on it, the cunt.

'Wha'ever'.

'That's right', he says slowly. 'You made bad choices, you hung around with bad people on the wrong side of the law, you decided to engage in disgusting tantric sexual games, finding a way out for that Reformer, that Resister of Exchange, that swindler, and together you burnt down that beacon of Employment, prosperity, aspiration and fairness'.

If I didn't have this fucking brace on my jaw would fucking drop.

'Wha' the FUCK you fuckin' talkinabout?'

'We know exactly what you've been up. Had a little Bonnie and Clyde thing going with tha rascal, did you?'

'WHA?'

He prods his ze-pod and up comes hologram after hologram of news content about me and fucking Singe fucking.

'According to all the information we have acquired, I believe you were both embroiled in a plot to burn down and damage precious economical financial infrastructure of the UK whilst indulging in strange sexually motivated displays and rituals. Finally, I believe the whole thing was being puppeted and orchestrated by the madcap freakoid Daniel or Malga or whatever he calls himself'.

'Are ya kidding?'

'No. The story has taken off'.

'It'sa shit. Utter shit. You are fuckin'insane'.

'But you have been in the environs of both of these men?'

'Intha what?'

'In the vicinity or the company or the PRESENCE. You silly ignoramus'.

No idea what that is.

'Yeah but nothin, nothin like'a this!'

If they're going to get me and drag me into fucking Strangeways then they can at least get it fucking right.

'The fire...' I begin.

'Yes?'

'I did it. It wasa me'.

'Just as I thought', the PM says, snapping his digits. 'And the Reformer?'

'Had nothin'tado with it'.

'Nothing?'

'Nothin'.

He looks disappointed that his tantric sex theory is dud.

'So why did you burn down that building?'

'I'd hada bad day. MaEmployer, he'd no'paid suppliers, they cameadown to the buildin, theyawere violen' brought ina gu-'

'I'm going to have to interrupt you there', he says, holding up his hand in my mug.

'Why?' I squeak.

'I have the feeling you are about to reveal confidential information regarding your Employer's Business to me and that is not acceptable'.

'Wha' do you mean?'

'My role as Prison Manager, as with all other areas of Business and law and politics etc. is to not get involved with anything that is remotely infringing on Business rights to confidentiality and privacy. You do not have the right to reveal to me the machinations of your Employer's Business and the way in which it is conducted'.

JSNZHZU720EOKDKD'S#PCJMNSBGYFNOL;PJDL SSPWW523Q;.KLFFYUFD

'Bu'then how can'I tell yathe truth?'

'That right has to be suspended'.

'So Imma tryna tell you thisisa whole big misun'erstandin and you'rea tellin'me I can't?'

'Yes'.

'Rich and fuckin'Rick and that lot are more importan'than me tellin'ya right now that Imma not as bad as you think I am? ThaTROOF?'

'Yes'.

Marissa shoots into my mind.

'Bu' I have a witness!' I shout.

'And?'

'She'sin the other buildin'. Unrecognised, she's jus'over

there, she'll backa me up! Go anfind her, we can strai'en this out'.

'That won't be possible because again, it could result in a divulgence of private Business matters and that is hardly fair to your Employer. This country has strict laws on deregulation'.

'That is fuckinOUTOF ORDER', I yell and stomp my plim. There is nowhere near as much power coming from this lame hunk of rubber as from a beautiful steely bovver but it'll have to do.

'Excuse me-' the PM starts.

'FUCKINBULLSHITFUCKFUCK', I screech through the metallic brace holding my gob together.

'If you do not calm down at once I will call for a medical professional to come in to sedate you'. His globes glint a me.

I want to smash up his entire fucking office. But I don't want those zombie fucks to get their mitts on me. It's weird because I'm not scared of anything normally. I don't care if I get squished smashed or stomped on. I don't care about fucking about with other bods and turning them into pulp and expecting them to do the same for me. But now, with this lot. I can't do anything. I CAN'T DO ANYTHING.

I shut up.

'I thought so', he says, smirking.

I don't say anything.

'Now. This is what we are going to do. Until we agree a course of Reformation, you will remain a Threat to Society in this special compound. As far as we can tell and medically prove, you have dallied both with a highly wanted and heavily tracked Reformer who makes it his business, so to speak, to outrun the UK, the officials who are trying to track him and keep the rest of the population safe. You have also wantonly dallied with a Reformer who has run away from his duty and place here and whose trackers have somehow magically ended up in your system. Both evidently have questionable politics and ideas. Most terrible of all, you burnt down a Business and evaded due legal process. Therefore, you are hereby considered to be a Threat to Society and you will remain in this wing, which you must admit is pretty nice'.

I glare at him. It's nice and pretty and stuff but it is lonely and way way way too quiet. With that story, I'll never be getting out of Cream Castle.

'Is that OK?'

'No'.

'Well you're just going to have to acquiesce'.

'I don't wanna aqua'fuckin anything'.

His globes flash. 'Careful', he says waggling his digit in my mug. 'I will be in constant correspondence with your medical professionals and we will assess Reforms and treatments for you'.

'I don'need treatments'.

'I disagree'.

Fuck fuck fucking fuck fuck this fucking shit.

'To give you a slight insight, your Reformation programme will most likely consist of multiple regular bodily assessments, attitude adjustment and weeding'.

Sounds like fucking crap.

'I have hopes that we can form a fruitful partnership with you. I think Reformation will provide a unique opportunity for you to improve yourself'.

I really don't need improving.

'Oh and one more thing'.

'What?'

'You will not yet be granted access to the library'.

What the fuck. Why is there a library here?

'Wha?' I spit out.

'Now don't act so surprised, of course we wouldn't let you into the library, what with your current issues and instabilities'.

'Whyawoul' I wannago there?'

'All the other Threats to Society have access to the library because they are on Reformation programmes that are helping them to develop cultural assimilation. You can't carry on being a Threat to Society after all, that's a one way street!'

'So?'

'So the library is a place where Reformers can learn about the past and plan their Reform characterisation for the future, in a way that is cohesive to the aims and objectives of the UK, the best country in the world'.

Right.

'An'why can'I Reform? Go to the libry'an learn?'

'Because I am worried that you are still in your earliest primary stage of Reform and all you will get from reading and watching the materials in the library are ideas. You're too unstable. And immature'.

'Ideas?'

'Ideas'.

'But I don'care about ideas'.

'Don't you?'

'No. I don'care about anything'.

'Exactly', he says scratching his head. 'No it won't do, I am determined that your admission to the library will be postponed indefinitely unless you can improve yourself, drop this mad, bad behaviour and show a real desire to align yourself with our core values'.

'Core values...?'

He presses his watch and there's almost instantly a knock on the door. Great. Zombie company.

'You will now return to your room'.

'Right'.

'It's getting late-'

'Are you kiddin?' I scoff.

'LATE and I don't want you getting into anymore trouble. Don't think we don't know about that little chat you managed to sneak with that Unrecognised Reformer. We gave you an inch and you ran a mile'.

'Behind a tree', I mutter.

'Come in!' the PM calls to the zombie looming about

outside.

It comes in. The aggressive short one in white from earlier, its mask covering its mug except for its pale forehead and peeky globes.

'Please escort our visitor back to her room'.

I think I might make life difficult again and sit still like a big blobby stone but the zombie behind me makes me feel like it probably won't be worth it. I screech my chair back as loudly as possible making the PM wince. It's sublime.

The professionally medical zombie moves in but I'm already nodding saying I will follow it and out we step.

'It was just too easy really', sighs the PM.

'Whaddya mean?' I ask.

'It wasn't the game I wanted it to be. And I really did try'.

Right.

He pauses.

'It's always the way with the ones who bulldoze their way through life. You're just a little bit too easy. That's why I have high hopes for you and your Reformation'.

Whatever mate. I don't give a fuck.

We traipse back along the corridor and up the grand old staircase with the ruby rain dripping airy drops all about.

If I'm going to be cooped up in my Cream Castle box all night and forced to sleep or be sedated or whatever I might as well think of something to do. I don't want to Reform. I'm not going to make life easy and I'm not going to let them let me stick around. They're not going to do anything. Reform means rot. I've had enough. It's down to me and I will not go gentle.

We get back to my box.

The zombie slaps the door open with its expertly gloved hand. It stomps into the box, uncuffs me roughly and starts faffing about.

This one in white is definitely slightly younger than the ones in black. Still dead looking, but there seems to be something a bit hesitant about it to match the aggro.

I sit on the bed and watch.

It brushes its glovey digits against its mask repeatedly whilst jiggling about with a long plastic tube. It looks like the glove has scrunched up and slipped off its pale purple hand and it's trying to cheek it back onto its digits. It's making a hash out of it and it's actually quite funny.

All of a sudden, both the mask and the glove ping right off.

'Shhhhhhhhhhhckkkkkklaaaaaaapppppppppppp', they say, flapping. They land splat on the floor.

I snort with laughter.

It's a he. He is young, spotty with a thick jaw and a coleslaw coldsore on his gob. His dark globes are darting about, embarrassed, annoyed and afraid that the mask has popped off and revealed his mug.

I blink up at him.

He yanks the mask off the floor and back onto his mug.

'Dinner, later', he says. As if that's some kind of punishment that's going to have me grovelling at his feet.

'OK Bu'ercup', I say.

His globes flash at me and I smirk.

He lunges forward as if to tighten my brace. I swing my head gingerly out of the way and raise my plim.

'OK OK sorr'soz', I say.

He tilts his head back like a smug fuck and saunters out. Bun Bun really would have done well as one of that lot.

Poor Singe. The Devil's Arse? Fucking shit.

Everything I touch seems to turn to shit, which is fine but bods have been hurt and now the PM thinks I'm a sex-mad witchy loon who wants to blow the whole country up. I mean tbh that sounds quite fun. But he's got all sorts of weird ideas and fantasies flying about that aren't true. I don't know. He gives me the creeps, in the worst Rickish sense.

The door slams and locks behind zombie Medic Buttercup as he stomps out of the box and only a certified handprint will let me out. I'm alone and trapped in this airy fairy hell hole.

I lie back on the bed to begin to stare up at all the fascist flowers. As I shift my globes past the end of my bed I clock his other glove on the floor.

Oh goodie.

Now then.

It doesn't look like I'm going to get out of here in one piece. I'd be a fucking twonk to think that at some point they're going to be all like yayyyyyyyy you've doth Reformed let's have a party, here's freedom. I don't have it in me to Reform, whatever that means. And what fucking freedom anyway? The UK? As if. I'm not going to fucking bother. I might as well fuck shit up as much as I can whilst I can, before whatever happens next. Get it over and fucking done with.

Maybe it's because I've been shat on so many times now. Maybe it's because I'm deadly afraid but I don't have any more energy to deal with it; no will or deepest desire to resist and wait it out. Nope. No thank you. Maybe nothing's so much of a shock or surprise anymore. Honestly. All this fucking shit. How bad is it really going to be when they chop me up? Maybe it's all inevitable anyway and why should I wait around for them to set me up to fail. I will bulldoze right into the thumper of it thanks very much.

It is all so boring and entirely predictable. If they think I'm a witchy loon, fucking all the guy and girl bods and causing racket and riot everywhere I go, I'm going to be the witchiest loon they have ever seen. It's not so very far from the truth anyway.

I grab a bit of my sheet and scoop up the glove, careful not to contaminate it with my mucky paws.

All I can see for myself is Mara.

I think a little night time trip to that library is in order. They couldn't dangle a tasty little piece of potential mischief in front of me like that if they didn't want me to BITE.

3.2

I wait about for a long time. Even when I think I've waited a long time I wait even longer and then I wait until it's no longer even a bit light outside and the blue electric moon is beaming brightly into my box.

The glove is stuffed in my pillow case.

Waiting is boring as fuck.

Boredom is fine when you're supposed to be doing something else and you're wasting some other bod's time and money being bored and unproductive and you get that queasiness where you're all oh-fuck-I-should-have-been-productive-and-oh-what-a-waste-I-doth-done-never-mind.

Now it's just meh. Wait about for the chop. I feel a bit sick. I feel a bit like I don't give a fuck. I feel a bit highly strung. Just sick string.

I get up and then I sit back down again. Pace about for a bit in the blue. One of those zombs will be along for my midnight feast, poking and jabbing me with all sorts of crap. Do I wait until they all piss off again or go before and let them catch me in the act?

Because this is it. There's no way I'm not getting caught. I want to be caught. It all feels very clear. This is terminal shit.

I decide that the best thing to do is to wait until after the midnight checks.

I peel off the boilersuit and clamber into the neatly folded night shirt that I've been ignoring for the past few hours. I jump into bed but carefully place my head on the pillow as if I'm fucking royalish or dead or something. The brace stops me from rolling about as much as I would like so instead I content myself with kicking and shuffling about. The sheets are surprisingly soft. You'd have thought that they were going to be rough and horrible and make you itchy scratchy but they're actually super duper soft.

I haven't slept in such nice sheets for a long time, if ever.

No. The sheets are playing games like that bloody mooncup. They're trying to make me think that I'm being looked after and that this is for my own good, that I'm in the right place and that I'm a poor little Reformer who's made bad choices and needs to change their ways. No sheets. You are soft but I'm not stupid, you can't bewitch me with your silken touch and your nice smell.

I kick about a bit for good measure so that they are well and truly crumpled up and creased.

Serves you right sheets.

Suddenly there's a slap on the door and the short young mardy Buttercup zomb in white barges in. Thank fuck it's not the High Zombie in black.

I snap my globes shut and pretend to be asleep.

I can feel it peering into my mug and it's taking everything I have not to start grinning. Everything is always five hundred times funnier when you're not supposed to be laughing. The only thing I can do is chew the side of my cheek that isn't facing him and try to make myself hurt as much as possible which isn't actually too difficult because this fucking brace is so painful and makes lying down the absolute worst.

Medic Buttercup grabs and yanks my arm. He's entirely unconvinced that I am asleep and starts doing all sorts of strange crap. He sticks a needle in and starts pumping foodstuffs into my blood, which is painful and I really want to squeal but I don't want to give him the satisfaction, I'll keep up my sleepy charade in the hopes that it'll piss him off more.

I don't care if it hurts.

Any mere sharp pointy pain is better than this achy crap around my jaw. It's just that it makes me feel sick and all whooze. Ick. This must have been the point when I did actually throw up all over my front and that zomb manic crazy thing was grinning at me. If that bit was even real.

I suppress the sicky, I take a deep breath and then snort as though I'm sleeping, just for good measure.

He really doesn't buy it. He twists the tube into my arm

harder for good measure. Fuck fucking OW.

Then comes the wide band that squeezes the shit out of my arm and makes it throb.

Then there's some kind of weird scanner thing he casts over my bod that makes barely detectable whirrings and must be counting my little trackers like little fishies.

Finally he slaps some cream on my poor crusty singed head and then unhooks me entirely.

I exhale deeply and murmur. I smack my chops together as if in sleep.

'Cut it out', he drawls.

'Hmmmumm, what?' I say sleepily.

'Behave'.

'Hmmmyessum Buttercup'.

This time he does tighten my brace and he does it really bloody tight.

He then starts pacing around the box in a flighty and frantic way. He looks out of the window and under my bed. He paces around some more.

Fuck. He must be looking for the glove.

He looks at me and I look back quizzically. I really hope he believes my quizziness because my whole flimsy little plan revolves around this little glove and I can't have him finding out and fucking everything up.

He huffs and he puffs for a while.

Nope no glovey.

I try and keep natural which is easier said than done and all my joints are getting slightly sweaty at the thought of his thinking to yank up my head and snatch the glove from under my pillow. I feel like the glove in its gloveness is burning an image of itself through the pillow, glowing and waving at Buttercup to get his attention. I keep my limbs relaxed and calm, stiffness will show.

He's about to give up.

He slaps his left gloved hand on the door. He's gonna be in troubleeeeeeee when the High Zombie finds out.

He gives me one last menacing look and I just feel like whatever mate. That look is really beginning to lose its spice. I don't give a fuck.

I leave it for five or ten and then start to get up. First I take the glove out of the pillow case with the sheet over my digits and lay it on the pillow. Then I slip into my red boiler suit.

Medic Buttercup bursts back in with panic in his globes.

He clocks the glove on the pillow.

I blink back.

His panic turns to rage and he stomps over. My limbies freeze still.

He looks into my globes and grabs my ear and twists my head up.

'AhahahahOWWWWWWWWWWWWWW', I shout, clutching at my jaw.

He pulls my head up.

'HA!' he shrieks into my mug.

Fuck.

'Think you could outwit me huh?' he sneers, peering into my globes. 'I'm smarter than you, more powerful than you and there is nothing you can do that I'm not going to suss out'.

I bet he's got a really small thing.

I look at his tum and it's a sack of flab.

I look back into his globes and growl.

He pinches and tightens his grip and I realise it's my favourite kind of stabby pain.

I boot my foot into his flab and it immediately winds him and he exhales into my mug and his breath is rank and smells like cheesy cheese crisps. I kick again and then use my knee to nut him. His knees cave in and he bends over on top of me and I think he's going to crush me because he is so fucking heavy. My arm is sore because he just stabbed it with food but I grind my gnashers and push push push him up with all my might and I manage to get him off. He rolls over wheezing and I jump up as quickly as I can. He pants and pants but he manages to swing himself up and round and lunges towards me. I'm prepared but the stinging slap I get on my mug is harder than I thought it would be and I go flying towards the window. I use the momentum to bounce off it and immediately boot him in the chest. He splats on the floor and I pounce on him, forcing him onto his front and grab the back of his head and whack his mug into the ground a couple of times with a thwack, crunch, thud thud thud thud thud. He moans and groans with each blow until I let his head fall and smack and he can barely move. I spot the shackle hanging from the bed and I grab it, latching it to his wrist with a bleep bleep bleep bl-bleep and I don't think a shackle has ever sounded so good. Medic Buttercup whimpers and whines and I get close to his ear and hiss, 'I'll give you some sussing'.

I reach down to his trousers and start to unbutton them and roll them down. His whines turn to squeaks and I roll down his pants until his bum is the white moon that this electric blue night box has been missing. I crack my knuckles and flatten my palm and start to smack him and smack him and smack him and then I use my foot and then I crunch my hand into a fist and pummel him and then I use my palm again to smack and smack and smack and smack to teach this stuck up brat a lesson and the fire in my tum feels so good and my hand is red from the force but it's not as red as his flabby rear and it is so good to teach this fuck a lesson, so good to humiliate and leave for shit. I feel like I've got my creative juices flowing and flushing about. In the end, I'm out of puff and I can't hear anything coming from his end. I roll him over and his mug is a mangled bloody mess, his conk bent and squashed out of joint and his chops split and puffed up. His globes are barely open and there are tear tracks running down his mug. I roll his trousers down a little more and there his thing is.

Tut tut tut tut tut tut tut.

'You do have a small thing', I say.

I leave his trousers down and calmly reach for my plims. I park next to him and lace them up expertly. His breathing is shallow like his fucking personality.

I again carefully reach for the glove with my hand in the sheet so that I don't get my mucky prints on it. It has stayed pristine in spite of all the scuffling.

It's actually pretty fucking hard to put a glove on when you're not holding it properly so even though I want to keep my movements serene and calm whilst I go on my lap of glory, I'm actually fumbling and flailing about awkwardly and this bloody sheet is going everywhere and I nearly drop the glove and to be perfectly honest it's pretty fucking typical and maybe I wouldn't have it any other way.

Finally I reach in.

Huh. Buttercup has really small hands.

That figures.

The glove really doesn't fit but it doesn't matter. I've squished my knuckles into it so that it looks knuckly and contorted in the sheeny second skin rubber glowing in the bright bright blue.

I step over the pale moonish lump of Medic Buttercup, who isn't making much noise at all now, and gently pat the door. My knots tighten for a second because I've just assumed all along that this is going to work and I'm not even sure if it will but then I hear those yummy clicks and I push the door and it swings open.

The corridor is empty.

My jaw really fucking hurts. The bone-deep aches come oozing back and I bend over to stop myself from vomming.

There must be all kinds of lasers and ze-cams and shit that are keeping a close eye on every single movement and breath. They'll know what I'm up to in seconds. Whatever. I will act as casual as if this is the most natural thing in the world and the pride, the pride of it will piss them off into action. There's nothing like pissing off bods who already have shit shoved up their arse by acting as cool as a cunt. I would know because it's usually me who's off her rocker.

I pad down the corridor and pass by the other room boxes. I wonder who's in there, lounging about trying to Reform. I bet there are bods in here who have stuck their things about, chopped bods, blown things up and all sorts of other nasties. But then, I wouldn't be surprised if they weren't downright poor sods who have found themselves in a scrap because of things they couldn't control. I'm not saying that I'm the nicest bod about because I set fire to a building and chopped Rich and Ryan but it's not like I'm a cold-blooded whatsit. Maybe this lot are the same. If they're banging and bunging bods up for not wearing the right Uniform or nicking tins of soup then something not so serious could actually be serious. They've got weird standards. Who knows. I haven't seen any of this lot, and probably never will. It sounds like they're all Reforming whatever that means so they all must be behaving themselves and playing by the rules. Quiet bunch. Haven't heard or seen any of them. I wonder if they know about the racket I've been making? Who knows how good the soundproofing is, here in pretty Cream Castle Downton Dungheap.

Door after door after door.

I knock on one. My tum leaps.

No reply.

Boring.

I reach the ze-pad.

I jab my gloved digit at it and it unlocks.

The screen sits on a boring homepage with a few tabs open. One is The Money News, which is a mandatory window that's open on every ze-pad or phone or technological whatever. It's the most important news you know, and it's only right that we track every single wave in the currensea.

Then there's a secure page linking to some Reformer or other that's password protected. Not even my glove is going to get me in there which is a bit of a bum because I fancy a bit of a looky.

I need some kind of map or blueprint.

I scan around the home drive to see if there's some doc or PDF that will show me about.

It's interesting. Even though there's all this high-tech palm reading security and mad medics and tubes and trackers and whatnot, the programme being used on this ze-pad is at least 5 years out of date. Monk would choke on her disgust. She's a right techy.

Funny that somewhere so secure is so behind with their IT systems.

I search for a map and there isn't one.

Fucking fuck.

I'm just going to have to wander about. The risk is that some zomb will pick me up before I actually manage to find this fucking library. Or pick up Medic Buttercup and than charge after me. Either way, I don't have much time.

But it's worth a try. Plus it's fucking cold out here and I want to get a move on.

It won't be on the same floor as us lot. It'll be further away so it feels like a big thing to go and visit it. A privilege. Something they don't actually think you're up to or deserve, like the one at the Academy. That's how Reform works right? The kind of Reform where the word sounds like it's going to help you out and make your life better but actually it's just masking the fact that you're going to get shat on and then forced to eat it.

The Academy. Now there's an idea.

I often thought the Academy felt like a prison. That big sliding metal door preventing us from getting out, those clammy classroom boxes, penned in at play time, concrete everything and nothing. Crap crap crap.

The library was barely a library because there are restrictions on what kiddies can and can't be exposed to but it was still thought of as a treat to go there.

Lots of Academies didn't even bother with libraries

anymore because they are so old-fashioned. That's why ours was seen as even more of a treat. Fuck knows why because our Academy was in the arse-end of nowhere. Our Head was a sentimental old bodger. I ripped up loads of books in my time there and I wasn't the only one but she still wanted us to have a library. Turning everything digital helped to spur the crude vandalism and the arsebucketry. It was fun while it lasted.

But anyways. The library at the Academy was on the far left hand side of the Academy hub on the fifth floor.

I go through the door next to the ze-pad.

The courtyard steps were on the ground floor two floors down from here and the PM's office was one further down in the basement. So I follow the stairs up.

The blue moonlight is shimmering through the red droplets of the stained glass window creating a strange mixture of colours that are beaming in all diamond-shaped directions. It really is very bright and purple and weird.

I pad up the stairs and my plims aren't making a sound. Good plims.

It is bloody cold though. I should have brought that duvet with me. I think I should always just have my duvet with me.

I hold my scrunched glovey hand out in front of me so that I don't contaminate it with my grubby self. It's probably useful but it also bloody hurts because I've chosen the same hand whose arm that had that fucking tube stuck in it which is achey and bruised. But it has to stay up. Normally, I make a mess out of trying to keep things neat, tidy and in their place. I don't think I've ever painted my nails without smudging and fucking it up. Monk's the same. We're the right sort of bods. Not like bloody Lauren who had perfect painting skills on her digits and look what she did to Marissa. Squish under the trammsmuter. At least she'll get out soon, but not as soon as me. Plus she's cramped in that awful stuffy block. I am roaming free.

Hand up. No company yet. I plod on. I have perpetual

sickness and my globes are ringing in the silence but I feel fucking buzzed. The Rick-knots are always there, I'm achey and shakey but all in all the rest of my limbies are feeling pretty fucking fine.

I get to the next floor.

This window is bloody ginormous.

I get to the next floor.

I get to the next floor.

There's a corridor leading to the left. Good sign. That doesn't happen on the floor I live on. I look down it. Very very dark. I cross over to the door leading to the right hand side, directly above the corridor with all the Reformer room boxes. It's brighter down there. There's a warning sign on the door. Medical equipment, lots of chemmies and other sorts of stuff. Nope.

I turn back to left hand side. It's dark and remote. Doesn't get much action. This is pretty promising.

I press my hand to the door and it lets me through.

Fucking bingo.

I am the smartest fuck I have ever seen.

WHUM.

The door thuds shut behind me and I nearly shit myself.

Fuck. Noisy bargey cunt that I am.

I pad pad pad with my noiseless plims down the corridor. I will never really feel comfortable without my bovvers, but these are alright. I feel all sly and sneaky. Makes a nice change.

I get right to the end of the corridor and it leads to a door with a thin glass pane running down the middle. There's no tech for entry. I wave my gloved hand around to try and catch something but there isn't a ze-pad or anything. I nudge the door with my plim and it eases open.

Huh. Not very secure. Probably don't think of the library as a desired destination. Not a dangerous place after all. Weird that the PM doesn't want to let me have proper access then.

I squeeze through the door, whacking my stupid fucking brace as I go which is really fucking painful.

I really want to shake the fucking thing off my fucking head.

I step into the bowels of the library.

It's very dark in here. No windows.

Fucking freezing.

The only light shining about is coming from the pale blue numbers and titles lining the shelves. There are a few map books and history books but everything else is digital. Vids and recordings, things like that. Can't see any story books but there may be films and you never know.

This lib looks like it extends back a long long way. There are blue numbers at the end of each aisle hovering in mid-air stretching all the way back. Everything's stacked in rows and columns and rows and it feels very uniform and familiar.

I look behind me and pause for a moment. I can't hear anybod coming. Then again those zombs sort of glide about silently like the ghosty things they are. How would I know.

It's really very dark. Too dark. My Rick-knots are getting too tight again.

I came into this all RARARARARA and I have to make a decision now.

I hug my elbows.

I could just go back.

It's easy not to be nervous and agitated and anxious when you're tucked up nice and warm in silken sheets and you can take the piss out of the medic and everything feels pseudo-safe. I could go back and they would know I've been out and about but they'll know that even though I got here, I decided to go back. I could Reform, I could survive. Yes, I did beat up Medic Buttercup and he fucking deserved it but I have seen the errorz of my wayz. I don't have to subject to whatever kind of hell they'll cook up if they realise I'm not prepared to aqua-whatever.

I don't know. Maybe Singe was on the right track. Get out anyway you can. Obviously I would not like to end up dead next to the Devil's Arse but I don't want to waste away like

Mara or end up resisting for nothing like Rosée and Sam. Me? The PM could stick to his promise of aspiration and good days rolling around but I will most probably end up back where I started because everything and everyone else in the UK is a fucking shit.

It's only Malga who has the right way of going about things. Perpetually piss them off and never get caught. Dance and shimmy and shake your way through and always keep them scratching the itch. Even though his plan to break the Internet is lame. That poly-versity lot never do get rid of those delusions of grandeur however much they shimmy and shake.

That's just not me though. I always get found out. I'm not the subtle one.

I feel trapped. Well, obviously I'm trapped because I'm in this National Trust shitshow, but right now, right this minute, I'm tangled in a big old Rick-knot in my head. It's icy bloody cold and I could just give up. In fact that's exactly what I'll do. I turn around.

I blink at all the numbers. That's the thing though, and I can't forget it: I am giving up; but also not. I'm giving up making a hoo-ha. Don't forget the hoo-ha. The hoo-ha makes all the difference. I'm giving up my way dammit.

I kneel down on the floor with my legs tightly pressed together.

It's a wooden floor. Creaky.

I can't slip my digits into this jumpsuit easily so I just clench and press my clit against my thighs and I start to wank.

There's nothing better.

Having a big orgasm is the best way to clear your mind. Everything just makes perfect sense. You feel calmer and more precise about your decisions, about everything.

Plus I want to imagine their horror that I've entered their precious little lib and I'm being all sexual about it. In fact, it's quite the turn on.

It's not going to take long.

****

I get up.

My knees crack but it's fine. It's still the old jaw that's being a bastard.

I feel so much better. I find my stomp again and thump straight down the centre of the lib. All these rows are bloody the same. I have no idea how they're ordered or what's been shoved down each so I might as well pick any old number to go down.

3.7.5005J

That'll do.

I give one look back and plod down the aisle.

I stop about half way down because why not and then turn to a random screen. There are some wireless headphones next to it. I pop them on, keeping one ear uncovered so that I can listen out for any zombs who arrive to chop me.

I use the gloved hand to jab at the screen. I'm not sure if I need to use the glove but I might as well, seeing as it's jammed onto my hand.

Thinking about it, it's pretty bloody weird that they use designated computer ports for each numbered item. A modern system would have each file remotely accessible from anywhere in the lib. This place is so old-fashioned. Corruptible if you know what is what.

The screen lights up really fucking bright and I have to shield my globes. Going from gloom to garish is a bit of a shock to the system.

The film starts out quite grainy but begins to settle. Really low budget. Whoever is filming this was not using the best digitals. This must have been made about twenty something years ago.

Some words pop up.

'Part 3. Physical Hyper-Reformation. LAW FORCE 1.0'.

OK.

The ze-cam is fixed and still. I'm looking at a smallish box. It's dark outside. There's no one in shot. It's not as I would imagine, professional and Strangeways. The quality is crude, almost homemade looking.

After a few seconds there's a crash as a door swings and slams open.

A small boy is dragged into to the centre by some thuggy looking brutes. They must be the original LAW FORCE before they were developed into mechanized bots. This lot are Recognisable with their red caps and smart T-shirts and jeans Uniform. Normal looking. They actually look scarier than LAW FORCE now, even though LAW FORCE seems scary when you first see them because they communicate in beeps and you can't see their mugs and they're built up with plastic and metal. It's like Marissa said, they're just stupid weaponised thugs. This 1.0 lot look so normal. I haven't seen anybod dressed like that since I was little. It makes me shudder. I'm glad that lot are gone. I can deal with a mugless monster, easier to get riled up about and kick and thump about. Something that's not trying to be your mate with a nice cap on and a big toothy smile. Snide all the way to the top. All the more to punch. Not to be trusted. Like that PM fuck. Coming to think of it, he's must be early LAW FORCE leftovers.

They drag the little tot to the middle and he's only a little skinny thing and he's very upset.

'Like we agreed', says one of the Caps, 'this will be filmed to provide an educational legacy for future generations of LAW FORCE guards. Agreed?'

The boy whimpers.

'Now, why are you here?' says a Cap who is crouched down in front of the boy.

'I don't know', squeaks the child.

'OK, let's try something different, shall we?'

The boy sniffs and rubs his conk. He's very snotty.

'Shall we?'

He shrugs.

'DON'T SHRUG AT ME BOY. LOOK AT ME WHEN I'M SPEAKING TO YOU'.

The boy snaps his mug up to the Cap and his gob is open in shock and fear.

'That's better. Now remember, you are here to help with a prospective training programme. You are helping us with some extremely important matters of principle and moral character. There's no need for any more tears. This is your duty as a man. Stop crying'.

The little boy nods but he still looks shit scared.

'Now. Tell me about your parents'.

He blinks.

'M-my parents?'

'Yes your parents'.

'W-what about them?'

'Well what are their names for starters?'

'Joshua and Leroy'.

'Joshua and Leroy', says the Cap sighing.

The other Caps all start clucking in unison with tuts and titters to follow.

'Yes, Joshua and Leroy' says the boy.

'What do you call them?'

'Dad and Daddy'.

'That's ludicrous'.

The Caps laugh.

'W-why?' the boy asks wiping his globes.

'Because you can't have two Dads'.

'I do, I'm not lying or anything', says the boy shaking his head earnestly.

'Oh believe me, I know you're not lying. You poor little thing', he says, ruffling his hair. The boy looks confused.

'Then why can't I have Dads?'

'Because you need a Mum and a Dad, not two of one'.

'No, n-no', says the boy sitting up straighter as if he's remembered something. 'You don't. You just need two people who are in love. Doesn't matter if they are girls or boys'.

'I'm afraid it does', says the Cap.

'I don't think so', says the boy. 'I love my Dads'.

'That's because they've led you down the merry garden path of moral chaos and calamity. It's not right'.

'But, b-but'-

'NO BUTS. Now are your parents... I mean parents, really?' says the Cap turning to the other Caps and scoffing. 'Are your 'parents' active in their support of gay rights?'

'Um...'

'Do they campaign a lot, go on the street, go out together in public'.

'Yeah', says the boy frowning.

'And you go with them?'

'Yes, all the time. They give out leaflets and I help'.

'Why would you do that?'

'Because some people don't like them and I want people to like them because they're my Dads and I love them'.

'Do people respond well?'

'Yeah'.

'No one gets violent with them or you?'

'No, not with me...'

'Ah see', says the Cap softly, 'they are using the boy as a human shield. No one's going to hurt a child whilst they're spreading their nasty propaganda'.

'Proper...?'

'Propaganda'.

'What's that?'

'The spreading of the ideas of a certain ideology using visual and aural means. To persuade and convince people to agree with you'.

'I don't know anything about idolgee but they weren't convincing anyone of anything', says the boy shaking his head. 'They just wanted to share love'.

'Share love? How revolting'.

'B-but love is wonderful', says the boy edging to the front of his chair. 'That's all it is'.

'Not the kind of love your parents share'.

'Why...?'

'Enough. Young man. It is a revolting, counterfeit form of love and it isn't legitimate or acceptable. Not in the UK that we are trying to build'.

'Maybe you don't understand?'

The Cap pauses.

'No YOU don't understand', he growls, prodding the boy in the chest. 'And that is what we're going to rectify. Right here, right now'.

Panic flashes over the boy's mug.

'Where are they? I want them, I want to go home now. Please'.

'Oh, you'll not be going home anymore'.

The boy starts to cry and he's trying to stifle his sobs but they keep rolling up through him, his chops quivering.

'P-please let me go home'.

'You are in the hands of the UK Management now. Even if I did let you go home, your parents wouldn't be there'.

'No no no, please, I want my Dads I want them please'.

'Calm down. Stop crying. Start being a proper man. None of this queer emotional nonsense'.

'I c-can't', the boy stammers. 'I want to go home, I want to go home!'

'It has been decided that you are going to be fast-tracked to Employment as compensation for the loss of your parents and then you can start making money sooner than everyone else. You have a great life ahead of you already'.

'But I don't want a great life', shakes the boy, 'I want my Dads'.

'That's the problem', says the Cap. He signals to two other Caps and they bring a big bottle and a cup into the shot. 'We're going to wash away all the dirt from your life. We could have tracked down where your Dads got you from in the first place, because two dicks don't make a right', he glances at the other Caps and they all chortle. 'But that requires too many resources. Instead, you're going to start afresh and we're going to help you'.

'How?'

'You keep rubbing your globes don't you son'.

'I'm sad', he says.

'Let us help with that, let's get all the dirt out'.

All of a sudden, two of the Caps pounce on the boy and hold his shoulders. He starts screaming and wriggling and the next Cap clamps his gob shut with a big leathery hand. The two Caps holding his shoulders use one hand each to force the boy's lids shut. His poor little legs are flashing and scrapping about. He's only little so they don't need to use that much force but they obviously use more force than they need to because they're fucking cunts. The boy's globes are clamped shut and then liquid from the bottle is poured into the cup and thrown over his globes.

The boy screams. He screams and screams and screams. There's smokey steamy stuff rising from his globes and he's kicking about with all his might screaming and screaming and screaming.

The lead Cap brandishes a knife over the racket.

'GET THE TOOLS. WE NEED TO GET HIS DING DONG OFF'.

I jab the screen hard making it stop.

It wobbles like mad.

My breathing is shallow. I don't think I've actually breathed properly for about five minutes.

My Rick-knots tighten and I really feel like I might be sick or shit myself or both. That kiddo, that poor poor tot.

My digits go to my stupid busted jaw and I gnash at my nails and it hurts but oh fuck I don't feel it, it barely scratches the surface.

I exit the screen and I type the floating blue number into the search directory. My hands are shaking.

The description is succinct and small.

Training video: Part 3. Physical Hyper-Reformation. LAW FORCE 1.0

The Reform methodology used in this video footage was prototyped for 12 months but quashed after negative press attention. The aim going forward was to negotiate with media cultures on the presentation of the queer problem. If this sort of practice was outlawed in the court of public opinion, public opinion would have to be changed. This will take considerable time. This footage is kept on file as a historical document of a practice that was trialled and can be re-visited when consensus is seen to be more in line with that of the UK's proposed institutional framework. It is a key Reformation learning material.

For further reference, LAW FORCE 1.0 training videos can be found at numbers blah blah blah blah blah blah blah blah blah blah blah blah blah blah blah blah blah blah.

How disgusting.

So this is Reformation. Reformation is THAT. Getting on board with THAT.

Fuck no. Fuck never.

Poor little tyke. Poor little titchy.

What a fucking uberhorrorshitshow.

And Lucy.

Scars on her lids.

Acid could do that. That was acid. Her parents... she ended up in Clinking and Clanking.

YEEEEEEEEEEEEEEUUUUUURRRRRKKKKKKKK.

I hurl up all the food that Buttercup had pummelled into

me earlier all over the screen.

I want to beat the shit out of all of them. Picking on little twitches, those fucking disgusting Red Cap fucks.

I scrabble back to the screen and start trying to wipe the vom off. It smells fucking rank. It makes me retch even more. Doesn't even smell like my normal sick after a binge on bubbles brown and clear. It tastes and smells like dog cack.

I try and scrape it away at it but I just YEEEEEEEEEEEEEEUUUUUURRRRRKKKKKKKKK.

Fuck. I've been using the wrong fucking hand. There's vom all over the glove and now the prints are going to be drowned in my chunks.

Who fucking cares anyway.

My Rick-knots are cramping and my whole tum feels like it's going to crawl out of my choker and empty itself all over the poison I have just been watching.

I wonder if anybod knows about this. It's probably just been shoved straight down the drain so that no one has access to it, except Threats to Society.

I shiver. They're using the most dog-eared bods to re-wire their violence into their Strangeways vein. It stinks. Bods out there won't stand for this shit will they? If they knew, they wouldn't stand for it.

The zombs will come soon.

There must be some way I can get this vid out. Leak it. Send it to The Money News and they can shut this place down.

I jab and tap and swish around the screen but it's no use. My yucky vom has clogged the entire thing. The screen is all frozen and all I can see is the little kid's gob shaped into a big wide O as he screams and screams. Can't even see the rest of his mug, just his little arms clinging to the Caps trying to rip them off him.

I stare at the still in utter horror. It's disgusting. Nasty mean unfair disgusting.

I can't look at it anymore.

I slam my paw across the screen causing it to crash and smash.

There was no way I was going to be able to leak it anyway. I bet there's a huge firewall and I bet even if it did get into cyber-space, the UK will find some way to shut it down or catch it in some kind of world wide web where it will get stuck and gobbled up so that it couldn't get anywhere anyway.

If bods knew...

But, Lucy.

There must be more like her around and about, with scarred globes. Bods must know that this shit has been going on.

It hits me like a fucking trammsmuter. Nope. Nobod cares. They're just funnelled into Conscription. Nobod cares, nothing nothing nothing. And the thing is Lucy wasn't doing anything either. Just sitting around arguing with Bun Bun. Probably because the whole sitch was so fucked up and terrifying that the only thing she could do was try to not let it affect her at all. Develop new skills, new things, a new way to define herself. Picking fights with Bun Bun seems like a much better idea than picking fights with the UK.

I don't know what to do.

I'm angry but I'm tired. I don't have any honey-oil and even if I did I don't have that flashy whooshing feeling in my tum that makes me want to set this place on fire or smack Buttercup's bum for fun.

I don't even want to smash any of these fuck-awful screens up. Vids in this lib should not be lost or destroyed because then it would be like the whole thing hadn't happened.

But then I want to smash them up because I feel so fucking sick about what I've seen going on. This horror.

I can't even breathe.

I get onto my hands and knees and try to calm myself. Forcing the breath to slowly move in and out.

If Reformation has anything to do with watching and

syncing with that kind of utter shit then I want to be disposed of. I've made the fucking best decision ever. I don't want to play a part in this thing anymore. There's nowhere left to go. I don't want to go round and round the same old circles. Relive the same old shit and get knotted into the same old mess.

I start hammering the floor with my fists.

I use my knees to make a racket.

My plims are fucking useless rubber fucks.

I hop up as quickly as I can and start trying to rip this stupid brace from my head.

YAHHHHHAHHHHHHHHHHHHRGGHHHHHHH HHHHHHHH I howl in pain. Followed by a YEEEEEEE-EEEEEEEEEEEEEEEEEEEEEEEEEEEEK of manic laughter.

I twist it and yank it. I bend it enough so that it's completely misshapen and a fucking wonky state.

I throw it on the floor and stamp on it. This would be so delicious in my bovvers. I grunt grunt grunt like a fat old pig as I heave it about.

I smack my digits on my head.

My jaw is fucking KILLING.

I take the screwed up metal brace and scrape it along the creaky wooden floor making ziggy zaggy lines and limits scratching and dashing and whacking. There's all sorts of weird cuts and grooves it's making and wood bits are chipping and floating and feathering about.

I have so much violence in me and I want to fuck the shit out of everything in this stupid fuckdamn place.

I whack and shriek and whack and shriek and eeeeeeeeeek and yaaaaaaaaaack and thwaaaaaaaaaaack around with my metally metal.

My Rick-knots are all screwed up and I feel like I could even take a big shit on the floor right here. Defecate and destroy.

I take the brace and swing it a few times around my head and I launch it into the gloom to let it clatter and clunk and echo and echo all around.

Fuck them all.

I turn around and WMMMFFFFF I throw up all over the High Zombie who has materialised out of literally fucking nowhere and scared me before I even realised it.

My Rick-knots screw and scrunch as I lock globes with it. Brace off, vom all over my gob and my boilersuit, I stare it down as well and as much as I can.

It doesn't say anything.

It lowers its mask to reveal its switchblade smile and starts to click its tongue about.

Its globes flash.

I lift my plim with a deftness I never even knew I had and I boot it in the tum. It's becoming my signature move. Bods should care about their tums more.

It staggers back with an UMPH.

All of sudden there are zombies everywhere popping out of the dark and they seize my arms and legs and my head.

I have no strength because I feel so sick and my jaw is pounding and I don't care what happens next. I let them, I let them. In the dark, blue numbers hovering about. This is it.

Then the PM's there.

He's, yep, he's wearing a velvet dressing gown. I would know that from a mile away.

Fucking sad fuck, looks like he bloody lives here. How sad. I mean he's PM but he might as well be in Employment like the rest of us.

It's pretty fucking weird seeing an oldish man in his jammies. I kind of don't want to see it but then I kind of do and it's weird and entirely appropriate for this fuck-knows-what-the-fuck-is-happening sitch. He's still wearing his watch. It goes perfectly with the rest of his ensemble.

He's got a crusty saliva gob from sleep and his globes are dewy and wet. Don't cry for me bitch.

He looks at me squarely and says nothing.

'What?' I grunt.

'I gave you a chance', he says starting to grin, looking mad, 'to Reform. To change and become a better person'.

'Whatever', I grumble, nodding to the destroyed vom monitor.

'A real chance', he says shaking his head and smiling smugly.

'No chance', I snap.

'What makes you say that?' he says.

'Tha'shitshow'.

He leans close to my mug. 'Wash that foulness out of your gob and speak properly'.

'OK!'

I spit in his mug.

He recoils and nods at the zomb.

He looks back at me. 'There's nothing more I can do with you'.

'Good'.

'Good?'

'Ge'it over withya dopeydoss'unt'.

His globes flash. He gets right up and takes his nails and scratches along the length of poor singed skull.

AAAAAAAAAAAAEEEEEEEEEEEEEEEEEEEEEEIIIIIII IIIIIIIIIIIIIIIIIIILLLLLLLLLLLLLLLIIIIIIIIIIIIIIIIIIIIIIIIINNN NNNNNNNNNNNOOOOOOOOOOOOOOONNNNNNN NNNNN

He rakes up skin and grime and gunk and he's chapping and spluttering the blisters and it HURTSHURTSHURTS-HURTSHURTS and I'm glad I can't see the top of my head because it feels like he's left actual tracks up there. It HTURS and it really fucking HRUTS but hope he finds every bit of mm disgusting and manky just so that it'll piss him off.

'Such an angry, vile little girl', he whispers in a very condescending way. 'So dissatisfied, so rejecting of those who might help'.

Little girl. Whatever.

Shrug shrug shrug shrug shrug shrug.

'You're a disgusting thing and you deserve nothing. I want you silenced and out of my sight'.

Fine fine fine fine fine.

'I did tell you very clearly not to come in here', he says knowingly, because we both remember the conversation and we both knew mm was going to get in here anyway, he's probably just pissed off that it took mm such a short amount of time to actually do it. Buttercup will need a talking to. And another spanking if he's lucky.

Stick mm chops out as a piss-take. Poor PM. Poor you, mmmm disobeyed you and broke into your lib. Fuck offfffffff finish me offffffffffff had enough. Not even scared. One last thing, one last release is needed. A spit? A swear word? Vom? A shriek? An O O O? Wish there was honey-oil.

No. No more destruction. Best until last.

Globes widen as mm shit mmself and the stench envelopes everything. Dirty mad fucker.

PM's globes flash in panic as the smell fills the air and he gags like mm shoved mm gammy fist down his choker.

'YUM YUM YUM', mm bellow.

'ENOUGH', he roars, jingling and jangling his watch around as he waves his digits in front of his conk.

Thrusts a zomb in mm way and even that icy exterior has been undone by the unquenchable fruity sniff stuff. Its conk is wrinkled. Never really looked at its conk before. Scary things are never so scary when you take in their conkish extremities and you see just how weird and un-scary they actually are. Conks are proper funny.

It wrinkles its conk some more and mm laugh in its mug.

They shouldn't act so surprised. They put shit in mm, shit's going to come out.

What next?

It hisses.

'Lobotomised. Buried alive'.

Let mm limbs go all floppy. Succumb to their grabs and gropes. Look up and they're tustling and making it very uncomfortable but that's OK. Been in tumbling tustling hands all this while, so it's really no different.

It's not the fading away that mm once thought for mmself. Feel like mm sparking like fuse.

We leave the dark shitty gloom of the grottiest grotty grib lib and they take mm down all the stairs to the bottom floor.

All the walk down, stare at the blood drops of red glass that dance in the air. It's happy and sad that once the drops hit mm they disappear because mm wearing such a ruby reddy red, although the nice blooming dark patch near mm cunt and mm bum is beginning to make a nice contrast.

Medics are all completely ridiculous. Staggering about because they don't want to touch mm or smell mm and mm juggled expertly to avoid it.

Oh if only everyone else in Strangeways and beyond could see them now. They're scaredy bums. Scared of bums.

Marissa and the rest should all just shit themselves and then Strangeways would turn upside down.

It makes mm chuckle all the way down the stairs. Chuckle chuckle chuckle silly billy bods.

Pretty red diamonds glistening and floating all about.

The rest is turning into blur. Shitty blur.

Trehe's a geradn you konw.

Flehctr Msos.

Mhesntaecr. Sotuh.

Rlealy ncie.

All rkcorey, felwreos, teres, sbrhus, lal teh culoors. Pryittesh wdlernesis.

Ew took hte ptah. Ew wnet dwon hte ptah, runod teh tienns curots dan dwon nowd itno het roekcry.

Autumn.

Aywals lkeid taht msesed pu jblmubed pu word.

Cloour coolur cuoolr lal dfifreent lla oevr het pacle hggelidy pdiglgey gdoo rof a sanp. Oen lsat fnial hrruah.

Dwon dnow teh ptah ew took. Dnow, nowd down. Em adn het bcalk dgo.

Balck god ldaineg het wya. Tial pu dna snigiwng aobut. Boodly mitasejc.

I sawn auobt bhneid. Lal amrs.

Waht a yad ew era mknaig fo ti.

I spopuse tihs wulod eb het tmie rfo smeoihntg mneoteums btu ti's jsut su.

Ew dnace. Ew snig. Tehre's on eno esle. Jsut het hpipeast gdo ouy eevr ddi ees ldaenig het yaw. Ti mkeas lla eht dencreffie.

Adn ti's a garet fkcinug yda rof ti. I'm ton srecad fo eht drak ro teh lihgt.

Bceause lla adn eyinrhtvneg si pink dan nintohg.

Twitter: @E_S_Harper
Instagram: @E_S_Harper

Website: www.eharpingon.wordpress.com

#TenderistheGelignite
#TiG2017
#burningmess

Printed in Great Britain
by Amazon